THE CANARSIE CONNECTION

A Novel By Divine G

Also by Divine G

Novels:

Baby Doll (Published by Q-Boro Books)

Money-Grip (Published by Street Knowledge Publishing)

Money-Grip 2 (Published by Createspace)

Enigma of Love (Published by Divine G Entertainment)

No Other Love (Published by Divine G Entertainment)

Short Stories:

Averted Hearts (appearing in *The Game*, published by Triple Crown Publications)

Stage Plays:

Peak-Zone (appearing in *Exiled Voices, Portals of Discovery*, published by New England College Press)

THE CANARSIE CONNECTION ®

ISBN-10: 1940765102
ISBN-13: 978-1-940765-10-5
Createspace Edition

Paperback and ebook editiona published by Divine G Entertainment
Written by: Divine G
Edited by John "Divine G" Whitfield
Cover layout/Design by Divine G Entertainment

For information contact:

Divine G Entertainment
Website: www.divinegentertainment.com
Email: divinegentertainment@gmail.com

Dedication

This novel is dedicated to the numerous family members, friends and associates who were very instrumental in helping me to get this novel written, edited and published. The list of supporters is so huge and extensive, I am very apprehensive about attempting to mention names, because from past experience, if anyone is inadvertently left out and feels he or she should have been mentioned, it creates a lot of bad feelings. So, this time, I am taking the safe road by sending out a universal dedication to all those who played a part in the success of this novel, without itemizing each individual name. If you were there, by my side, had my back, and was supportive, then you are the person I am referring to when I send out this dedication. This novel is dedicated to you for being there when times got extremely rough, rocky and raw. Once again, thanks for all the support, love and understanding.

CHAPTER # 1

Shamara Fox walked slowly down the street as the sickly glow of the street lamps cast an eerie image upon the dilapidated Newark New Jersey houses. Her heart was pounding heavily in her chest and was pumping hard enough to be felt pulsating in her eardrums. There was also a faint ringing sound that confused her because she never knew fear could make the body respond in this fashion. Tonight her beauty was to be her strongest asset. She was hoping the skintight jeans she wore really made her heart shaped ass look as big and juicy as it felt, since she needed their target to put his guards down and keep them down long enough for them to get off a first strike.

Shamara looked across the street and saw her home-girl, partner, and life long friend, Fashawn Corcino, a caramel complexioned big boned sister with hips for days, walking with her hood covering her head, and her hands stuffed in the front pocket of her forest green hoodie. Shamara knew Fashawn was caressing a concealed 9mm in the same fashion as she was.

Moments later, Shamara saw the house they had been scoping out up ahead; she picked up speed, and as planned, she took a seat on the hood of the nearby gray car and waited for the signal. Why did she insist she be the lead shooter!? Her nervousness wouldn't let up. She answered her question when that voice said, *because you need to bust your cherry if you gonna be a hit woman! Calm down, girl,* she repeatedly told himself, *this is gonna be like skating on ice.* She and Fashawn had rehearsed this run in their heads repeatedly; they even did a walk through three times and the routine was basically engraved in her memory bank, so there was nothing to worry about.

1

Shamara cut her eyes and saw Fashawn leaning up against the grocery store gate as two crack-heads scurried pass her, apparently on their way to cop some crack from the crack spot about two blocks away. Shamara pulled her hand from the pocket of her hoodie and stole another nervous peek at her wrist watch. It was ten minutes to eleven o'clock. She stuffed her hand back inside the pocket, looking around at the windows of the nearby houses, hoping it was late enough. Then, she realized, according to regular people's sense of time it was late, but for those in the game it was standard work time, and since Newark was a city not much different from New York City, it too was a city that never slept. But, then again, Shamara thought as she saw a skinny crack head slide down the stairs of a three family house next to the house she was watching, no drug infested community could ever sleep, since the monkey on the back of any motherfucker naïve enough to consume drugs would not permit it.

Shamara sighed frustratedly as she nervously snatched her hands from her pocket and wiped her sweaty palms on the front of her pants. There was no question she was scared half to death, she realized as she stuffed her hands back into her hoodie pocket and gripped the huge handle of her 9mm. She'd never killed anyone before, and wondered if Fashawn felt the same way she was currently feeling when she caught her first body oversees in Iraq.

Out of nowhere the Bible quote dealing with the question of committing murder slid back onto the surface of her thought process, and she hastily kicked the thought to the back of her mind, because she'd already grappled with that issue and had finally got pass it. *Why are all these crazy ass thoughts popping into my head!?*

Suddenly, the headlights of a car entering the street swept over the immediate area. She looked at Fashawn, saw the hand signal and her heart leaped in her chest. It was time. It was time to do the damn thing and she slid onto her trembling feet. She tried to move, but realized the fear literally had he stuck. She looked over and saw Fashawn had stopped walking and was staring at her, apparently wondering what she was waiting for. Although she couldn't see Fashawn's face clearly, Shamara knew she was grilling her with a rage-laden expression. Shamara sucked in a lung full of air, and forced herself to move. She picked up speed, realizing her hesitation had put the plan in jeopardy.

When Shamara saw the two typical urban thugs getting out of the black Audi, she panicked because there was supposed to be only one. Her mind was jumping all over the place now; she had forgotten that she and Fashawn had discussed this possibility, and had a contingency plan in place for it. The nervousness and fear was about to overwhelm her. Then, she remembered what Fashawn had told her repeatedly: "If you ever fell yourself gettin' nervous and it's about to interfere with you completing this mission, think about how Tommy brutally murdered your mom and dad; how that motherfucker mowed them down and then got away Scott free. That'll be enough to get you on track."

As Fashawn's words echoed in her memory bank, Shamara pulled up that nightmarish mental image of the drive-by shooting; a horror-stricken image that had been haunting her for the pass fifteen years and her hand instantly reacted. The gun sprung from her pocket and was trained on the two thugs wearing baggy pants, typical hoodlum grills, and were about to approach the house. Shamara felt her confidence coming back when she saw their target, Ray Ray, was one of the two; he was a brown skinned dude with shifty eyes, and numerous jailhouse razor cuts on his face. The pictures they received from Malik were remarkably accurate.

"You know what the fuck this is, niggas!?" Shamara announced as she saw Fashawn through the corner of her eye moving rapidly towards the two. She was supposed to simply open fire, and didn't understand why she was procrastinating. The plan was simple; no talking, roll up, and start shooting. Fuck the drug money they were carrying, just shoot these muthafuckas! "Put your fuckin' hands up so I can see them!" She shouted and didn't understand why she couldn't pull the trigger.

Fashawn had her 9mm aimed at Ray Ray and his man as her anger mounted with each rapid step she took towards the situation. She wanted to yell, "Shoot them motherfuckers!" but knew that wouldn't help the situation. In fact, it would make it worst because then Ray Ray and his man would know this was a hit and not a robbery. Then, she saw Ray Ray's partner frantically reaching for his weapon and Fashawn caught an instant Marine Corps flashback.

BOOM! BOOM! BOOM!

Fashawn's weapon roared as her first two bullets cut down the reacher while the other bullet struck Ray Ray in the neck.

The thug who reached for his weapon managed to squeeze off a shot that wheezed pass Shamara, cauing Shamara to frantically take cover. The moment Fashawn's bullets ripped at the street thugs, Shamara noticed her fear brought her straight to her hands and knees and nearly caused her to wet her pants.

Fashawn was in a shooting stance as she fired two more rounds, carefully aimed at Ray-Ray as he crumbled to the pavement. She raced over to the back of Ray Ray's car, peeked around the back of the vehicle and saw the two were down. She could hear them moaning, and so she briskly moved towards them and fired a shot to each of their heads, execution style. She yelled as she ran towards Shamara, "Bitch, get the fuck up! Let's go!"

Shamara scrambled to her feet and before she was fully standing, Fashawn latched onto the sleeve of her hoodie, and dragged her down the street as they fled the scene at breakneck speed.

Five minutes later, Shamara and Fashawn were in the back seat of the get-away car, breathing hard as Kenyetta, a baby-face light brown skin brother with sparkling brown eyes, and a meticulously thin goatee, with matching side burns, maneuvered the supped up black Ford Mustang down the Newark streets. One of 50 Cent's latest, hard-hitting rap songs was whispering through the car's stereo system.

Fashawn sighed exhaustedly as she looked over at Shamara and smiled at her. "I'm sorry for yelling at you back there." The last thing she wanted to do was break her spirit at a time like this. She understood what Shamara was going through, since she could remember feeling the same way when she made her first kill, even though she ultimately had no serious problem putting some hot ones in her target. "Shamara, don't worry." She reached over and massaged Shamara's shoulder. "This is normal. Killing is not an easy thing. Don't let it discourage you."

Shamara felt a mixture of embarrassment and insecurity. "I—I don't know what the fuck happened, Fay. I swear--I—I don't know." She had bragged profusely about being able to handle this like a trooper, and now she had chumped herself in the worse way. She now realized this was nothing like committing an arm robbery, since the intent to steal was way different from the intent to kill. She wondered if she could ever get beyond this inhibition.

Kenyetta said without taking his eyes off the road, "I'm not gonna beat you in the head with the I told you so, but it sounds like you violated the first rule." He paused for dramatic effect. "Never, ever hesitate. One blink and lights out. Permanently." He glanced at the rearview mirror and made eye contact with Shamara. "Now you see what I'm saying when I

5

said this is the real deal." He instantly noticed her depressed state. "Don't worry about what happened back there; what you went through is the best kinda lesson you can get."

Shamara sucked her teeth loudly.

Kenyetta continued, "You fell, now get back up, brush yourself off and keep it movin'."

Shamara felt herself becoming more insecure by the seconds, and wasn't surprise Kenyetta was beating her in the head, especially in light of her cockiness. She mumbled under her breath. "Y'all probably ain't train me right."

Fashawn heard what she mumbled and was about to say something, but realized Shamara didn't mean what she was saying since she was just venting.

Kenyetta saw through the rearview that Shamara looked like she was about to cry. "We here for you, baby girl; we know what you been through, but if you going to play the field, you gotta remember it's kill or be killed. You ain't totally new to the game, so use what you already know. Tap into all that good energy you got going on inside you."

Shamara was tired of Kenyetta's broken record speeches. "Yeah, I know what time it is, being that you told me that shit a hundred times already."

"And I'll say it another hundred times," Kenyetta sensed she was about to catch an attitude because he was making sure she didn't mess up again. "We ain't trying to beat up on you, Shamara." He also knew Shamara was notorious for blaming folks for her own fuck ups, once she got a roll going. "I'm just making sure you understand that what we're getting into ain't no game. This shit ain't no mufuckin' movie script where we can call cut and do it over again if we ain't satisfied with the results."

"Alright, alright," Fashawn saw an argument about to ignite. "Your position is well taken, Kenyetta. Let's not make this bigger than what it is. The hit was a success and that's all that matters. What you need to do, Kenyetta, is make sure we get inside Tommy's crew. Let your man Malik know we serious about that full time spot. Keep drilling it every chance you get."

"And especially, don't forget the money," Shamara said, realizing the shit load of bills and the two outstanding rent payments would disappear once their hands touched the rest of that money.

"The money is all good," Kenyetta glanced at the rearview mirror. "Once Malik confirms the kill, I'll pick up the cheddar. But, I doubt Tommy'll put y'all down with his team on account of this one hit."

"Well, let him know we can handle whatever he got for us," Shamara said, vowing to redeem herself during the next run. "I didn't come through like I wanted this time, but the next time I'm gonna go all the way with this shit, and that's my word is bond," She mumbled her next comment more to herself than to Fashawn and Kenyetta. "We gotta get inside there and get close enough to this chump to push his fuckin' wig back."

Fashawn and Kenyetta's eyes made contact in the rearview mirror and they both constrained the smiles that were trying to come to life.

7

CHAPTER # 2

Tommy Bossett sat on the sofa next to his seven-year-old son, Tommy Jr., with a joystick in his hands, playing the latest Play-Station video game. The two were really into the game, but Tommy Sr. seemed to be having difficulty controlling the karate figure on the TV screen.

With nonchalant energy Tommy Jr. duffed off his dad's karate man, and laughed joyfully. "I got you again, daddy."

"Hey, that wasn't fair," Tommy Sr. sighed playfully. "You didn't give me a chance to get ready. How you make the guy jump and kick like that?"

"Naw, I ain't telling you my secrets," Tommy Jr. said as he hit the button to start a new game.

"Oh, so you gone just beat up on me like that, huh?" Tommy Sr. said, gearing up for another game. He turned his head when he saw Kahmel entered along with Malik on his trail. He said to his son. "Uh oh, look who just popped up." He rose to his feet and sat the joystick down on the coffee table. "You know what this means. Yeap, it's work time."

"Yeah, yeah," Tommy Jr. said as he activated the single player button and got brain-locked into the game.

Tommy exited the living room, heading for the backyard patio of his four million dollar mansion. He said nothing to Malik or Kahmel as his muscular physique moved through the mansion; he made a detour into his huge study room that was the size of a small gymnasium and had all sorts of awards and gold records hanging on the wall. Also on the walls were old rap posters; the biggest one of all was the one of Tommy when he was much younger, holding a microphone, while dressed in back in the day hip hop attire, with the Kangol hat, Addidas sneakers, huge rope gold chains dripping from his neck, and the whole sha-bang. At the bottom of the poster in big letters was the statement: More Power to the People.

Tommy went to his gun cabinet that had shelves full of all sorts of antique weapons. There was an old fashion Tommy Gun from the Roaring Twenties, a Civil War one shot revolver, a complete set of silver plated automatics of all conceivable calibers, a WWII assault rifle, a Russian sub-machine gun, a Japanese WWII handgun and his most precious and prized possession: a gold plated Glock eighteen shot 9mm. Smiling proudly, Tommy opened the glass door, and retrieved the golden 9mm. Every time he laid eyes on this sheer work of art, it brought back a wave of memories.

After Tommy started touching major paper, he decided to fulfill one of his dreams, which was to one day own a golden gun. This compelled him to purchase this tailor made "Golden 9." After Skeeter and his mob had made an attempt on his life a few months back as he was exiting a business office in Elizabeth and a brief exchange of gunfire erupted, Tommy made it an ingrained habit of keeping this Golden 9 with him at all times (with the exception of when he spent quality time with his son). Likewise, Tommy not only kept twenty four hour bodyguard protection on himself, but he also slept with his Golden 9 under his pillow, despite constant protest from his wife, Ashanta.

Tommy shook loose of the reverie, tucked the Golden 9 in the back waist area of his pants, and exited the study room. Kahmel and Malik were waiting right outside the study room, and followed in Tommy's footstep as he continued onto the patio. They both knew what Tommy retrieved from the study room.

A minute later, the three were sitting in lounge chairs with ice cold drinks in their hands talking as the early June sun beamed down upon the area. The water in the huge in ground pool about fifteen feet away cooled the atmosphere as the currents of the breeze bounced off of it. About several dozen feet from the patio two other bodyguards, Caddy and Slick, were dressed in street thug attire, and were patrolling the mansion grounds. By the way all of Tommy's bodyguards were dressed no one would have believed they were professional security personnel, especially since they weren't the huge muscular type bodyguards. However, the weaponry they carried at all times more than made up for their lack of body mass.

Tommy sipped on his Hennessey and ginger ale and said, "So your little killer hood rat crew came through?" He saw Malik nod his head. "And I see they laid down his homie, Snake, in the process. We got two for one outta this deal."

"Yeah, it's a good thing I held back giving them any instructions to hit only Ray Ray," Malik said, "Not that they would've followed it, but it's good they laid down another foe of ours."

"In this game you never leave witnesses behind." Tommy added. "And I'm sure you're schooling them on that fact." He saw Malik nod his head. "How much gun play was there?"

"Wasn't any actually," Malik said as he picked up his drink. "Snake busted off a shot, and that was all she wrote." He sipped on his glass of Hennessey.

Tommy shook his head as he screwed up his face at Kahmel. "You hear that shit, Kahmel. Them bitches smoked both of them niggas and only one shot was let off." He was still furious with Kahmel and Caddy for butchering the hit they attempted on Ray Ray, turning a simple job into a full blown fiasco, equipped with a massive shoot out, a car chase, and the lost of two dedicated street workers to the Criminal Justice System. He wasn't the type to belittle his staff in the presence of others, but this was simply too irresistible; plus, it was an opportunity to compel

Kahmel to tighten up his game. "Maybe you should have a sit down with these broads, and learn some of their tactics. If they could air this chump out with only one shot being fired, there was no reason for you and your peeps not to do the same."

Kahmel cracked a good natured smiled, but deep down he wanted to spazz out. He hated when Tommy shitted on him with Malik around. In his humblest tone of voice he said, "In all fairness, Tommy, they had an advantage from the jump, since they obviously were able to get right up on them niggas."

"That's right!" Tommy shouted excitedly. "They got some things y'all niggas around me don't got! They got pussys and military training. Most ballers in the game don't expect bitches to bust their gun like that." For years Tommy had been trying to recruit a team of killer bitches and all he could find was a bunch of dizzy, come slurping tramps that couldn't even fuck straight, much less handle hardware. "With this shit brewing between us and Skeeter's click, we're gonna need some hitters that can get up on a mufucka." He stared off into the oblivion, dreamingly imaging how Shamara and Fashawn were going to change the conflict between him and Skeeter. "Man, as fine ass these. . . what's their names again?"

Malik said unemotionally, "Shamara and Fashawn."

"Yeah, Shamara and Fashawn." Tommy pulled up the image of their faces and banging bodies (he had viewed a couple of video recordings of their meeting with Malik and Kenyetta), and knew their beauty could get them in places no man could get inside of. "As fine as those bitches are, we'll be able to turn this beef around, and slide Skeeter's bitch ass right out of the game."

Kahmel felt a ping of jealousy erupting; the thought of finding these two bitches and smoking their ass before they forced him out of a job was

11

strong. "You might be right, Boss, but it's way too earlier to start counting cash on them."

Tommy stared at Kahmel and then said impatiently. "That's obvious, nigga. What the fuck you think, I'ma just roll these broads up in here without making absolutely certain they're down with us 110%?"

"Naw, dawg, I—"

"After all the attempts made on my life, you playin' yourself talking like that, Kahmel." Tommy saw Kahmel shift nervously in his seat. "You of all people know I don't even trust my mufuckin' self, much less a few gun slinging chicks. You talking like I'm about to take a chance with a thirteen million dollar a year empire just 'cause a few fine bitches show up at his door step." Tommy was into everything from drug dealing, legal and illegal gaming, and prostitution to money laundering, music producing and luxury car smuggling. "You hear this shit Malik?"

Malik cracked a smile while nodding his head, enjoying what Tommy was doing. He'd been rolling with Tommy since his music industry days when Tommy dropped a rap album that didn't do well on the market, and even back then Tommy was notorious for riding Kahmel. But, he had to admit; this treatment was well deserved in light Kahmel's very brutal, vindictive and vicious personality. Malik often commended Tommy for knowing that Kahmel was the type of cat that had to be constantly reminded of who was in charge, since Kahmel stayed bullying the help as if he was running the show.

Tommy said to Kahmel, "So, basically you think I'm slipping? Is that what you implying?"

"Naw, I didn't mean it like that," Kahmel said easily. "I'm just doing what I do best, and that is watch your back. You know I always look at everything from another angle, you know."

Tommy couldn't argue with that. There was no doubt Kahmel watched his back with hawk-eyed precision, and kept all the troops in line like a deranged Parris Island Marine drill sergeant. Although his pessimism was irritating at times, it was a healthy pain in the ass because it made him pause and look at everything very closely. There were countless instances since he'd teamed up with Kahmel over twenty years ago where Kahmel had prevented disastrous courses of action by throwing his pessimistic ideas into the equation. In fact, Kahmel had been rolling with Tommy ever since he was a street D-jay, playing music in the parks, clubs, community centers, house parties, and battling other D-jay groups. Kahmel was the crew's strong arm and protection man, carrying the guns and waiting for cats like stick up kids to get out of line, so he could brutalize them. When Tommy dropped the D-jaying bit and got into the drug game, Kahmel was right there by his side. A few years after that, Tommy had backed tracked a little and produced his own rap album entitled, "More Power to the People", and sure enough, Kahmel was dead on his heels. Even when Tommy eventually became a street lieutenant for a Brooklyn drug crew ran by two ruthless cats named Eternal and Remus (God bless the dead) Kahmel was with him and was one of his best soldiers. As Tommy gnawed, grind, and struggle up the ladder of ghetto glamour and glory, Kahmel stuck to him like glue, and to this day as Tommy reached true big boy status, Kahmel had never once crossed him, which was truly a very unique and phenomenal thing for ballers from hood. In short, seventy million dollars later, and Kahmel was still with him.

Tommy instantly realized he was being too hard on his life long comrade, and said, "Kahmel, I'm only fucking with you, dawg. I'm just trying to keep you on your toes." He throw up his fist to give him some dap.

Kahmel felt a hundred times better as he gave Tommy some dap, and said, "We fam, and fam hold fam down no matter what."

Tommy said to Malik, "Now that they passed the first initiation test, I guess we can agree that they ain't no deep-cover agents, or some kinda super snitches trying to slide through the back door of our operation. Dropping bodies like that tells me they the real deal. I also had Bobby do a few paper and record checks on them and everything came back with flying colors."

"They just wanna make some money," Malik said as he shrugged his shoulders. "Like I said before, Fashawn just came home from the Iraq War; she was a professional sharp shooter; the military fucked her around, and now she's ready to make some serious dough doing what she does best. And that is . . . kill people. The other one, Shamara, did some heavy time upstate for arm robbery, and possession of a weapon. These broads just wanna make some real money, and ain't got no problem laying motherfuckers down. If you want my opinion, they're the kind of hitters an organization like ours should bend over backwards to get 'em on our team. You better make sure Skeeter don't get wind of them, because he'll snatch 'em up with the quickness."

"Oh, you can believe we ain't lettin' 'em slip through our fingers. I got a couple more jobs for them. If they pass these tests, we'll talk about bringing them in." Tommy saw Kahmel screw up his face and sighed impatiently. "Be easy, Kahmel; you gonna always be my head of security. You acting like these broads are about to take your position or something."

"Naw, dawg, it's just that I don't trust these bitches," Kahmel said as he stared at Malik to give emphasis to what he was saying. "Out of all the crews getting cheddar in hoods all over the tri-state, why these bitches wanna vibe with us? It just don't feel right to me."

Malik smirked up his face and said calmly, "What, you don't think the streets are talking? You don't think mufuckas know we the biggest and most organized underworld crew in the tri-state? Kahmel, these bitches got plenty sense and know if they gonna roll with a mufucka, it might as well be with the best, or at least a crew that's destine to take that position. Yeah, there may be some other crews that can compete with us, like Skeeter, the Diablo Brothers and a few of those Dominican clicks, but they don't got what we got, and that's diversity. We ain't just into the drug game. We got gaming spots, stolen car operations, clubs where a cat can get his shit off. We've reached a level the average crew will never touch. If you were an up and raising hitter, wouldn't you wanna roll with a team like that?"

Tommy smiled proudly. It was always a pleasure to know people were recognizing the advancements his mob was making in the game. His smile faded when he locked eyes with Kahmel, because Malik's comments were right on target, and it was clear Kahmel was getting on some emotional bullshit. "Check it, Kahmel. Stop letting your insecurity get in the way. Just 'cause they completed a job you couldn't, don't mean I'll put them before you, so chill out with all this sensitive bullshit. Look at their coming on the team as you having more folks to beat up on." He laughed along with Malik, but was disappointed when Kahmel didn't find the joke funny. "Come on, Kahmel, you know we fuck with the best, and we do groundbreaking shit. If these chicks can get us where we wanna be and stay where we at, then they will be on this team."

Kahmel sighed as he nodded his head, "Hey, big papa, this is your ship; if you want 'em down with the team, you got 'em. I'm with you wherever this ship goes."

"Now, that's what I wanna hear," Tommy said as he downed the last of his drink and poured himself another shot.

"So what's up with the payment for this last job?" Malik said as he gulped down the last of his drink, and sat the glass down. That was it for him.

Tommy gave Kahmel a head nod, and he headed towards the mansion after giving Caddy the signal that he was leaving, apparently to retrieve the money. Tommy locked eyes with Malik and said, "This next job is gonna be a lot different from the last one. In fact, it's a job I don't even think a mob of true thorough niggas could pull off. How much they charge for a job with a body count of at least four?"

Malik almost lit up with delight. After he got his cut off of a four body run, he'd have himself a nice chuck of extra paper. He'd have more than enough to buy that fur coat he'd promised his main girl, Diana. He was breaking himself off a cut of the money he was giving Kenyetta, who in turn hit off the chicks. Off the last job he had clipped off five gees. With this next job it was obvious he could squeeze himself about fifteen gees. Then, Malik suddenly realized Tommy was asking him to make sure he got a play with this next job, since it was obvious that the standard fee was supposed to be multiplied by four (70 gees x 4 = 280 gees), and if he had intentions of paying that much he wouldn't have brought up the issue of cost. Malik was about to blurt out a number, but decided to play it safe. "I'll shoot it pass Kenyetta. Give me a couple of hours and I'll holla at you. For the record, he said they were giving up discounts for certain type of jobs. A four men run would probably qualify for such a discount. However, I need to know if all four are gonna be together?"

"Yeah, all four will be together." Tommy said as he reflected back on the last transaction while gazing at the acres of open space he owned. He had paid thirty five gees up front and now was about to give up another thirty five gees since the job was completed. Seventy gees wasn't a bad deal, in light of the fact now he could take over Ray Ray's territory and his customers, a set up that brought in about fifty gees a week. Although money was a major motivator for knocking Ray Ray off, another reason Tommy felt obligated to cancel his contract was because he hired a drug crew of kids as young as eight years old to sell his drugs. Tommy had stepped to Ray Ray and asked him to be easy with the kids, and Ray Ray got on some real arrogant shit, talking about nobody had a right to tell him how to make his money, and started grandstanding like he was Al Capone or untouchable. Everybody knew the rules of drug dealing was getting grimier by the minutes, but even the most corrupt minded individual could agree that there had to be lines drawn that couldn't be crossed, and as far as Tommy was concerned, fucking with the babies was one of those limitations.

Malik saw Tommy was in the zone with his current daydream, and decided to acquire some clarification with the next job before Kahmel returned. "I guess it's fair to say this next run involves that dude Gangsta over in Jersey City? Since he's the only one I know that rolls with three other homies at all times, it's gotta be him."

"Yeap, Gangsta's gettin' too big for his breeches." Tommy said. "He gave me his word that he would always use my connects, and would piece me off, and now that he's moving major weight and got himself an army of workers, and gunslingers, he thinks he can say fuck me without there being consequences. Plus, I got a few peeps on standby waiting to move in once he's out of the picture." He turned when he saw Kahmel approaching with a suitcase.

After Kahmel sat the opened suitcase filled with money in front of Malik and Malik glanced at the content, Tommy continued, "I hope you make it clear to Shamara and Fashawn, and Kenyetta that in order to hit this cat, Gangsta, they gotta go real deep into some extreme hostile enemy territory." Tommy liked the way that sounded; it sounded like some real military shit: extreme hostile enemy territory. "He's literally got an army of young, wild mufuckas holding him down, and wherever he moves, at least three of them are his shadow. This is the type of hit, I can't even consider sending my crew inside, since they'll probably swallow them up before they get within twenty yard of their clubhouse." He looked over at Kahmel with a smirk and smiled, "You might get your wish after all Kah, 'cause if they slip up in any way when they step to Gansta, you can bet your ass he's gonna do them real dirty."

Malik understood clearly what Tommy was pointing out, since he was all too familiar with Gangsta, and his team. Besides the fact Gangsta's gang had an arsenal of high tech military weaponry, and plenty of young fools dying to use them, but they were also notorious for banging out with the police. In the game, it went without saying that if a crew didn't give a flying fuck about the police, it was evident that they would bring sheer hell to anyone else, especially two pretty hood rats, venturing off into a dirty and dangerous business like contract killing.

CHAPTER # 3

Shamara sat behind the admission counter of the "Flatlands Dental Clinic" on Flatlands Avenue and East 92nd Street, filling out a patient report of a Mrs. Madeline Rogers. She was a first time patient, and therefore Shamara had to start a whole new folder for her. Shamara had been working here at this Clinic for about a year, ever since her release from Bedford Hills Prison, and couldn't imagine working here another year. It didn't take long for her to realize that she wasn't built for secretarial work, although she could type a perfect sixty words a minute, could organize files with expert precision, and had extraordinary people skills. Her heart yearned for self-sufficiency. She'd always dreamed of owning her own business, like a restaurant or a huge shopping mall.

Suddenly, the head dentist, Dr. Moore came from the back of the Clinic with a folder in his hand. He was a clean-shaven black man with a low cut Afro, a lean physique and had a Jamaican accent.

He said to Shamara as he handed her the folder, "I need you to prepare a bill for this patient, and send it over to Medicare." He was about to zip back to this office, but noticed Shamara looked fatigued and worn out. "Hey, Shamara, is everything all right? You look tired."

With a lovely smile, Shamara said, "I'm fine, Dr. Moore. I had a rough time going to sleep last night." She couldn't dare tell him the truth; she was practicing firing her 9mm inside Fashawn's soundproof basement, and lost track of the time. "Plus, I'm trying to cut down on my caffeine intake, so I didn't have my usual cups of coffee today."

"You have a few sick days you know; like I told you before; if you ever need to use them, don't be afraid to ask." He smiled and continued back to his office.

19

Shamara really wanted to take a permanent leave of absence, but bills had to be paid, and her parole obligations had to be met. Although she no longer had to go see a parole officer, employment was still a basic prerequisite to being free of parole supervision.

Shamara resumed what she was doing and her mind instantly reflected on the fact that tonight she and Fashawn were scheduled to have a meeting with Kenyetta. He also had the rest of their money and news about their next job. Her stomach became woozy just thinking about this next "mission" (as Fashawn liked to call them). She was eager to prove she was built for this business, especially since Fashawn and Kenyetta were putting their lives on the line in order to help her. Here it was, all this was about helping her punish the man that murdered her mom and dad in cold blood and got away with it, and she was the one who couldn't bust a single shot.

Shamara sighed as she shook loose of this negative energy like Fashawn instructed her to do when her stress started acting up; she started focusing on helpful and reassuring things, like how they were going to make sure they impressed Tommy enough to guarantee they got inside of his organization, so they could get right up on his ass. However, she couldn't help but brood over the fact they weren't able to simply shoot Tommy from a distance, and end it right there. She and Fashawn had followed Tommy's entourage for two weeks as Tommy visited various places in New Jersey and saw he was basically untouchable. He never put himself in a situation where he could be scoped out by a hidden sharpshooter, and Kenyetta had tried to tell them it couldn't be done because of a major beef Tommy had with some cat named Skeeter; Tommy's guards were up as high as they could go, and he permanently kept them at that level of full alert. But, it didn't matter anyway, because Shamara vowed that Tommy was going to get what was coming to him, which resulted in them deciding to infiltrate Tommy's organization by posing as hit women.

Shamara looked up from her work when an elderly man entered the Clinic. After she got Mr. Bosky set up, ready to fulfill his appointment, and instructed him to have a seat until Dr. Moore was ready to see him, Shamara's mind was back at it again. She still couldn't believe she was taking her thirst for justice this far. She was actually killing criminals in order to convince another criminal to let her and her home girl inside of his organization, so she could in turn murder him. It was crazy, but it was something she believed she had to do. What she saw when she was ten years old transformed her life into something beyond a living hell, and merely knowing the person responsible didn't serve a single day in prison because people were scared to come forth, haunted her endlessly like a restless spirit. The harm this un-addressed issue caused had showed itself in many self-destructive ways as Shamara grew up.

Even the years of therapy Shamara received as a result of witnessing her mom and dad being murdered right before her eyes was useless. Needless to say, the side effects of witnessing this traumatic ordeal were plenty and many, which caused her involvement with the streets, drugs, gangs, the acquisition of fast money, the fear of serious relationships, a phobia of getting married, since marriage seemed to be synonymous with death, and a rebellious attitude towards authority figures, which culminated with her going to prison. But, to her utter surprise, it wasn't until Fashawn suggested that she personally punish Tommy for what he did, that she noticed she began to feel mentally, emotionally, and psychologically healthy. Just the mere thought of her being the one to punish Tommy had an affect on her that was truly empowering and highly liberating.

Now that she was also touching thousands of dollars, she realized being a hit woman wasn't as bad as she initially thought it would be, being that one of the side effects was financial stability. It sure felt good to finally know how if felt to have enough money to say she had a year's worth of rent already in the bag. The thirty thousand dollars up front money they received two weeks ago was split three ways, which meant they got ten gees each. Now, tonight they would receive another ten gees each and for a few hours of work, she had to admit that this amount wasn't bad at all.

At the end of her work tour (five o'clock), she was cruising down Flatlands Avenue in her hooptie, a gray Toyota, with rust stains everywhere; she was on her way to pick up Fashawn from her job over on Seaview Avenue and Rockaway Parkway.

As she cruised down Rockaway Parkway and pass Avenue K, Shamara saw Kojak and his fellow street corner bums, hanging out on the corner near the grocery store, drinking beer, while begging and borrowing from anyone trying to enter the neighborhood convenient store. For the life of her, Shamara could not understand how these losers could spend a lifetime living on a street corner. They were on this same street corner as far back as she could remember, and there was no doubt they were going to be in this same location for many years to come. Kojak and his crew were so ingrained into the landscape of the neighborhood they had even found a way to evade the new quality of life laws that made it an offense to hang out (loiter) on the streets.

Moments later, Shamara pulled into the Seaview Shoppers Mart Shopping Center parking lot and to her surprise she saw Fashawn was sitting on the hood of a red car smoking a cigarette. A few feet from where Fashawn sat was the store she worked named, "Seaview Hardware

Store." Fashawn was a stock clerk, and had been working there about as long as Shamara was working at the Dentist Office.

Shamara brought the car to a stop and Fashawn rushed over and got in on the passenger side. "What's up, Fay, I see James cut you loose earlier today." She maneuvered the car back onto the Parkway.

"I told him I needed to break out early," Fashawn flicked ashes into the ashtray. "We gotta get ready for tonight." She took another drag on the cigarette. "Once we get the details of this next run, we gotta get on it. Start scoping shit out, so you can pop that cherry of yours."

"Oh, I'm gone be alright this time, bet that," Shamara was about to start showboating with her words, but quickly caught herself. She always felt better when she showed confidence, however, after her last blunder she vowed it was better to show than tell. "Spark me up one of them cigarettes."

"I thought you said you was trying to stop."

"Yeah, well, I changed my mind," Shamara had been trying to stop smoking since she was in prison, and still hadn't gotten anywhere. The longest she stopped was two weeks, and it drove her crazy. She needed something to strive for in order to be successful in this endeavor, and so she created her own personal incentive. "I've decided once I blaze Tommy's bitch ass, that's when I'll stop."

"That's a good motivator," Fashawn said as she pulled her pack of Newport cigarettes, flicked a fresh one out of the pack, touched the lit tip of the cigarette she was smoking to the fresh one while pulling on the fresh one, and then handed it to Shamara. "We need to get to the Jersey spot a little earlier than planned. I'm a run in, grab my shit, and we can do the same with you."

"What about Kenyetta?" Shamara flicked ashes in the tray.

"I already called him. He was bitching, but he knows how I do shit. If there's one thing I learned from the military, and will give them big ups for, is they taught me that proper planning always prevent poor performance."

"No more of that booth camp shit again, please," Shamara whined playfully. Ever since they decided to step to Tommy, Fashawn had her and Kenyetta on some soldier shit, working out, exercising, lifting weights, and target practicing as if they were about to embark on a real military mission. It was a pain in the ass at first, but Shamara really started enjoying it after a while, especially the target practice part.

"The way we had to kick up dust during the last run, I'm surprised you still don't see the need to get your body right."

Shamara smiled at her life long friend since third grade, and said. "Girl, you know I'm only messin' with you. I'm grateful to have a friend like you holdin' me down. You were the only one that was willing to step up and help me make things right." It was the honest to God truth she felt blessed to have someone like Fashawn by her side. Their relationship exemplified the meaning of best friends to such a degree that after Shamara got arrested and sentenced to one to three years in prison for robbing a grocery store in Brownsville with her so-called boyfriend, Shabazz Thompson, Fashawn was so devastated she enrolled in the military, even though the US was at war with Afghanistan and the Taliban as a result of the 911 attacks and there was talk of President Bush going to war with Iraq. Anyone could see it was a terrible time to start talking about enrolling in the military, but Fashawn wasn't like most other people. Besides the fact she was almost insanely patriotic when it came to the good old red, white and blue, but she was also fascinated with soldiers and issues involving the military. She also knew Fashawn was always the adventurous, chance-taking, fearless type, but upon hearing she enrolled in the Marines, Shamara thought her home-girl was straight buggin'.

After making a stop at Fashawn's crib on Avenue J near the corner of East 93rd Street, they then raced over to Shamara's crib a few blocks away on Avenue L and East 91st Street. As they got out of the hooptie, Shamara heard loud music; Jay-Z and Beyonce were rapping and singing about being loyal to each other. It took a split second for her to realize the music was apparently coming from her apartment; she was on fire with something much stronger than anger as she stomped towards the crib. Her current boyfriend, Jalil, was doing exactly what the fuck she told him not to ever do again; using her crib as a hang out while playing loud music.

Fashawn saw Shamara was pissed and realized this was an opportunity to put some shit in the game as she followed Shamara towards the crib. "Why you fuckin' with that loser ass nigga, Shamara? Jalil don't respect you. He ain't got no job, ain't looking for one, he's ungrateful, and don't look like he got a serious pipe game." Fashawn caressed her 9mm, since she saw this time it was going down. "You need to kick his ass the fuck out your piece. I don't know why you be fuckin' with these clown ass niggas."

"Not now, Fashawn," Shamara said as she furiously searched her purse for her house keys. She felt steam seeping from every pore on her body; she was beyond furious, and saw a red glow hovering before her eyes. This was the last straw, she decided. She had told this motherfucker that the neighbors, and the cops were beefing about him playing loud music, and this inconsiderate, broke ass, leech mentality having ass motherfucker completely ignored every thing she told him, and was now blasting a fuckin' Jay-Z song like he lost his goddamn mind! Now that she was about to start rolling in dough, she was definitely ready to throw

Jalil's ass to the waste side, even though the dick was half ass decent, which was the only reason she let this chump ride this long.

Shamara found her key, opened the door, rushed inside and saw Jalil with four other street corner niggas, sitting around on her crush velvet sofa and matching chairs smoking weed and drinking 40s. Shamara stomped over to the stereo as Fashawn leaned up against the wall with her hands stuffed in the front pocket of her black hoodie.

Shamara damn near broke her CD player when she hit the off button. "Motherfucker, didn't I tell you not to play that fuckin' loud ass music in this apartment!?"

Jalil's ego flared up instantly. "Who the fuck you yelling at!?" He sprung to his feet; he had to let his boys know he wasn't a bitch.

Shamara rolled her head on her neck while waving her hand in Shanana fashion. "I'm talking to you! I told you the neighbors been bitchin' about this music and you know they called the police."

"That don't mean you gotta come in here disrespecting me—"

"Don't fuckin' play yourself, Jalil! Go on and act like you don't know. Fuck around and get your feelings hurt in front of your boys."

Jalil wanted to act like he was going to get physical, but he saw through the corner of his eyes, Fashawn standing with her hands in her hoodie pockets. Everybody knew this broad was off the hook and he didn't fell like clashing with her again. "Yo', you need to check your mouth, Shamara."

Shamara's rage was about to reach a boil. This arrogant motherfucker was acting like she was in the wrong. "That's it, Jalil. I'm tired of your shit. Pack your shit and get the fuck out of my crib!"

Jalil came at her with malice in his heart. "What type of bullshit you gettin' on Shamara—"

Shamara pushed him when he got too close, and was about to follow up with a jab to his face until she heard Fashawn loudly inject a bullet into the chamber of her gun. Jalil heard it as well and stopped in mid motion when he was about to push Shamara back.

"Jalil, why you like playin' yourself?" Fashawn said smoothly with her arms folded across her voluptuous breasts while the gun was boldly displayed for all to see. "Why is it so fuckin' hard for you to follow instructions?"

Jalil was about to panic. He desperately fought to hold on to his manhood, and desperately wanted to step to his business by putting Shamara's ass in check, but he knew lashing out violently would be suicidal. "Alright, alright." He inched towards the bedroom. "I'm leaving. You got that. But don't call me when that ass get lonely and you need somebody to scratch that itch."

"What!?" Shamara laughed at him. "That must be some strong shit y'all was drinking and smoking." She laughed even harder, causing Jalil's boys to snicker under their breath. "Nigga, don't flatter your fuckin' self." She said to Jalil's back. "You ain't built like that downstairs."

Fashawn winked at Shamara while nodding her head at Jalil's homies.

Shamara instantly caught on. "Yo', Dupreme, y'all gotta go. Wait for your boy outside."

Dupreme sprung into action; he wisely knew this wasn't the time to start joking and playing with Shamara like he usually did. He led the others toward the door, squeezing pass Fashawn as though he was scared shitless of her. The others looked even more nervous. They all heard the rumors that Fashawn Corcino got kicked out of the Marines because the bitch was crazy. They also knew she was half African American (her mother, Barbara), and half Italian (her father, Bobby), and that her father was a made mafia man for the Genovese crime family. Although her father, Bobby "the Hatchet" Corcino disappeared without a trance, nobody had enough heart to find out if Bobby the Hatchet loved Fashawn enough to come back (or send one of his soldiers) to do some terrible things to someone bold enough to put a hand on his daughter. In any event, Dupreme and the others had no intentions of tangling with Fashawn or Shamara.

When Dupreme and the others exited the apartment, Shamara went to the back room to watch Jalil pack his shit. The last thing she needed was this trifling ass dude stealing her shit and forcing her to go looking for him.

Five minutes later, Jalil had his stuff packed, crammed into two hefty garbage bags, and was dragging his shit towards the door with a long face. He stopped to say something to Shamara, but she immediately held up her hand, and Jalil knew for sure he had fucked up for real this time.

Jalil stopped with his hand on the doorknob, and said to Shamara. "I'm asking you to please don't throw my mail away until I can get it re-routed."

"I don't get down like that Jalil, and you know that. I'll hold onto your mail if it comes here."

Jalil zipped out the door.

It took Shamara and Fashawn twenty minutes to eat a quick meal (turkey and Swiss cheese sandwiches with lettuce, tomatoes and pickles) and pack a few things for their trip to Newark New Jersey. As they exited the house, Shamara and Fashawn saw Jalil and his crew were gone. They got in the hooptie and pulled off.

About an hour and a half later, Shamara pulled her hooptie in front of the house they rented in Newark to serve as their home away from home, and their headquarters when they were planning and doing their hits. As far as Malik and any others from this area were concerned, Shamara and Fashawn lived in this house, and the plan was to make sure no one knew they lived in Canarsie. They saw Kenyetta's Ford Mustang was park in the driveway and they parked in back of his ride, got out of the hooptie and entered the house with their own set of keys.

They saw Kenyetta looking over a map and Fashawn smiled because the sight reminded her of what a General did as he planned and coordinated a complicated military strike.

Without looking up, Kenyetta said, "This is the reason why y'all need to move out of Canarsie. Y'all late as usual."

"Shut up, Kenyetta," Shamara came up along side of him, and started tickling his armpits and his stomach. "You know we ain't never leaving Canarsie."

Kenyetta giggled as he wiggled away from Shamara and put her in a playful headlock.

"Come on y'all, this ain't the time," Fashawn said in accordance with her bossy and strictly business personality.

Shamara and Kenyetta stopped joking around.

"So how's our big bro doing?" Shamara asked seriously.

"Tryin' get this thing poppin' for my true Homies." Kenyetta said as he continued looking over the map. He loved Shamara and Fashawn just like they were his real little sisters. He'd been vibing with the both of them since they were in the seventh grade in 211 Junior High School. Although Kenyetta was two years older than Shamara and Fashawn (he'd gotten left back twice in public school), the three were in the same classes up until he dropped out in the eleventh grade while they were attending Canarsie High school together. They had lost communications when Kenyetta moved to the Bronx, and re-connected recently when they tracked him down with a proposal, asking him to help them get at Tommy Bossett. Somehow they had discovered he had prior dealing with one of Tommy's closest friends, Malik, and because of this fact they wanted Kenyetta to help them reach out and touch Tommy.

Since Kenyetta was living in Canarsie when Tommy killed Shamara's mom and dad, and knew how that incident had literally destroyed Shamara--it showed in her destructive behavior as she was growing up--he was more than willing to give his two baby girls a helping hand, especially considering the fact he was getting a third of everything they touched. He had left the game a couple years back, but when he was doing the damn thing he had built a vicious reputation for being a die hard hustler, which was the reason Malik was so willing to roll with Kenyetta on this proposition of having a team of hit women down with his organization.

Fashawn said to Kenyetta as she examined the map. "And for your information, we ain't never leaving Canarsie. We were born and raised there, and will probably die there."

"Unlike you," Shamara smiled. "We ain't into selling out, and you know better than to ask us to jump ship on the hood we love." As this topic hurled her into a deep reflection, she agreed that there was no question she and Fashawn loved Canarise. Their parents were raised in Canarsie and they in turn were born and raised in this area of East Brooklyn. Around the time when their parents were growing up in Canarsie it was predominately Italian, and unlike the nearby areas like Brownville, East Flatbush, and East New York, Canarsie was always considered a clean, smooth area of Brooklyn. Shamara and Fashawn loved Canarsie so much that even when they moved out of their parents' homes they chose to remain in Canarsie. Shamara's uncle Earl Reid who was now an Ordain Minister at the Holy Cross Church of the Lord over on Flatlands Avenue and Rockaway Parkaway (the very church where her mom and dad lost their lives in front of), and had raised her after her mom and dad were murdered, was also a die hard Canarsian. He used to often tell Shamara when she was young that Canarsie was a community she should "stay loyal to."

Her uncle Earl stayed trying to force that Church stuff on her, and although she attended church on Sunday since she didn't have much of a choice in the matter (Minister Uncle Earl made it a rule that anybody living under his roof had to attend church on Sunday), Shamara never truly embraced that biblical stuff, primarily because she didn't believe her Uncle was sincere about being a man doing God's work.

Despite the fact uncle Earl was an ex-gang banger, and a man with a very violent temper, who turned his life around by embracing church doctrine, he seemed to be using the church to make money, and get rich off of poor folks that were trying to get to heaven by paying tides to clean up all the dirt they were doing and would continue doing. There were also a number of other reasons she was absolutely not feeling her uncle Earl, but Shamara decided to force her thoughts to focus on the issues at hand.

Fashawn said to Kenyetta, "How accurate is this map?"

"About as accurate as we gonna get. It's a Rand McNally joint, the best on the market. It got street names, house numbers, Government buildings, the whole nine."

Shamara looked at them as thought they were out of their minds. "Come y'all, I know y'all ain't serious."

They looked at Shamara as though they had no idea what the hell she was talking about.

"You know we deal with first things first." Shamara saw they still didn't catch on. "What's up with the rest of the money from the last job? Let's close that out before we go diving into this next job."

Kenyetta smiled as he went to the other side of the room and retrieved the huge brown paper bag. "Clear that map off the table."

Fashawn folded the map and laid it on the near by chair as Kenyetta spilled the bundles of money onto the table.

"Thirty gees." Kenyetta said with delight. "Spit three ways, that's ten gees each. As you know, Malik got his commission fee of five gees." He started stacking bundles. "Each bundle is two gees; everybody gets five bundles."

Shamara was grinning from ear to ear as she stacked her bundles. She enjoyed when Kenyetta engaged in this little ritual of his; he said he did it this way so everybody could collectively take part in the sharing of the proceeds. The symbolism according to him was that it showed supreme and open equality. Shamara looked over and saw Fashawn was nonchalantly scooping up her bundles as if she was bored with this part of the process, and she knew Fashawn actually was because she made it clear that money wasn't what motivated her with this mission.

After everybody took possession of their bundles of money and put them in individual plastic bags, the map was put back on the table and the three started looking at the red marks.

"Now, let's run through this shit again," Fashawn said. "You said this cat Gangsta's main hangout is right here." She pointed.

"Yeah," Kenyetta said, realizing he forgot to give them the bad news.

"Is there any other—"

"Before we get deep into this planning," Kenyetta hated to cut in like that. "I just got some new info on this cat, Gangsta. This dude got an army of young wild heads rollin' with him."

Fashawn looked at him as if to say and . . .

Kenyetta continued. "This ain't no regular street corner crew we dealing with here, and from what I was able to scope out so far, these dudes got their shit tight and together. Now check it; this nigga is sharp, and he got his headquarters hooked up to where it's in the middle of a circle of other spots they control. It's like he got himself surrounded. And I was surprised when I found out they got specialized walkie talkies and shit, and communicate with each other like they on some serious organized shit. This ain't gonna be one of those simple hits where we can walk in and start shooting cats like the last one, and then just slide off the scene and out the back door. The minute a shot in fired I heard his peeps roll in from all directions and will box a mufucka in with the quickness. They did it to some cat out there who tried to get at one of them, and I heard they straight mashed this fool out. Since they about seventy deep, this ain't something we can take lightly. Nor can we rely on your previous facts."

There was a moment of silence while everyone chewed on what Kenyetta and just hit them with.

A moment later, Shamara realized they jumped another hurdle, and figured she might as well get this thing on track and in order. "What you saying is very serious, Kenyetta, but once again, let's deal with first things first. How much are we getting for dropping these four cats? You said Tommy wanted us to give him a play. We told you to use your judgment on this, and obviously we would like to know what the outcome was."

Kenyetta smiled at Shamara. "That's why I love you so much, Shamara. You always keep first things first, especially when it comes to the cheddar." He sighed because he knew they were going to be very upset. "He's giving us two hundred grand. I dropped eighty gees." He saw Shamara screw up her face, while Fashawn simply shrugged her shoulders. "Don't worry, it'll all come back. In this game you gotta know when to give a little, 'cause in the long run we'll get a whole lot back in return."

Fashawn was getting irritated with all this money talk, while putting the mission on the backburner. "Listen, y'all, the money is a secondary issue." She loved Shamara, but her fascination with money could get irritating. "We here to punish this motherfucker, Tommy. Let's not lose focus of why we're out here putting hot ones in a bunch of low life drug dealers, and other fucked up fools who society won't miss anyway." Her hatred for drug dealers was about to flare up, and she had to concentrate not to let it overwhelm her thinking. She lost three cousins to crack cocaine, and saw way too much pain and suffering not to hate this drug business. It was clear there were other motives for Fashawn highly enthusiastic attitude for getting down with this program, but she'd decided that her comrades didn't have to know. "Okay, we get two hundred grand; we loss eighty gees. Even that's enough to get us right when we split it three ways."

"You right," Shamara submitted to the truth. "I'm on this money thing because if one of us get popped, we're gonna need some serious legal representation, and I'm serious when I said we're going to have to start saving up just in case something goes wrong. It's always better to be prepared, than not prepared." She glared at Fashawn to place emphasis to her comment.

Fashawn nodded her head; she liked that. Her homie was definitely learning. "That's my girl. Now that's the way we supposed to be thinking. Proper preparation always prevents poor performance!" She was about to get all riled up and start beating them in the head with a long, drawn out speech on the necessity for being ready for anything, but she tamed her energy with a slight struggle. "Now that that's out of the way, let's get back to this problem we got."

Kenyetta continued, "The way I see it, we need to hit the field again. Get another look at this thing before we lock into an approach. Tomorrow, I told Malik I'll give him a definite decision whether or not we'll take this track. He warned me that if we take the up front money, there's no turning back."

"Who said we were planning on turning back?" Shamara said.

"I'm not saying we're gonna turn back, I'm just letting you know that this is what is known in this business as a nonrefundable contract. If we take this tract, touch any money and don't come through, we become the job."

There was a moment of silence.

Kenyetta continued, "Basically our entire plan has to be revised—"

"What's wrong with the plan we already hooked up?" Shamara said seriously.

"It won't work, Shamara," Fashawn said softly as if she was a teacher talking to a confused student. "If they got outposts strategically situated to box in an adversary, they can easily withstand a head-on strike." Fashawn was staring off into nowhere, slowly inching towards a Marine Corps flashback. "They got communication devices; they'll neutralize us the second a shot is fired. This type of hit is new territory for you, but trust me, Kenyetta's right, we gotta hit the field again." She started gathering her belongings, scooping up her black hoodie as she looked at her watch. "We can take a look at the area again, and be out of here by one o'clock. Let's get it movin'."

Shamara followed their lead, "And for the record, you can let your man, Malik, know we taking this hit."

Fashawn gave her an impatient look, and merely shook her head as they got ready to hit the road.

As the three prepared to exit the house, Shamara felt a consuming and terrifying vibe growing in the pit of her stomach. She didn't like the way this felt. By the tone of Kenyetta and Fashawn's evaluation of the situation, she knew this run was not going to be as easy as she was hoping it would be. For the first time since agreeing to do this particular hit, she suddenly started to truly grasp the magnitude of the situation they were getting themselves into, and it clearly indicated they all could be killed if they slipped up in the slightest way. She didn't want to acknowledge it, but that little voice in the back of her head was telling her that one of them was about to die. After years of mastering the art of selective amnesia, she was able to ignore this screaming voice and premonition without even realizing she was doing it.

CHAPTER # 4

Kenyetta eased the Mustang down the late night streets of Jersey City while Fashawn was in the passenger seat and Shamara was in the back. This was the second night they were scanning Gangsta's Hood and still couldn't find a hole in his armor big enough for them to squeeze through.

Kenyetta pulled the car to a stop at the red light and said, "I think we bit off more than we can chew." He cut his eyes at the rearview mirror and saw Shamara scanning the streets. He felt like messing with her head. "We shouldn't have taken that up front money. I told y'all we should've locked into a strategy before we decided—"

"We gonna find a fuckin' way around this shit!" Shamara said defensively, since she was the one who insisted they take the money before constructing a plan; she hated to be wrong, and especially hated it when Kenyetta threw it in her face when it was obvious she fucked up. "There's no way you can tell me these dudes are untouchable—"

"Not now y'all, please!" Fashawn said at a normal voice level, but with clear frustration. "We're not going to start bickering among yourselves and become our own worse enemy." She paused for a moment and then continued. "We got that money, and now we gotta keep looking for a way to pull this shit off." She wanted to tell them the truth that there was no way they were going to run up on Gangsta, kill him and his closest homies, and get away without also being killed. She'd looked at this thing from every conceivable angle and it was clear as day that his set up was too fortified to penetrate. Of course they could do the hit, but the problem was getting out alive. She sighed and said, "Please, y'all gotta stay focus!"

The light turned green and Kenyetta hit the gas pedal.

Shamara hated the ear shattering silence that consumed their surroundings; she wanted to demand that they turn on the radio to Hot 97, so she could hear her man, Funk Master Flex, but both Fashawn and Kenyetta agreed that they didn't need any distractions of any kind as they checked out Gangsta's Hood. Little did they know, she functioned better when she had music playing. When she was in high school she couldn't even begin to study unless she had some kind of background noise and music playing.

Realizing the music issue was dead, since she was out voted across the board, Shamara shook loose of her urge and focused on the mission at hand. She started rocking back and forth to an imagery Wu-Tang beat in her head as she thought about their predicament. Even she could see that stepping to Gangsta on his turf would transform this run into a suicide mission. She allowed this one particular fact to tumble around in her mind, letting it bounce back and forth with the freedom of an uncaged bird.

A moment later, it hit her. Maybe they shouldn't step to him on his turf, and come up with a whole new approach that had nothing to do with his turf. The eagerness to share her sudden revelation with the others grew with awesome speed and urgency. She said with excitment, "Yo' check this out." She waited until she felt she had their full attention. "Since it's obvious we can't touch this cat on his turf, why don't we touch him somewhere else?"

Fashawn allowed this info to circulate in her mind. Then something clicked inside her third eye. She shook her head because it apparently was a good idea. "You know something, Shamara, you are 100% right."

Kenyetta caught it as well. "Word up, you know something, we all brain locked on stepping to this nigga on some head-on shit, and didn't even think about going about it another way. So what you got in mind Shamara, since you brought it up?"

Shamara thought about it and said, "Maybe we can follow him around during the day for a couple of weeks, see if he got a routine that takes him away fromhis headquarters. If he does, we might have to even do a broad day light hit or something in a public place."

Fashawn smiled; twice she had thought about such a hit, but didn't think the others were ready for it. The cover of night always had a reassuring affect on lawbreakers, especially for a new hitter that still hadn't bust her cherry. Since Shamara was suggesting this approach, it was all game now. "Kenyetta, take us back to the house. We need to talk about this with some maps and shit in front of us."

Kenyetta turned right and navigated the Mustang towards the expressway. About a half hour later, they pulled into their driveway in back of Shamara's new ride, a used sparkling blue Honda Accord. He was glad his baby sis was using sound discretion by not buying a brand new luxury car, or splurging money on other expensive items. The last thing they needed was to start drawing attention to themselves by making people think they had money. In any event, he was planning to buy him a new, sensible ride after they got the rest of the money for this run, and intended to use the ride for none work purposes.

They entered the house and talked for about two hours. When they were finished, they decided to take turns following Gangsta with rental cars. The plan was simple. They would rent two cars a week, follow him around while switching up every now and then so he wouldn't catch on, and when they figured out his pattern, they would then coordinate the hit.

When the first week rolled in and they saw Gangsta didn't do a lot of traveling by car and didn't have any kind of consistent pattern that involved him going to public places outside of his hood, they started becoming extremely nervous. Even Malik was getting impatient, and Tommy was beyond impatient since he knew Gangsta's head was swelling with each day that slid by without there being hell to pay as Tommy had warned him would happen.

During the second week they decided to return to the drawing board. They went back and forth, and argued with each other until Shamara suggested they try to pull off an inside job. "Maybe we can pay somebody to lure his ass into the open, and then step to our business." Shamara had said, but Fashawn and Kenyetta instantly shot this proposal down, insisting that such a course of action would cause them to expose themselves, and by exposing themselves that would put everything in jeopardy. After two days of beefing and bickering, they decided to ask Malik for some assistance. They ended up taking a crack at Shamara's suggestion, which was to find an inside person who could pull Gangsta into the open.

To their surprise, Malik did know a girl who was cool with Gangsta's main girl, and was about as trifling and foul as they came. Nesha was all for convincing Gangsta's girl, Monique to get Gangsta to take her shopping. For a cool five gees Nesha was ready to lay down her acting game, and after only one cell phone call the plan was in play. Tomorrow, Gangsta was taking Monique and Nesha to the Jersey City Mall, and as usual he was bringing along his three shadows.

*   *   *   *

Shamara stood near the entrance of the Mall, trembling even worse than she had done during the Ray Ray hit. She was dressed in a convincing disguise, the dreadlock wig, fake moustache, and bummed out clothing turned her into a homeless Rastafarian man, and she was certain even her uncle Earl wouldn't have recognized her if he walked up on her right this minute. Earlier, she and Fashawn had taped down their tities to conceal their womanhood, and now Shamara noticed this shit was hurting like hell. If it weren't for the crippling fear of getting caught or killed, the pain of having her breast tightly taped down would have driven her insane.

Shamara leaned against the wall and saw Fashawn was about ten yards away sitting near a shoe store along with a real, genuine bum, keeping her eyes open for Gangsta's crew who had parked their ride somewhere around the corner. Twenty minutes ago, they saw Gangsta and the girls (Monique and Nesha) pull up in front of the Mall, got out of the cream colored Mercedes Benz, and approached the store as the Benz pulled off. Shamara and Fashawn were waiting down the street and had immediately got in position.

Shamara turned with flinching speed when a couple stepped through the electric doors. It wasn't them. She sighed and kept telling herself to calm down, but noticed she simply couldn't control her anxiety no matter how much she tried. Then, she wondered could she actually shoot Gangsta? She remembered what Kenyetta kept pounding in her head, time and time again: "In this business it's kill or be killed." She knew if she pulled the gun and didn't use it, Gangsta would wet her ass up so fast she wouldn't know what hit her. That much she was certain of, and she was confident, she wasn't going to let that happen. But despite all that was going on inside of her head, she wondered for the hundredth time, could she really do it!? She sat down on the trash laden pavement in order to really get into her bum role, and to move so as to contain her nervousness.

Fashawn was sitting on the sidewalk with her back to the wall of a shoe store as the bad breath, pissie smelling bum drunkenly talked to her. She pretended to be a deaf mute and made convincing ah sounds and signs with her hands to throw off the bum and any pedestrians. When she saw the cream colored Mercedes ease around the corner, she turned to get Shamara's attention while giving her the signal, and noticed Shamara was looking in the opposite direction. Fashawn stood with her hands in her dirty brown hoodie, and caressed the mini Mac 10 machine gun tucked in the waist of her pants. *This fuckin' bitch is daydreaming again*, she cursed inwardly as she continued staring at Shamara, hoping she looked this way.

Shamara looked up and saw Fashawn's screw face and the Mercedes. Seconds after she realized it was about to go down, the electrical doors slid open. Shamara's heart leaped into her throat when she saw Monique, then Nesha, and coming up the rear was . . . Gangsta. Her entire body felt frozen solid as he walked pass her. *Oh, God, I can't do this*, she suddenly realized. She panicked as she jetted onto her feet and forced her hand to going for the 9mm. Everything seemed to be going in slow motion, and Shamara allowed that image of her mom and dad screaming as the bullets tore at their innocent bodies to guide her.

With a terror-stricken struggle, Shamara moved briskly behind Gangsta. The doubt was proliferating at a remarkable speed. She drew in a deep breath of air and allowed the years of frustration, rage, bitterness, loneliness and the missed opportunity of experiencing the comfort and care of her parents, to galvanize her into action. She pulled the weapon and took aim.

BOOM! BOOM!

Shamara pulled the trigger twice and saw huge red chucks of Gangsta's head fly every which away.

The crowd of pedestrians screamed as they frantically ran for cover.

When Gangsta fell face first to the pavement, Shamara did exactly what Fashawn instructed her to do just as she heard the Uzi gunfire exploding a few feet away from her.

BOOM! BOOM!

Shamara pumped another two bullets into Gangsta's head. She was amazed how these two additional bullets had made it look like most of Gangsta's head had disappeared. Without a second's pause, Shamara ran as instructed.

Moments earlier, seconds after Shamara fired her weapon, Fashawn pulled her Mac 10 machine gun, ran towards the Mercedes, and unleashed several spurts of Mac 10 bullets into one of the soldiers who was rushing out of the car. Before he fell, Fashawn continued spraying bullets inside the open door of the Benz, and saw her bullets were eating at the other two. Blood sprayed, splattered and spewed as the 9mm bullets made sure they didn't give her targets a chance to squeeze off a single shot. The target in the back seat had stupidly ducked down just as a barrage of bullets sliced through the seat and pulverized his body. Even after Fashawn was certain her bullets had done what they were intended to do, she reached the fully automatic weapon inside the Benz and expended the remaining bullets in the clip into their motionless bodies, just in case.

Just when Fashawn had completed emptying her clip, Shamara was running towards her, and they both bolted down the street towards the Yamaha motorcycle about twenty yards away. Since the bike was already running, they leap on the bike and zipped down the street with Fashawn driving, not caring who were able to identify them.

*   *   *   *

Five hours later, Tommy sat in his conference room with Malik sitting across from him. Tommy was dressed in one of his designer suits with Stacey Adams on his feet, since he was getting ready for a meeting in Atlantic City. Tommy was all smiles.

"They dropped all four of them," Malik said as he shook his head, still amazed at how they were able to pull it off in one of the busiest

Shopping Malls in New Jersey. "They did the old Rasta man costume trick."

"Naw! Are you serious!?" Tommy was truly shocked. "I thought they burnt that one out back in the nineties. How about that bitch Nesha? You think that bitch'll really keep her mouth shut?"

"That's hard to say."

"I still say you should've forced them to lay her down along with Gangsta. They had her ass right there for the taking."

"I tried to get them to do it," Malik insisted. "But they were dead ass serious about not hurting her. I even offered to let them keep the money I made them give up for us finding her, but they wouldn't bend. Actually, the broad Shamara was supposed to be giving me a warning, talking about nobody better not touch her."

"Word!?" Tommy was really surprised now.

"She's the sensitize one that's serious about not hurting folks not in the game."

"That bitch Nesha ain't no goddamn angel in this shit." Tommy felt a bout of anger formulating. "She's just as guilty as the person pulling the trigger, and if this bitch start talking she could do some serious damage."

"But the good thing is, Willie don't got any direct connections to you," Malik paused, and then suddenly felt the urge to give an honest analogy of the situation. "But then again, we both know that won't mean much if a serious criminal investigation for multiple murders was to get underway."

Tommy leaned back in his chair. He didn't like loose ends. Even though Malik sent a nobody to talk to Nesha, and there was no obvious way to connection him to Willie, but in this game, he knew tracks should always be covered when murder was involved. Eternal and Remus had indeed taught him well when it came to shit like this. Likewise, there were more than enough horror stories of gunners failing to tie up loose ends and ended up in prison with life bids. It took a few seconds to decide how to handle this. He would send Kahmel to deal with Nesha. Since she was a typical thirsty ass hood rat, this would be a bullshit run.

Tommy rose to his feet, causing Malik to do the same, and said, "Alright, don't worry about Nesha. I'll figure something out later. I spoke to Kahmel, and he's got the rest of their money ready."

Malik was about to leave.

"Check it," Tommy said. "Let them know I got another run. This time it's a breeze. I'll holla at you with the details when I get back from this meeting. Just ask our little killer bitches, do they like to travel, since this is gonna be an out of State run."

"If the money's right, they'll ride with us. Since the money's right, you can count 'em as a guarantee."

"Between you and me," Tommy added. "If they do the right thing with this next run, I wanna meet them personally. Keep that between us, alright?" He saw Malik nod his head. "Give me a holla in the morning. Peace."

"Peace." Malik gave Tommy a clinched fist salute and headed towards the door.

As Malik exited the conference room, Tommy wondered if killing Nesha was the right thing to do. For some odd reason, he was feeling a bad vibe about killing her. By the way Shamara and Fashawn refused to gun her down, while throwing around warnings, he wondered if they got wind he killed Nesha, would they get on some bullshit?

CHAPTER # 5

Shamara was behind the wheel of her Honda Accord cruising down Flatlands Avenue with her radio tuned to Hot 97 as her girl Angie Martinez was dominating the airwaves. It was twenty minutes to seven o'clock and the July sun was still frying everything in sight. Dressed in a terry cloth short set that showcased all of her voluptuous goodies, Shamara was handling the heat-wave like a veteran, since her air conditioner was on full blast, and she was in a reasonably good mood. Besides the fact she was thrilled by the fact she had finally bust her cherry (as Fashawn so eloquent put it), and completed the run with flying colors all across the board, she also discovered it wasn't as emotionally damaging as she thought it would be.

She was on her way to pick up Fashawn so they could do their bi-monthly grocery shopping at the Pathmark near Breukelene Projects, an area known as the Canarsie/East New York borderline. In fact, it was believed that one half of the projects was considered East New York, while the other half was Canarsie.

Shamara was also in a very good mood because she had finally sent her girl, Wanda Biggs, who was doing a twenty five year to life sentence for a murder she clearly didn't commit a few hundred dollars to help her get another Private Investigator. Wanda was trapped in Bedford Hills Prison until the sun burned out, despite the fact she had found a shit load of newly discovered evidence demonstrating that she wasn't the shooter, and yet the courts, the Governor's Office, and all the others in authority knew this woman was innocent, and was straight ignoring this gross miscarriage of justice.

Before she left Bedford Hills, Shamara got real cool with Wanda, and after Wanda showed her all the evidence of her innocence and was

46

still stuck in that place, it had touched something inside of Shamara that was powerful enough to make her promise Wanda she would try to help her one day.   Shamara was apprehensive about making such a promise because she was the type that always kept her word, and at the time she wasn't certain whether she could provide Wanda with the type of help she really needed.   Also, in prison, it was all too common for full-of-shit-folks to sit around flinging all sort of promises at fellow prisoners, promises they never intended to honor, and didn't realize that all those lies usually always caught up with them, one way or another.

There was no doubt it was a small world, and Shamara had saw first hand how one prisoner had made a thousand promises, didn't keep them, and when she returned back to the prison system, she couldn't get any love from anybody since she was dubbed a fake ass fraud with a propensity for selling dreams. In any event, Shamara perceived herself as one of those rare and real prisoners, the ones that never made such promises unless she had full intentions of keeping them, and Wanda saw this was the case as well, which was why it felt so good sending Wanda a seven hundred dollar money order.

As Shamara tapped her foot to the new rap song by Ja-Rule, she realized she and Fashawn had to start planning for the next hit. Fashawn didn't go into details over the phone, but she did say Kenyetta told her it was an out of state job.

Shamara reached for her purse, found the pack of Newport, and sparked up a cigarette. *Damn, I'm now an official killer*, she thought, wondering was this something to be proud of or embarrassed by. *I guess it depends on who your audience is*, she concluded as she savored the Newport smoke filling her lungs.   The sight of Gangsta's head disappearing was still fucking with her head, she noticed, and it was making her feel sick to her stomach whenever she flashed back to that image of the bullets disintegrating his dome piece. She never knew bullets could do that sort of damage to a human body. In fact, she realized all that was actually needed was one shot to the head and four shots was definitely overkill. Fashawn was buggin' when she told her to put two more in him when he hit the ground. But, then again, she realized her home girl Fashawn had an overkill type of personality; she was about as extreme as they came, and it was no wonder she wasn't able to keep a man. It was only natural for her to make sure Gangsta was dead, and there was no better way to do that than to put some extra bullets in his ass.

Shamara also noticed that immediately after that shooting she had a nightmare the same night; she had even woke up abruptly in a cold sweat like she used to do all the time when she was a teenager. Just when she thought she was about to relive the living hell of not being able to sleep because her dreams were driving her crazy, she went to sleep the following night and everything was all right. Even this morning she woke up and realized she didn't have a nightmare.

Shamara blew out a cloud of smoke and realized just thinking about all the hell Tommy put her through, made her drive to kill that son of bitch that much more virulent. Because of Tommy she experienced countless sleepless nights, ended up dropping out of school, messing with drugs, going to prison, developing anti-social behaviors, and even grew to despise her Uncle Earl and the rest of her so-call family members. Because of Tommy she hated damn near everything and everybody. When he killed her mom and dad, he literally killed her; not physically, of course, but in another way that was hard to explain. Her hatred for Tommy was truly of a blinding quality; he was going to pay for what he did, and that was that.

As she stopped at the red light on East 90th Street, the image of the bloody chucks of Gangsta's brains blowing apart returned, and she instantly noticed if it wasn't for the reality that Gangsta was a murderous, drug dealer, she might not have been able to get beyond knowing she had violated the first commandment, "Thou shall not kill." She knew if her Uncle Earl found out about this he would literally hit the Church ceiling, and shit fifteen bricks.

When the light turned green, Shamara hit the gas pedal as the Ja-Rule song ended and Angie was announcing the next song. Shamara made the turn onto East 93rd Street, and saw her old running partner Kadedra Riley sitting on her porch with a glass in her hands, apparently enjoying the heat. Shamara honked the horn, and Kadedra waved excitedly as Shamara kept it moving. A few minutes later, she pulled up in front of Fashawn's house, double parked the car, and hit the horn four rapid times. This was their personal Morse code signal.

As she bobbed her head to the beat of the rap tune by Busta Rhyme, Shamara wondered if something was wrong with her because she genuinely felt nothing as a result of killing Gangsta. *Damn, did this make me a monster?* At the moment she decided to become a hit woman, she just knew after she made her first hit she was going to go crazy with guilt, sorrow, and severe remorse. But, strangely, she didn't feel anything. Her inner voice told her it was because she was only killing bad people who had killed people themselves, were selling drugs to innocent men, women and children, and were getting their just deserts anyway.

Another conscience soothing fact was that she and Fashawn agreed that they would never kill innocent people, or anyone who was not in the game, and they proved this when Malik tried to get them to blaze Nesha. She still couldn't believe this nigga had the nerve to even fix his fuckin' mouth to ask them to kill Nesha, especially when Nesha helped them get to Gangsta's bitch ass. This issue was making her mad as hell! If anything she was an ally.

Shamara sighed as she snuffed out the cigarette in the ashtray, realizing just how foul, grimy, ungrateful, and cutthroat this game was. She just hoped Malik took heed their warning that they better not put a finger on Nesha. Although Malik promised that nothing was going to happen to Nesha, she knew they would have to get Kenyetta to do some snooping around to keep tabs on the situation to make sure they didn't renege on that agreement. The thought of a non drug dealer victim getting murdered on account of her would definitely twist her up emotionally, even if Nesha was grimy herself, since she set-up Gangsta, knowing he was probably going to get murdered.

Suddenly, Shamara saw Fashawn exit her house, lock the door and approached.

As Fashawn got in the car through the passenger side, she said, "I need you to stop at the cleaners first." She slammed the door with bone breaking force. "Oops! Sorry about that." She saw Shamara was pissed off.

"Damn, Fay, why every time you get in my ride, you just gotta slam the door like you ain't got no damn sense?" She pulled the car onto the roadway.

"I guess I still haven't gotten that Marine Corps stuff outta my system. Slamming doors on a military vehicle was safety protocol. You never know when that ass'll hit a sharp turn and that ass a go flying outta that piece."

They both laughed.

Five minutes later, Shamara pulled in front of the cleaners on Farragut Road and Rockaway Parkway, and Fashawn zipped out of the car, got her clothing, and returned within five minutes.

As they cruised down Flatlands, Shamara decided to find out more about the next hit, "So what Kenyetta say about this next job? When is it?"

"Next Saturday. We gonna jump on a plane Friday night, and fly—"

"A plane!? Girl, you know I ain't into no damn flying." Shamara was dead ass serious. "Especially with all this terrorist shit going on. That's like asking for trouble, jumping on a plane—"

"Flying ain't all that bad, Shamara. There ain't been a terrorist attack in this country since 911. Actually, they say flying is probably safer than riding in this car."

"Well, I don't know about all that. Maybe we can drive there or something. We gonna have to talk about this shit some more. So where this hit going down?"

"Cleveland Ohio. The price is the same, and it's a one man hit."

"Who's this guy we supposed to be blazing? Is he a drug dealer or a—"

"Kenyetta said we'll go into all of that next week." Fashawn knew she had to shut Shamara down quickly or she'll be asking questions all evening. "Everything I just told you is all I know."

Shamara felt her anxiety percolate back to life. She knew nothing about Cleveland Ohio, other than the football team the Cleveland Browns. Walking into the unknown was something that always scared her silly, and now she saw she was going to have to fight once again to keep her anticipation from causing stress.

"So how you holding up?" Fashawn asked as she lit up a Newport. "Them nightmares are gone or what?"

"All gone," Shamara smiled. "I think I'm good to go now, girl. And how about you and them military people? Are they still messing with you every two weeks? You still didn't tell me why they still got you coming in twice a month?"

"It's nothing, I told you." Fashawn felt like she was about to hyperventilate. "It's the way the military works when a person gets a certain type of honorable discharge. They like to keep track of their solders and the way they do it is have us come in and talk to us every couple of weeks."

Shamara saw there was no way she was going to get a clearer answer. Ever time she asked Fashawn about these meeting she got very defensive. Shamara was about to push Fashawn to give a detailed answer, but realized it would only make her uncomfortable and agitated, since ever time they talked about this issue she could see the anxiety literally twinkling in Fashawn's eyes and bodily gestures.

Ten minutes later, they pulled into a parking space inside the Pathmark parking lot. They got out the car and was surfing the aisles with shopping carts minutes later.

As Shamara was picking up a box of laundry detergent, she heard someone at the end of the aisle calling her and Fashawn's names. Shamara turned and saw a light skinned, big boned woman approaching; afer a second or two she noticed it was Denise Jones.

"Damn, I knew that y'all." Denise said with a shopping cart full of items, along with a little snotty nose rug rat tucked in the child's seat compartment. The little boy was a spitting image of Denise. "What y'all been up to? I ain't seen y'all in a month of Sunday."

The three talked as they strolled through the supermarket, catching up on so-called new developments, consisting of who got married, who died, who was fucking who, who had this dude's baby, who had a fight with this one, who stole who's man, who was sneaking around fucking this one, who got locked up, who robbed this one, who had AIDS, who looked like they had AIDS, who did this, who did that, and so on and so on, and so on.

By the time they finished shopping and were waiting on the check out line, Denise said, "Hey, listen, I got mad juice at this club over on East New York Avenue and Rockaway Parkway. Girl, they got some fine ass brothers up in there, and they pockets got the mumps too. Y'all need to come hang out with me this Friday."

"I'm with it, girl," Shamara said without hesitation, since after kicking Jalil's ass out of her crib she noticed that little itch was coming back, and needed a way to scratch it without bringing Jalil's ass back into her life. "Come on, Fashawn, don't even go there, 'cause this Friday we ain't doing shit. And you and I both know you and I need us a break." Shamara gave her an expression that said after all this running around shooting up a bunch of drug dealing ass niggas in New Jersey definitely entitled them to treat themselves to at least one night out.

When Fashawn saw Shamara and Denise looking at her with expressions that indicated they weren't taking no for an answer, she gave in and said, "Alright, alright, let's do it. We'll go out and have us a good time, like back in the days."

*   *   *   *

"Why you do some shit like that without talking to me first!?" Tommy shouted as he sat on the side of the huge King size bed dressed in his pajamas.

Ashanta was standing in front of the mirror attached to the expensive dresser; she was a slim, light brown skinned woman with a short Halle Berry hairstyle, and had huge shapely breasts that looked fake, but were the real deal. Underneath her white, see-through silk nightgown, she also possessed a body fit for a super model.

"Two hundred gees ain't no light weight money to be throwing around."

"You don't control me!" Ashanta spat back at Tommy as she put on her lip-gloss. "I work; I bring in a paycheck, and I got the right to invest money in a business project—"

"Not with my money! And not without talking to me!" Tommy was literally seconds from beating the shit out of her, but sensed this might be Ashanta's way of softening him up for one of her crazy sexual episodes; she was in the mirror trying to look pretty and he knew this was a tell tale sign that she was ready to get freaky tonight. But, the thought of her fucking around with his money without talking to him first was destined to get her far more than a serious ass whipping, and she had to know this by now.

"Half this shit is technically mine," Ashanta said as she pranced over to her side of the bed and sat down as she smiled deviously. She was in the mood tonight and knew this topic would touch a major nerve. "Keep fuckin' with me and I'll—"

Tommy reached over and grabbed her by the neck. "Don't play your motherfuckin' self, Ashanta." He was on fire now. "I told you don't go there with me." He shoved her and saw she was still smiling. "That's my word!" Tommy clenched his fists as the rage began to mount. The smile on her face told him she was trying to fuck with his head. He could never understand why when she wanted to have kinky sex she just didn't say so. Why all the head games and conniving tactics? The answer hit him just as the question appeared inside his head. He decided two could play at that game. "How many times we gotta go over this? Just 'cause we married, don't entitle you to shit you don't earn. It'll be differ if you were putting in some real wifey work. You don't spend time with little

Tommy. You can't cook at lick. You won't go to church with me and Tommy and—"

Ashanta sucked her teeth loudly as she felt the blow to her heart.

Tommy looked over and saw she was steaming now. "And most of all, your son wants you and you can't even—"

"I told you I wasn't ready for a kid!" She sat up in bed with attitude. Just like he told her not to talk about messing with his money, she told him not to throw that unfit mother shit in her face. "You forced me to have him and I told you he's your responsibility when he comes, and you were all for it. So don't throw that shit in my fuckin' face when I warned you." Ashanta wanted to kick herself in the ass for allowing him to talk her into having Tommy.

Tommy despised her remarkable ability to be so callous and uncaring when it came to Tommy Jr. "That child needs a mother in his life who's gonna—"

"Listen, Tommy, please let's not start this shit again. You wanted him, you got him, and you're gonna have to be his mom and dad. I got my career—"

"That boy wants to be with you!" Tommy said with deadly venom in his voice. The tone announced that serious violence was imminent. He turned his head and stared into Ashanta's eyes. "And you're gonna spend some time with him!"

Ashanta felt a chill crawl up down her back. The seriousness in Tommy's words caused a vicious alteration of the atmospheric pressure in the room, and she knew it was time to take a few steps back. She wanted to get him riled up, but not to this degree. She sighed loudly. "Alright, I'll take him out this weekend." She laid back down on the bed, realizing he was forcing her to do things she didn't want to do. "I don't need to be here fighting you over this shit." Her anger was about to flare up and she fought it back; making sure it didn't shatter her sexual mood. She started thinking about all the upcoming events in her life.

After a moment of reflecting on future events, Ashanta smiled wickedly because her plan was about to take off anyway. She'd been creeping with this white millionaire cat from West Palm Beach Florida, and she almost had him where she wanted. John Brady was the owner of Amera-Foods, a Food Conglomerate Company, and she had been fucking him for the last year and a half. Despite the years of being with Tommy, John had showered her in more riches than Tommy had done in eight years. He had even purchased her a house down in Florida and a Benz, and was going to let her take part in his business operations. Most of all, he was straight legit through and through. She was tried of living day to day wondering when all this underworld bullshit was going to come crashing down around them and her ass would once again be in the poor house or maybe even the big house. John had recently hinted about marriage, which compelled Ashanta to start trying to make Tommy think she was about to start up a real estate business in Florida in order to justify her constant contact she was going to be having with John at his main office until the marriage was confirmed. Although John had a home in New Jersey (where they did most of their sneaking around), he was planning to spend more time at his home base, and Ashanta promised him that she would be there with him.

Tommy was on fire at the thought of this bitch not wanting to spend any time with Tommy Jr. Every time she did this, it fucked up his mood. He sensed she wanted him to break her off some dick, but her neglecting their son was infuriating him. Tommy was about to slide under the covers until Ashanta grabbed his hand.

Ashanta was itching downtown; plus, she hadn't given him some in about a week, and didn't need to start creating any problems at this particular moment. In any event, she loved rough sex, and since Tommy knew her body like no other man, she reached over and slapped him in the face.

Tommy smiled with an evil grin and said, "So, you fuckin' with my money 'cause you feelin' freaky tonight." He reached over, grabbed her by the neck as she squirmed while swinging her arms, and strategically came in close to prevent her from striking his face. He tactically choked her ever so slightly until he was convinced she was woozy, and then roughly flipped her onto her stomach, ripped her silk gown off, exposing her voluptuous, naked body, and he slid his manhood inside of her womanhood in doggy style position with one stuff plunge as she struggled and fought like a wild beast.

As Tommy pounded inside of her, warding off her hands from scratching his face as she moaned and groaned with squeals of delight, he wondered one again, why did he find these super freaky broads so sexually attractive.

*   *   *   *

Shamara, Fashawn and Denise sat in a booth with drinks in front of them as Biggie Small and Lil Kim were booming through the club speakers, repeatedly talking about "Get money."

Shamara looked up and saw a crew of four fine looking brothers dressed in the latest wares enter the club; they had money written all over them, and by their mannerisms, it was clear they came to this joint looking for dates. She saw Denise's radar was on full alert as she noticed Shamara scoping out the brothers. As if the four brothers had picked up Shamara and Denise's mental transmissions indicating they were very interested in getting to know them on an up-close level, the four brothers approached.

The four brothers introduced themselves, and immediately honing in on who was riding with who. Shamara and Hakiem naturally gravitated to each other, since they just looked like the epitome of a perfect couple, while Fashawn and Rahson hooked up, and Denise and Shawn were hugged up before they knew it. The left over brother, Michael, took it all in stride as he went out onto the dance floor, apparently on the prowl for a date. After some small talk, the whole group entered the VIP section, courtesy of the owner of the club who was a good friend of the four brothers.

Michael returned shortly with a date, a dark skin beautiful woman name Ramonda and the two blended perfectly with the group. They all drank expensive champagne, talked, danced, laughed, drank some more champagne, and by the time the night was coming to an end, they all were ready to be full participants in a one-night stand. Courtesy of the four brothers they decided to rent four rooms at the Marriott Hotel in downtown Brooklyn.

The minute Shamara and Hakiem entered the Hotel room they went straight to business. There wasn't any foreplay or any body massages. It was straight animal lust that took full control of the situation, and their clothing came off with an urgency similar to someone rushing from a fire (or into a sexual fire). Lying on her back, Shamara welcomed Hakiem's manly but gentle embraced as he laid down upon her. She sighed as Hakiem entered her with his condom-covered penis; her juices instantly flowed like the rushing waters of the Niagara upon noticing Hakiem was well equipped downstairs; he was hitting walls inside of her that hadn't been touched in a well.

As he pumped in and out of her, Shamara felt the stress from the previous weeks of adventure started to ease from every crevice of her body with the grace of a humming bird's awaking call. She cocked her legs, about to throw her stuff back at Hakiem, and the minute her legs were high in position, the urgency in Hakiem's pumping action told her tonight was not going to be one of those intercourses she would remember as a memorable sexual moment. Her anticipated fuck fest had officially turned into a dud fest, since Hakeim was a true blue minuteman.

Meanwhile, two rooms down the hall, Fashawn was peeling off her clothing as Rahson laid in bed with his hands behind his head, showing off because he had a huge, fat ten inch dick that was pulsating as it stood at attention. Fashawn was surprised she felt intensely sexually aroused, and the whole thirst for a hard throbbing bone inside of her was rapidly coming back as she took off her clothing. She was also woozy, and hoped the mixture of the alcohol with her medication didn't cause any dangerous side effects. She was forced to take the medication the other day, since she was scheduled for a therapy session; she made it a habit of keeping the medication in her system only during her sessions; just in case Doctor Richards tried to conduct a surprise blood test to see if she was taking the meds. Fashawn was really surprised she hadn't scared Rahson away when he saw the 9mm fell from her purse; she had nonchalantly picked it up and placed it back in her purse.

Once her clothing was off, she slid over towards Rahson. "Put that fuckin' condom on." She demanded, almost in military fashion.

Rahson obeyed and he tried to embrace Fashawn, but she pushed him down onto the bed. *Oh shit, I got me one of those chicks that like it rough*, he thought, as he savored Fashawn's caramel colored, amazingly shapely body.

"Lay down!" Fashawn said, her eyes becoming wide with excitement. She saw Rahson obeyed and she mounted him. She grabbed his condom-covered wood, inserted it inside of her, and began to ride him. Her mind instantly swirled with utter delight. She was a holler by nature, and had come to this hotel with no intentions of holding back. "Ohh! Yes!! Uhmm! Go daddy! Ahh, yeah!" Then, suddenly, she sensed Rahson was about to come, and she almost panicked because she didn't want him to come. She instantly went into combat mode. "You better not come! Hold that nut, man!" She shouted as though she was talking to her platoon. "Stay focused, Rahson! Now let's do this!" She started back riding Rahson, slowly bouncing up and down, and when she felt his dick become rock hard as he whispered, "I can't hold it any longer, Fashawn", her eyes got wide with rage; she almost became mentally unhinged, but realized suddenly she was coming as well. The euphoric sensation of the ejaculation explosively erupted and it instantly comforted her mind in ways that she couldn't describe.

In Unisom, they both unleashed their juices from their bodies, and it was all paradise until Rahson saw Fashawn get up off of him and laid down, staring up at the ceiling, while he reflected back on her extreme aggressiveness. He wondered what would've happened if she hadn't come when she did and he couldn't hold the nut as she violently instructed him to do. He sighed with nervousness, wondering if he could slide out of this situation before she got near her gun. He vowed this was the last time he would pick up strange, beautiful women and have sex with them. Something was terribly wrong with this chick, he told himself, and he prayed to God he made it out of this alive, since he didn't think his dick was going to get hard again.

*   *   *   *

Three days later, Shamara, Fashawn and Kenyetta were at their New Jersey hide out sitting in the living room talking as the TV was playing, but nobody was paying it any attention.

Kenyetta said, "The mark is a business man. They didn't go into all the details, but I did find out that he reneged on a multi-million dollar drug deal. He's some kinda International drug broker, who hooks up big time drug deals between drug producers and drug traffickers and distributors."

Shamara pulled on her Newport, and then said, "You mean to tell me this nigga Tommy is living that large in the game, to where he's got hook ups with big time cats into International shit?"

"I don't know for certain, but it's apparent he's plugged in some how. He might be doing this as a favor for some real big timers, and if he comes through they'll bring him and his organization into their network, or something. I don't know, but I do know this shit is so important, that he offered us a bonus if we do this thing right."

There was a moment of silence as Kenyetta started watching the TV as Shamara and Fashawn stared at him, waiting to hear the rest.

"Come on, Kenyetta!" Fashawn said, extremely irritated. "Why you gotta start this shit with us!" The realization that he was toying with the mission despite the seriousness of such an operation was making her delirious with rage. "We here to take care of business and get the low down on what's going on with this fuckin' mission, and—and you--Stop playing these fucking minds games with this mission!" Her anger was mounting by the seconds, and it forced Shamara and Kenyetta to stare at her gapingly as if she was insane. Their expressions also said "it's not that serious, girl" and "it's only a joke, for Christ sakes!"

Fashawn was almost foaming from the mouth. "You just trying to make us fuckin' beg your black ass like you some kinda motherfuckin—"

"Fashawn!" Shamara said with wide eyes. "What the hell's wrong with you, girl!? You know Kenyetta's only playing with us!? Are you all right!?" Her concern for her best friend was genuine, and what she just saw was scaring the shit out of her.

Fashawn bowed her head; she was about to cry, but swallowed it up. "I'm sorry y'all, I—I—I'm just a little stressed out today." She hated these damn side effects (severe mood swings) caused by the medication when she stopped using it abruptly and then would resume using it when she had to go to therapy. "Please, go ahead, don't mind me, I'll be all right."

Shamara and Kenyetta looked at each other as if they were unsure whether or not they should continue.

Kenyetta said, "He offered us a fifty thousand dollar bonus."

"Yeah!" Shamara said cheerfully. "That means we can add at least another fifteen gees each to our numbers."

Fashawn said, "There's one other thing you forgot to mention. So is this a long range target or are we going walk up on this cat?"

Kenyetta smiled, "It's a long range run. We got professional rifles with high tech scopes ready and waiting for y'all." He saw them both nodded their heads agreeingly. "And if everything works out, we'll finally get what we been gunning for."

Shamara smiled, "So he's ready to meet us?"

"That's right!"

Fashawn smiled as well, "Now that's the best news I heard all night." She couldn't wait to shoot this motherfucker.

Shamara leaned back on the sofa already imagining herself pushing Tommy's wig back. It felt good because she knew beyond all doubt that she wouldn't have that same problem she had with the other targets. She was a 100% sure that she could empty an entire clip in his head, and enjoy each and every bullet of it.

CHAPTER # 6

Shamara sat in the window seat on the Pam Am flight 740 to Cleveland International Airport. Fashawn sat next to her reading a Wall Street Journal newspaper she picked up at a Newsstand just before boarding the plane. It was seven o'clock in the evening, and the hot August sun looked as if it had no intentions of setting any time soon. Shamara said to herself for the tenth time, *how I let Fashawn and Kenyetta talk me into getting on this plane is beyond me.* The plane was seconds from take off and her stomach was bubbling with anxiety. She wondered about her symptoms. *What is it called, seasickness or airsickness?* Well, whatever it was called there was no doubt she had it, and she hated it.

"All passengers," A woman's sensuous voice said over the plane's speaker system. "Please fasten you seatbelts. We are moments from take off."

Shamara started nervously rocking in her seat and saw Fashawn crack a smile. She wanted to blow up on her because it was obvious she was enjoying seeing her nervous like this.

"Chill, Shamara," Fashawn said. "Watch, you'll see, flying is nothing."

Suddenly, the plane jerked into motion and Shamara nearly screamed in terror. She was about to hyperventilate, and had to force herself to calm down so as not to make a scene. Shamara saw Fashawn was now biting her lip, apparently trying to avoid laughing at her. She huffed and puffed, "Oh, so you think this shit is funny, huh?" She tried to force her eyes to their normal size, but they seemed glued into their wide position.

A few minutes later, the airplane was airborne. Shamara was sighing in relief. She figured if the plane was still in one piece after all the violent turbulence that made the plane jerked and shimmied moments ago, then everything was going to be all right. She looked out the window at the land below and was fascinated at the way it looked almost like a map.

About five minutes into the flight, Shamara and Fashawn ordered a couple of drinks and decided to talk about the job some more.

Fashawn pulled out the pictures of their target; the object of this activity was to engrave his face into their minds. She knew from military experience that repetition of virtually anything would produce good results. "What you think this chump is? What's his nationality?"

Shamara scanned the pictures spread out on Fashawn's lap and said, "He's Cuban or Columbian."

"Naw," Fashawn shook her head. "He looks Argentinean."

"With a name like Gomez?" Shamara shot back doubtfully. She then thought about the issue as she scrutinized his facial features, and realized either one of them could be right. "Actually, he could be from any one of them South American countries." Then she realized Antonio Gomez's nationality really didn't matter anyway and said, "Why should we care what this dude is?"

"I'm just making small talk, Shamara, and making sure we keep this chump on our minds. We gotta know this chump like we know ourselves until we finish this mission."

"Believe me," Shamara added as she sipped on her drink. "I've been following your instructions. I been looking at them damn pictures four or five times a day. I even had a dream about this mufucka." Shamara looked out the window again. A moment later, she turned to Fashawn and said, "So, you gonna let me be the lead shooter or what?"

Fashawn thought about the question. She had suggested Shamara not take that position, but left the question open until a later time. She had her doubts because Shamara wasn't anywhere near an expert sharpshooter. There was no question she could shoot and she was far from a slouch; her aim was half ass decent, but this wasn't a game. If they missed this mark, there could be some serious consequences, and Malik had made that very clear. She sighed because she knew from experience that the only true way to learn something was to give the student a chance in the field. She'd learned all sorts of military maneuvers this way, and learned them well because she had a commanding officer that gave her a shot, and took mad chances with her. Fuck it, she would give Shamara that shot. "You know what, Shamara. I think you should be the lead shooter. I know you can handle it. But just make sure you know if you blow it, our heads could end up on the chopping block."

Shamara smiled, but instantly felt a wave of mixed emotions, caused by Fashawn's last remark. This was a very big responsibility, and there was no question if they fucked up their asses would become the job. Despite her doubts, she was ready to take the lead. "Thanks for believing in me, Fay, I won't let us down."

About six hours later, Shamara and Fashawn were exiting the Cleveland Airport. Another twenty minutes later they were inside a blue rental car heading towards the area where the hit was to occur. An hour later, they arrived at the location and saw the building where Gomez would exit tomorrow afternoon looked exactly as it did in the photos; the only difference was pictures were taken during the day while it was currently nighttime. The building where they would be positioned was just as accurate. They drove around the block, and examined the buildings again. They then proceeded to a dilapidated area on the other side of town, retrieved their sharpshooters rifles from an abandoned building and went to their hotel room about two miles away. They ate, got familiar with their weapons, watched TV, relaxed, talked about the run again, and went to bed early.

*   *   *   *

The following day, Shamara sat on the hard gravel on top of the roof, peering through the high precision scope on a 30.06 rifle. The barrel of the silencer-laden weapon sat on top of the railing, and Shamara was watching the people entering and exiting the hotel across the street. Fashawn sat a few yards away from her; she was similarly positioned with an identical rifle and was apparently looking at the same location.

They both were dressed in dark, loose fitting clothing. Sitting next to them both were the miniature suitcases in which the rifles were stored along with a black nap sack that contained extra bullets, and their 9mms just in case something didn't go according to plan and they had to result to "close range combat" as Fashawn had so eloquently put it.

Shamara sighed as the nervousness surged through her body. The uneasiness made clear it had no intention of giving her a break, since it had been present from the moment they exited the hotel room. In other words, her anxiety flared up and stayed at full flow ever since. Shamara looked at her watch. It was seven minutes to five o'clock. It was almost time. She'd been in this aiming position for the pass fifteen minutes, and her back and arms were screaming with agony from sitting in this highly uncomfortable position so long.

She wondered was it a good idea for them to sat in this awkward position for such a long period of time and be expected to fire a rifle with perfect precision. It didn't seem like it was wise practice to her, but who was she to argue with a woman that won military awards for sharpshooting. Then, she realized Fashawn was used to this stuff and apparently didn't realize that she didn't have nowhere near the years of practice that she had. Some times she wanted to ring Fashawn's neck when she started bugging out with all this perfectionist, super solider bullshit, and expected her to be on the same level of competency as she was, even when she knew all this stuff was foreign to her.

Shamara couldn't take it anymore; the pain was simply too unbearable. She pulled away from the scope and moved her neck while shrugging her arms in order to get the blood circulating again. From the corner of her eyes she saw Fashawn give her the mad screw face as if to say, what the fuck are you doing!? Shamara sucked her teeth and peered through the scope again.

Shamara felt a flash of terror when she saw the Limousine had pulled up. It was Gomez's Limo she instantly realized and now saw why Fashawn was on it the way she was; she was correct when she said once they got on deck to start the show, they had to stay absolutely focused; so focused that they couldn't even blink or move to scratch their noses. She had pulled away for a mere few seconds and the limo had popped up just that quick. "One blink and the mission could be ruined." She remembered Fashawn had said.

As Shamara watched the limo driver get out of the stretched limo and moved to the passenger side of the vehicle, she got up and into her shooting stance. Kneeling on one knee with her elbows comfortably propped on the ledge of the roof, she saw Fashawn was already in the standard shooting stance. Shamara saw the driver leaned up against the Limo and lit up a cigarette. *Any second now*, she heard the inner voice in her head say, *any second now. Just be easy girl; just be real easy.* Shamara placed the driver's head in the center of the target sights, making sure her hand was steady. *Oh shit!* Her hands were trembling like crazy, she noticed, and it was obvious this type of trembling would interfere

67

with her pulling off a perfect shot. She pulled in several rapid, deep breaths of air, hoping the trembling would go away. She steadied her aim and saw it was a little better.

No sooner than she confirmed her target sights Gomez appeared. He was heading towards the limo and was accompanied by several bodyguards. An explosion of anxiety gripped her mind. That familiar voice told her she couldn't do this, but she struggled to ignore this pessimistic inner voice. She drew in a deep lung full of air, steadied her aim, and the target sights landed smack dead on the center of his chest. She still didn't agree with Fashawn's instructions that she aim for Gomez's heart, since she had a thing for headshots, which seemed far more lethal. Although Fashawn said it was always safer to aim for a large target when shooting from a distance, that analogy still didn't make sense to Shamara because they were using high precision scopes that made it real easy to hit their target.

As planned, the minute Gomez was about several feet from the Limo as the Limo driver opened the door, Shamara was about to pull the trigger, but stopped when one of the bodyguards stepped in the way. Shamara struggled not to panic as Gomez eased towards the Limo and the bodyguard continued blocking her shot. Suddenly, the bodyguard zipped out of her path, she positioned her target sights and pulled the trigger. Almost at the same time she heard the muffled sound coming from the barrel, she saw Gomez jerked, but she instantly noticed she had hit him in the shoulder; a non-lethal shot. Immediately on the heels of this jerking motion, as she frantically tried to reposition the rilfe for another shot, Shamara saw a huge red cloud explode from the back of his head and knew Fashawn had saved the day.

As Shamara frantically snatched up her belongings and saw Fashawn was already in motion, she felt totally inadequate since she apparently blew this easy shot. Her feelings were hurt, and her face showed it as she ran in Fashawn's tracks. As they raced through the stairwell door, and then down the stairs, Shamara couldn't understand why her shot was so far off its mark.

Moments later, when Shamara and Fashawn reached the ground floor, they crashed through the stairwell door, and ran face first into a janitor, who was mopping the floor.

Shamara almost knocked the man down, and grabbed at him as he stumbled into the wall, "Oh, I'm so sorry Mister. Please excuse me—"

"Watch where the fuck you going—" The Latino man said with serious broken English, while noticing he never saw these women before. They apparently were in an unusual hurry, and they were carrying suitcases. "Where you coming from!? I don't remember—" He looked at them and then at the entrance leading outside to where all the commotion had suddenly erupted moments ago. Earlier, he saw a man had been shot while coming out of the Hotel across the street, and he heard several observers said a sniper did it from a nearby rooftop. It didn't take long to put the pieces together, and the man started screaming as he ran towards the entrance. "Help! Help! . . .

Shamara saw her life flash before her eyes in that instance, and it wasn't hard to tell that she and Fashawn were in one hell of a fucked up situation. Their whole world was about to crumble down upon them if they didn't do something very quickly.

*   *   *   *

About four hours later, Tommy was in his living room playing Play-Station with his son, when Kahmel and Malik entered. Tommy looked up and sighed with clear irritation.

"What the hell is this!?" Tommy said as he continued toying with the joystick. "Can I get a minute with my kid around this place!?"

69

Malik and Kahmel were about to leave.

"Hold up!" Tommy was seriously into the game because he was finally about to beat his son. He was working the joystick with frantic energy. "After this game, I'll be with you. Just hold tight." He said without taking his eyes off the screen. "I . . . almost . . . got . . ." He was smiling now because he was almost there. "I almost got—"

Tommy Jr. quickly snuffed out his dad's play-figure with four swift kicks and laughed explosively. "I got you! Game over again! You can't beat me, daddy!"

"You know what," Tommy sighed defeatedly as he sat the joystick down. "I think you're right. I can't beat you at this crazy game." He tickled his son playfully, kissed him on the forehead and said, "But I can beat you in a whole lot of other stuff, bet that." He snatched his son up into a loving bear hug. His son giggled joyfully in response. He put Tommy Jr. down and headed towards Malik and Kahmel.

Tommy gave them the look of death, and said as he walked pass them, "This better be good." They were about to say something but he held up a hand stopping them.

Moments later the three entered the huge conference room on the other side of Tommy's mansion. With his golden gun tucked in the back waist of his pants, Tommy took a seat, and waved to the others to do the same. Tommy nodded at Malik for him to begin.

"I'm sorry for barraging in like this." Malik hated to be the bearer of bad news and didn't know where to begin. "But, I think this is something you would consider serious enough to—"

"Get to the fuckin' point, will you," Tommy was hoping this wasn't as bad as Malik was making it out to be.

"I just got word our hitters in Cleveland ran into some serious difficulties," Malik paused.

70

Tommy sighed animatedly. He saw his entry into the Columbian network had instantly gone down the drain. He knew he should've sent Kahmel and Caddy to handle this shit. *Damn it!* He decided he had to start following his first instincts.

Malik continued. "Our hitters completed the hit. Gomez is out of the picture."

Tommy sighed as he felt an instant wave of relief. He knew he had made the right decision when he chose the broads over Kahmel and his team.

Malik continued, "What happened is, as they were leaving the building where the shooting took place, they ran into some guy who thought they were the snipers and they ended up killing him. This is where it gets a little foggy and I'm unable to figure out what actually happened. From what I can tell, after they shot this guy, they fled the building, but a few people saw them. Now, they're stuck out there, since I hear the police got all the airports, major roads, tollbooths, and highways locked down. The police and Gomez's people are searching that area for two young black women. This is where we come in. Basically, Kenyetta wants you to pull some strings. He's suggesting that we give him a hand sneaking them out of there; maybe in a truck or something—"

Tommy started laughing. His laughter went on so long it caused Kahmel and then Malik to start laughing along with him. Tommy forced his laughter to a controllable level and said, "You tell Kenyetta, that if we step in it's gonna cost. If they give up the bonus money, then they got a deal." He looked over at Kahmel and saw he displayed no emotions. Then, it suddenly hit him. This was another opportunity. "Actually, this is a good thing when you really look at it; if they get through this on their own, it'll show and prove just how thorough they are. Look at it as a trial

71

by ordeal. If they get pass this on their own, I'll sign them up as top notch family." He laughed and Kahmel laughed along with him, because they both knew that wasn't going to happen.

Malik stared at Tommy, thinking hard about what he was about to say. After a moment, and after realizing that he had to take a stand since he knew he was in the right, he said, "No disrespect, but they supposed to be a part of our team. Now, what I'm about to say, you can fly off the handle if you want, but you know I keep it as real as real can get, and I ride with you no matter what the situation because we go back to the days when we was cutting rap songs at Dezoe's studio in his momma's basement, and even then we always kept it funky."

Malik let that ferment for a moment, and then continued. "We vowed when we got in this shit that once a team player is on the team, we would never abandon him as long as he's for the team, and that we would give him our full support. Straight like this, after laying down the number of bodies that they laid down, and at those reduced hit prices, those chicks are down with this team, and I say we should hold them down." Malik put special emphasis on his next remark. "Free of charge, and without all the head games."

There was a long moment of brutal silence.

Tommy felt deeply offended and definitely didn't like Malik's tone. He reflected back on the last time he had to set some examples within the ranks of his closest personnel and realized it had been quite a while since utilizing that kind of discipline, and by the looks of things, it was long over due for a nice little refresher course. Suddenly, another trust hindering reflection rekindled inside of his gut; the root was his suspicion dealing with Malik and Ashanta's creeping. Although there was no hard evidence to support this suspicion, his internal hostility always came to life at moments like this. In that moment, Tommy allowed his emotions to guide him and he did what he had to do.

CHAPTER # 7

Shamara sat looking at the evening news while Fashawn was doing push-ups, jumping jacks, and other military oriented exercises. They were inside a second floor room of an old beat down, super slummed out hotel in the ghetto part of Cleveland. Two days had gone by since they last heard from Kenyetta, and they were on the verge of giving up hope that an effort would be made to get them out of this city.

After they narrowly escaped the situation with the Latino janitor, they immediately called Kenyetta, and he started working on getting them out of here. A few hours later, he called them back, informing them that he brought the matter to Malik's attention and that he was working on it. That was the last they heard from him, even though they had been blowing up his cell phone daily.

Shamara's mind was all over the place, imaging every bad thing that could have gone wrong. The first disaster that came to mind was that they had killed Kenyetta, because the hit didn't go down as perfect as it should have. The mere fact that the police and Gomez's people knew it was two black women that did the shooting was enough to say that this hit was a failure. Not a complete failure, but a failure nonetheless.

The good thing she noticed was that they stopped talking about the shooting on the news programs. The first night after the shooting they were talking about the incident like crazy. Despite all the turmoil, Shamara realized she was truly grateful that the police didn't have a positive description of them. All they knew was that two women were seen fleeing the scene of shooting dressed in dark clothing. Shamara was also thankful she had someone like Fashawn on her side because Fashawn had several back up plans already in place, and didn't even tell her she had them all planned out. She had brought along an extra change of clothing, and when they reached an alleyway, they quickly changed. She also saw Fashawn had even had this Hotel scoped out beforehand. Not to mention Fashawn didn't hesitate to gun down the Latino man that blew up the spot and caused all this when he flipped out.

When the evening news went off, Shamara decided it was time they do something. She was never the type to sit around waiting for other people to do things for her, and realized there was no way she was going start getting all enmeshed in a welfare mentality. Shamara went over and sat on the chair a few feet from where Fashawn was exercising. "Yo' listen, Fashawn, we need to talk." She saw Fashawn stopped exercising.

Breathing hard Fashawn said, "What's up?"

"We need to get the fuck out of here. Something's wrong. I say we need to start looking for a way to get the fuck back to New York on our own."

"Kenyetta said he's working on it. You and I both know he would never turn his back on us."

Shamara didn't want to burst her bubble, but she had to say it. "How we know they ain't do something to Kenyetta? Name one time he ever ignored our calls this long?"

Fashawn stopped dead in her mental tracks. For the first time it hit her. She didn't know why she had refused to acknowledge this possibility before, but what Shamara had just said was indeed a strong possibility. "Let's not start jumping to conclusions." She refused to believe this mission had gotten that bad. "He's probable working overtime trying to get shit right." She stopped in her mental tracks again because it was obvious what Shamara was saying made a whole lot of sense. Based on the excessively long delay in Kenyetta's response, it was obvious something was wrong.

Shamara saw Fashawn's disturbed facial expression, and tried to calm her friend's nerves. "I'm not trying to upset you, Fay, but we gotta start taking matters into our own hands if we gonna make it out of here in one piece, and without going to jail. We got about a week's worth of money left, and after that we gonna be assed out. What're we gonna do once our money run out?"

Fashawn didn't have to answer that question because it was obvious what they would have to do.

"And what about our jobs? You can bet we'll be fired if we stay out here any longer. You and James are cool, but he ain't that cool to let you disappear for a whole week and keep you on the payroll, and you know it."

"Okay, okay, you right." Fashawn had to find herself a seat. She sat on the arm of the moth-eaten sofa. "We gotta make a move." She went into a deep trance thinking, *what would a commanding officer stuck behind enemy lines do in a situation like this*, she asked herself over and over again. Dissecting each internal answer with five star General precision as they flowed from the question, Fashawn noticed none of the possible approaches were making any sense.

Shamara was thinking of a way out of Cleveland as well, and knew it was always good to start with the simplest approaches, since most of the time the solution to difficult problems were usually sitting right there under your nose. After a moment, it hit her, and she blurted it out, "Why don't we just get in the rental car we got and drive our asses out of here? Maybe one of us can dress up like a man. That should be enough to throw them off."

"Naw, that's too risky," Fashawn blurted out, since this was how she always reacted to Shamara's suggestions, even when they made

76

sense. Seconds later, she back tracked a little and had to admit this one did make some sense.

"Why is this too risky?" Shamara knew the best way to handle Fashawn with issues like this was to force her to explain her position. "Don't nobody know our names, they didn't say anyone could positively ID us. When you rented the car I didn't go inside with you; they only saw you, and if they thought the car was involved in that drama, they would've gave you hints when you called them the other day to get an extension of time. I'm telling you, girl, we can get in that ride, drive to New York, and drop the car off at one of the company's nearby stores. Eco-car got stores at damn near every airport in the country, and you know they got one in Kennedy and LaGuardia."

Fashawn sighed because she didn't know why they didn't think of this earlier. It was obvious they didn't need Kenyetta, Malik or anybody to get them out of this. "Shamara, you know what? Let's pack our shit and get the fuck outta this place." She rushed over to her bags and started packing as Shamara did the same. "Since I'm doing the driving, I'll play the man role."

*   *   *   *

"This is a test to see if they're sharp enough to handle pressure," Malik said as he sat at the elegant restaurant table with a crystal wine glass in front of him, while dressed in a sleek business suit. "I know it sounds crazy, and it's foul for us to squeeze you like this, but really look at the logic in it."

Kenyetta sipped on his red wine. He was dressed casually and his bodily gestures were indicating he wasn't trying to hear anything Malik was saying. "This shit is some straight bullshit and you know it, Malik. Shamara and Fashawn are as real as they come, and there's no need to test their—"

"That's what you say," Malik tapped his fingers on the tabletop. "Me and you may be cool, and we go way back. But, let's keep it real, Kenyetta. Tommy don't know you or them broads from a fuckin' hole in the wall. Why should he trust y'all? Just 'cause you did a few hits and he paid you for your services? You told me y'all wouldn't mind rolling with us, and Tommy felt that might be a good idea. Now that they went out there and got trapped off, this implies sloppy work. If they serious about getting down, then they'll wiggle out of this situation they got themselves into."

There was a moment of silence.

Kenyetta sighed loudly. He wanted to remind him that he was sounding like a broken record, since he'd said this several times already.

Malik continued, "We know y'all bust your guns and everything, but Tommy's fuckin' with millionaires and know mad people in all sorts of businesses and places you couldn't begin to imagine. And you know he's got a couple of major beefs. There's mad hatin' mufuckas all over the place. He's not gonna surround himself with anybody unless he knows for sure they are sharp on their toes, can respond, think and maneuver under serious pressure."

"I'm just not feelin' this dude talking about he's gonna smoke me if I give them a hand," Kenyetta was totally fucked up when he got word that he was not to provide Shamara and Fashawn any assistance and to not even answer his cell phone when they called. "These women are like my little sisters, man." Kenyetta was boiling with anger because this shit was not only foul, but it was utterly ridiculous. Not to mention, it was down right dangerous. "I don't understand this shit. Since they completed this hit, what's wrong with helping them get back to New York, even if they ran into an unforeseeable problem? In this business, there's always gonna be unforeseeable things popping up. There's no such thing as a perfect track record of hits, and you know that. At some point, everybody runs into a few bad ones, even the best of the best."

"Have you been listening to anything I just said to you?" Malik was getting very impatient now. "I see what time it is. You just wanna see and hear what the fuck you wanna see and hear and everything else is not registering. It is what it is, and that's the way it is. We'll close this topic on this note. If they make it back in one piece they in for life."

"So what you saying? Tommy's gonna hire them?"

"He's not only going to hire them on a full time basis if they're interested, of course, but he wants them down with his closest bodyguard team. He knows the benefits of having a team of killer bitches around him. But, he wants to know if he's fucking with the real deal all across the board. They get through this without our assistance, then they the real deal as far as we concerned."

Kenyetta constrained the smile that was struggling to reveal itself. This was turning out to be a blessing in disguise. They were hoping to get close to Tommy, so that they could do their thing, but they didn't anticipate him making them a part of his closest bodyguard team. Being that close to Tommy there was no question they could pull off a perfect hit on him, and get away unscathed.

As the food arrived and he and Malik dug into their meal, Kenyetta felt a ping of anxiety erupt in his stomach when he thought about Shamara and Fashawn's situation. His anxiety grew ten folds, because he had made up his mind. The next time they reached out to him, he was giving them a hand. Whatever happened if and when Tommy and his team found out would be something he would just have to deal with.

CHAPTER # 8

Shamara sat in the passenger seat with her head leaned back on the headrest. Fashawn was behind the wheel maintaining a fifty five miles per hour speed limit as the rental car's radio was on a station that played R & B. Freddy Jackson was talking about "come on and rock me" for old time sakes and Shamara was surprised that folks in Cleveland were up on all the banging old songs. It was dark outside and they had been driving for about five straight hours. There were no words to describe how she felt when they made it out of Cleveland without any problems. Every time they came upon a tollbooth Shamara felt her anxiety about to burst through the seams of her mind.

Shamara looked at Fashawn and couldn't help feeling the urge to crack up laughing; she had on a fake moustache with her hair tied back into a knot with a black baseball cap on her head, and reminded Shamara of a busted ass, washed up El Debouage on his way home from an unpleasant fishing trip. To make herself look even manlier, Fashawn had put smudges of mascara under her eyes to make it appear as if she was suffering from chronic stress or a sleep disorder. That particular trick didn't make a lick of sense to Shamara, but who was she to judge.

Five minutes later, Shamara took a closer look at Fashawn's eyes and noticed they were looking real sleepy. Suddenly, she caught Fashawn's eyes slowly closing and springing back open. *Oh, no she didn't,* Shamara thought excitedly, and then shouted. "Hey! Fashawn!"

Fashawn snapped at attention as if she was caught stealing something.

"That's it, pull this car over. I'm driving for the next few hours while you sleep—"

"Naw, what you talking about! I'm not—"

"Fuck that! I ain't tryin' to hear it. I'll be damn if you gonna kill me up this mufucka, 'cause you tryin' to sleep and drive at the same time. Now pull this damn car over and let me drive."

Fashawn sighed and did as she was told since it was obvious she was tired ass hell. Within minutes the car was pulled over onto the breakdown lane, they swooped places and Shamara had the car rolling at a speed within the limit while Fashawn was snoring the moment her head touched the headrest.

Ten minutes into the drive, Shamara decided to hit Kenyetta's cell phone again. They hadn't tried it in hours, and figured what the hell. She punched in the number and put the phone to her ear as it rang. After four rings she was about to hang up until she heard his voice on the other end.

"What's the deal?" Kenyetta said from the other end of the line.

"Kenyetta!?" Shamara screamed and woke Fashawn up. "Man, where the hell you been? We've been hitting your ass up on this phone like crazy."

"Yeah, I know, I was—"

"You know!?" Shamara was about to go in real hard on him. "And you didn't answer our calls!?"

"Hear me out, Shamara, please. This bitch ass nigga Tommy told me not to interfere. This dude is on some real bullshit. He's trying to turn this shit into a test to see if y'all can handle pressure on y'all own—"

"What!?" Shamara saw Fashawn's eyes were wide with nosiness and she keep asking, what he said. "We damn near got busted and this nigga's playing fuckin' games?"

"Before you start spazzing out, it ain't all that bad. He said if y'all come through this drama with flying colors, we in for life. He'll put y'all down with his closest bodyguard squad."

"You serious!?" Shamara smiled with wide-eyed delight as Fashawn started reaching for the phone and she nudged her away with her elbow.

"And he told me if I say anything to y'all he would kill me, so you didn't talk to me, a'right."

"Yeah, you know it, this conversation never took place."

"So where y'all at? What you need me to do?"

"We on the highway eighty in Pennsylvania near a place called Tylersville. From the way it's going, we'll be in New Jersey before sunrise. Meet us at the Jersey crib. We'll kick it then. You wanna talk to Fashawn?"

"Yeah, put her on," Kenyetta said, realizing he would have to repeat everything he just told Shamara because Fashawn always wanted to hear it from the horse's mouth.

As Shamara handed Fashawn the phone and they talked, her mind went into a thought provoking daze. *So, Tommy is a real head gamer, huh?* She wanted to start her ritualistic cursing and blaming him for being the source of all her pain, misery and suffering, but realized he would finally get his justice real soon. As a member of his closest bodyguard team they could smoke this chump with ease. *Yes! This shit is going down*, she cheered inwardly.

Five hours later, Shamara, Fashawn and Kenyetta sat at the kitchen table in their Newark hide out, discussing their next move. The sun had just risen and already it was 99 degrees with a humidity factor of 90%. They kept this meeting short and sweet. They decided to meet with Malik as soon ass possible—Kenyetta assured them it would be tonight—and get home so they could catch up on some sleep. After calling into work, and burning out another sick day (since it was Tuesday they had only missed one day), they slept the rest of the morning and half of the afternoon.

By eight o'clock that evening, Shamara, Fashawn and Kenyetta sat in an elegant restaurant in Elizabeth New Jersey, waiting for Malik. The three weren't dressed for the occasion, since Malik didn't warn them that the restaurant was for executives. Shamara and Fashawn had on casual slack sets, while Kenyetta was totally thugged out with baggy pants, Timberland Construction boots, and the whole urban attire bit. When they arrived at the restaurant they didn't expect to get in, but the door waitress apparently were expecting them and had a table already set up.

When Malik entered Shamara didn't have to be told it was Malik, since he made a grand entrance, was wearing a black executive suit with gator skin shoes, walked like he was all that and some more, and had hood resonating from him. Although there were other black men in this restaurant wearing expensive suits, and Malik could have been connected to anyone of these other waiting customers, Shamara had a knack for spotting folks that had their roots in the hood, and had clawed their way out of the ghetto. It was like she had hood radar and she saw Malik had that look the moment she laid eyes on him.

Kenyetta introduced the three and Malik went straight to business, which was a good thing as far as Shamara was concerned. The night's schedule would go as follow, according to Malik. After they ate a meal, they would drive out to Tommy's mansion in Roselle, a suburban community in East New Jersey and meet Tommy Bossett. The plan was painfully simple and it irritated Shamara by the way Malik tried to turn it into an extraordinary event.

As they ate a French style chicken dinner that had a name no one could pronounce, Malik congratulated them on the excellent jobs they had done and tried to pry into their personal affairs; Shamara shut down politely, pointing out that their personal lives were an irrelevant topic.

By nine o'clock they exited the restaurant and got inside a black stretch limousine with tinted windows. About an hour later they approached a huge mansion that Shamara refused to believe was Tommy's. This place was about as huge as two baseball stadiums and had stylish shrubs and trees surrounding it. When the limo pulled to a stop in front of the giant front gate of this multi-million dollar mansion, Shamara's mind was saturated with sheer amazement as the gate slowly opened. She looked over at the others and saw they weren't moved, or at least they didn't show it.

The limo drove down a roadway towards the mansion for what felt like three city blocks before coming to a stop in front of the mansion that looked like something a movie star or corporate executive would live in.

Shamara felt her rage reaching a boil. Here it was a mufuckin' drug dealing murderer was living like a King while she was fighting to make ends meet. *This shit is crazy*, she concluded as she slid out of the limo when the driver opened the door.

Shamara made no attempt to conceal her amazement as she beamed at the white colored two-story mansion and its surroundings.

Malik peeped her amazement and said, "You like it, huh?" He smiled at Shamara.

"It's alright," Shamara said as though she wasn't fazed in the least. She snapped back into focus. *Never let 'em think they can razzle-dazzle you*, she told herself as she followed the group towards the front door. Just when they reached the entrance four bodyguards appeared from behind the door.

Kahmel said, "Peace y'all. I heard a lot about you guys. My name's Kahmel. I'm head of security. I gotta confiscate all weapons before you enter these premises. No weapons beyond this threshold." He gestured at the door.

Shamara instantly saw she wasn't going to like this cat. He had this foul, grimy look that announced he played by no rules, other than those of his boss, and would fuck over anybody—probably his own mother as well—with heartless enthusiasm. She gave Fashawn a quick glance because they knew a monkey wrench was already thrown into their plan. How were they gonna shoot this mufucka if they weren't allowed to carry hardware?

Malik said, "Hey, that's the rule. Tommy don't allow anybody to come near him holding heat. And that includes even me." Malik reached inside the back waist of his pants, retrieved his 9mm and handed it to Kahmel.

Shamara sighed as she reached in her back waist and handed over her weapon.

Kenyetta said, "I'm not holdin'." He held up both hands as one of the bodyguards approached him and performed a pat frisk.

Fashawn had on the mad screw face. She could hear her commanding officer inside her head saying, "Never give up your firearm at critical times, soldier! A true Marine will die with his weapon in his hands and smoke swirling from the barrel!" Fashawn noticed everyone was looking at her and she fought not to blow up the spot. She couldn't be the one to blow this mission, she told herself, and with a struggle she reached in the back of her waist and reluctantly handed Kahmel her weapon.

Two bodyguards stepped towards them with metal detector wands and waved them across each of their bodies from head to toe. Fashawn beeped.

"Please remove whatever that is from your leg," Kelvin said; he was a light skinned curly haired brother with a scar on his chin.

Fashawn screwed up her face as she kneeled, pulled up her pants leg, pulled the huge hunting knife from its holster and handed it to Kelvin. Fashawn saw Shamara was surprised and she inconspicuously winked her eye at her.

When they entered the mansion, Shamara saw the inside was even more beautiful than the outside. The smell of French Lavender mixed with Jasmine comforted her senses. She noticed her mixed emotions were flaring up; she didn't want to admit it, but she had hate in her blood. She wasn't hatin' solely because she wished she had all this high living, but her strongest aversion was because she knew Tommy didn't deserve all this good living. He killed her family, and he should be somewhere suffering, not living a luxurious life like this.

They entered a plush living room and took seats on the white colored sofa and matching armchairs made of an unknown fabric that was soft like cotton. Kahmel and Kelvin stood near the entrance acting like wooden soldiers on guard duty. Before Shamara and the others got comfortable, a waitress approached with champagne on a silver tray and handed each one a glass. Two minutes later Tommy made his grand entrance.

"What's happenin' y'all?" Tommy said with a confident smile as he eased into the room; he was dressed in casual attire.

Shamara saw Malik rose to his feet in the same fashion people rose to their feet when a Judge entered courtroom. She looked over at Fashawn and they shook their heads as Kenyetta reluctantly rose to his feet. She saw Kenyetta gave her a twisted smirk and she stood up with a clear nasty attitude, and Fashawn followed suit with the same mind-set.

Tommy saw Shamara and Fashawn were acting like they had a problem rising to their feet and showing him respect. He was about to make an issue of it, but he instantly realized these chicks were straight from the hood, apparently had killer mentalities, and this sort of gesture of respect was as foreign to them as Martian piss. Plus, he was totally distracted by Shamara's beauty. She had grabbed his attention when he saw her on the video recordings, but in real life she totally caught his eye, and he put no cut on how he felt when he went straight to her with a smile, gently took hold of her hand and kissed it. "Shamara, you look way better in real life. Those pictures and other images do you a great disservice."

Shamara was stumped. She noticed everybody was looking at her strangely. "Thank you, Tommy." *Ah shit,* she said internally, not knowing how to react to this outward display of attraction. She was also disturbed by the fact Tommy did have it going on, and he too looked far better in person than in his photos. He was built like he worked out constantly, his skin was clear, clean, and spotless, and there was even a glow hovering around him.

"And you're, Fashawn." Tommy gave her a smile and a head nod.

"How you doing, Tommy," Fashawn said softly, smiling back at him, really wanting to straight spazz on him.

"And you're Kenyetta, the middle man."

"That's me," Kenyetta said with a humble head nod.

Tommy inched pass Fashawn and took a seat next to Shamara, causing everybody else to sit down as well. Fashawn had to find another seat since Tommy hogged hers.

"First off," Tommy said. "I wanna thank y'all for such magnificent work! I've worked with a lot folks in the business and I will say, you are the first to earn my total and complete praise and respect." He looked up and saw Kahmel was getting sensitive again. "Another thing; I hope you understand what that last issue was all about. You know, not helping you guys get out of that last predicament." He knew it was wise to give them a clear explanation to defuse any hard feelings or misunderstandings, since he knew if he was in their shoes he would be very upset as well. "You see, I got this policy, that a real trooper is real not based on what he says, but based on what he does. A real trooper is also one who can handle shit on his own, and don't need anybody running to his rescue the minute there's a little bump in the road. And for the record, once I heard y'all got away and was laying up inside a hotel somewhere, I knew right then ya'll was all right. You got through the hardest part of the ordeal and wanted help?"

There was a moment of silence.

Tommy leaned back and looked at Fashawn. "That's the same thing so many people do when they're just this close to making history." He demonstrated with his thumb and index fingers. "They get right at the fuckin' front door of victory and fall short. It's an amazing phenomenon how folks start off strong, and run out of gas at the home stretch. Real troopers never run out of gas. I bet right now you feel a lot better, knowing you were able to pull yourself up by your own mufuckin' bootstraps, and save yourself. It just feels better knowing you can do it on your own, don't it?"

There was another moment of silence.

After Tommy saw he had their full attention, he continued, "Just know what I did wasn't personal. It was business, and it was done to test your thinking abilities and to let you see your own resourcefulness." He knew Fashawn was once in the military and would understand where he was coming from. "I only fuck with the best. Always did and always will."

The silence returned.

Tommy continued when he saw no questions were forthcoming, "Here's a rundown of what this job entails. If you ride with me, you ride only with me. No freelance work, no side jobs for other clicks. I got exclusive rights to your skills and talents. All tracks you pick up come from me and me only. How you feel about that?"

Shamara, Fashawn and Kenyetta looked at each other and nodded their heads.

Shamara took the spokesperson's position, "We can live with that if the price is right."

Tommy was feelin' shorty with every passing minute. He loved women that knew how to take charge. He nodded approvingly. "Okay, that's good. But before I shoot a price at you let me give you your entire job description. Basically, it's an easy job. I'm hiring y'all to watch my back first and foremost, do jobs when needed, and ride with this organization as our in house top cleaners."

"As far as watching your back," Fashawn said. "It looks like you already got an army doing that. What's the need for two more set of eyes?"

Tommy smiled genuinely. That was a very good observation. "Let's just say that watching my back is a smaller aspect of the job when it comes to y'all."

"Then it's fair to say the biggest aspect," Shamara chimed in. "Is that we continue doing what we been doing, the only difference is that you and only you have control over who we step to?"

"I couldn't have said it any better than that," Tommy rubbed his hands on his legs. "As far as how much I'll pay. Let's say I continue paying you what I been paying you for hits, but from now on I'll pay you a weekly salary of a thousand dollars each. All you gotta do is be on call whenever I need you. When I need you to attend special events, I'll add an additional five hundred dollars for each event. You can do whatever else you been doing as long as when I need you, you're there."

Shamara was ready to blurt out their agreement since this wasn't about money. She gave her comrades the eye to make it look good, and said, "Sign us up. We in and when do we begin?"

Right on the heels of this comment, Tommy Jr. raced into the living room dressed in pajamas, shouting "No! No! I ain't tired! I don't wanna go to bed!" A heavyset high yellow black woman was chasing him. The lady caught Tommy Jr. just as he reached his father.

Tommy shook his head, "Tommy, why you do this ever time I have company? Diana, I told you not to let him run wild."

"I didn't let him run. He stuck out of his room—"

"I don't wanna go to bed now!"

Tommy rose to his feet, scooped up his son into his arms, and politely said to his guests, "Everyone meet my son, Tommy Jr. He's the rambunctious type. I guess he gets that trait for his daddy." He laughed, causing Malik, Kahmel and Kelvin to laugh along. "Give me a minute, I'll be right back." Tommy headed out of the living room with Diana on his heels.

As Shamara watched Tommy exit the room, she subliminally realized the whole game had just changed. The minute she saw little Tommy something clicked inside her mind, and she noticed she had never contemplated Tommy having any children. She didn't know why but her heart was acting real crazy right about now, and it was talking to her in such a way that she wasn't trying to hear what it was saying. Not after all the hell she'd gone through to get this close to this creep. It was bad enough they would have to find a way to kill Tommy without a gun, but now she also had to deal with the reality that she was about to take little

Tommy's father away from him at such a very young age. He was evident Tommy Jr., was about a few years younger than she was when Tommy took her family from her.

But what frightened her most, and was hurting her in such a way that was becoming unbearable, was the indisputable fact that she saw herself in Tommy Jr., and Tommy Jr. inside of her. If she did what she planned to do to Tommy, then Tommy Jr. would be well within his right to do to her what she was going to do to his father.

CHAPTER # 9

The following day, Shamara, Fashawn and Kenyetta were at their Newark hide out locked in an emergency meeting.

"This shit is more than fucked up!" Shamara shouted as she paced the floor. "We went through all this shit just to get inside, and then can't touch this son of a bitch. This is straight fucked up—"

"Be easy, Shamara," Fashawn insisted as she leaned against the doorframe. "We're gonna come up with another plan to get around this, believe me."

"First things first," Kenyetta said as he sat on the nearby sofa with a bottle of Welchers grape juice in his hand. "Let's calm down and try to talk about this thing with a level head. All this scream and hollering and carrying on ain't gonna do much of anything, other than cloud our minds with a lot of negative energy."

Shamara realized he was right. After a moment, she realized she was probably blowing this whole thing out of proportion. She sucked in a lung full of air, let it out slowly, sat down in the armchair, bowed her head and massaged her temples in an attempt to relax. If they searched hard enough they could find a way around this hurdle. She kept telling herself this over and over. "Okay, you right let's calm down." She sat up at attention and started talking while waving her hands animatedly. "Let's lay out all the fucked up facts and then each one of us come up with a possible solution."

"The fucked up facts are simple," Fashawn said with an impatient attitude. "We can't get near this mufucka without any hardware, so it's gonna be impossible to blow this nigga's brains out or cut his throat. What else is there to get around?"

Kenyetta said, "There's also the fucked up fact that he keeps his bodyguards with him at all times. Even if we can hold heat in his midst, I'm sure we wanna get outta this thing alive. You know us black folks ain't never been into no suicide shit and I ain't tryin' be the exception to the rule, either."

There was a moment of silence. All three of them appeared to be in deep thought.

Fashawn had an idea but knew she was wasting her time to even suggest it. She swept it aside and continued searching for another idea. When no other suggestion came to the forefront of her mind, she realized she would have to at least try to push this idea that seemed to be stuck in her mind. "Listen, Shamara, I got a damn good idea. It's probably the only way to pull off this hit and guarantee that each of us get out of this thing alive. Now, it's gonna be a bit uncomfortable and you might not—"

"Tell us what it is," Shamara said impatiently. "We don't need you to put it in a nice neat package to sell it to us. Just lay it on the table and let's look at it."

"Alright," Fashawn said as she held onto another moment of silence. "I think you should go out with this chump, rock his ass to sleep—"

"Hell fuckin' no!" Shamara couldn't believe Fashawn even fix her mouth to utter such a crazy thing. "That motherfucker killed my family and you think I'll let that nigga touch me in an intimate way!?"

"Don't jump the gun, Shamara," Kenyetta said reluctantly. "I don't wanna burst you bubble, but Fashawn might be on to something."

"Well, she ain't on to nothing talking about taking it there. I can't imagine me dealing with this—"

"This'll be the perfect way to catch him with his drawls down, literally," Fashawn said. "The way he was drooling all over you, you won't even have much work to do getting his nose open. Even if you gotta fuck him, so what? At least you're working towards something we been trying to pull off for the past couple of years. Girl, we've murdered people to get this far, and I've risked life, limb, and life in prison holding you down. Don't tell me you'll murder someone, but won't fuck this fool to get him where you want him!? If you telling me that, than I regret to inform you that your priorities are totally fucked up."

There was a moment of deep, sullen silence.

Shamara sat locked in a state of disbelief, confusion, and dread. There was also another vibration that keep coming into her thinking process ever since she laid eyes on little Tommy Jr. This annoying vibe was scaring her more than all the others. She shook her head and massaged her temples again. What Fashawn was asking her to do was just plan crazy. How could she allow the man that murdered her family touch her in that kind of way? If she went out with him, she knew they would have to relate in an intimate way, or the whole approach wouldn't work. Shamara sighed loudly and shook her head, refusing to submit to such an insane suggestion.

"Girl, this ain't as bad as you making it out to be and you know it."

"You used to be my girl," Kenyetta said. "And I'm still jealous when I see you dealing with other cats even though our thing ended years ago. I ain't feeling too enthusiastic about promoting the fact that you should vibe with this creep ass dude, but looking at all the cards on the table. There's no other way to pull this off."

Shamara refused to believe this suggestion was the only way to get to Tommy. Her mind was working at rapid speeds, pulling, calibrating, configuring and then rearranging information. There had to be another way! Then, an idea hit her. She smiled as she spoke. "What if we try to snipper this chump again? Now that we're on the inside, we might be able to get him to put his guards down when he's in public. Since we'll have advanced notice of where he'll be going, we can plant a shooter in the perfect position."

There was a brief moment of silence.

"Think back to the time when we tried that," Fashawn said with an impatience that was rapidly growing into anger. "Don't you remember we followed this chump and not once he put himself in a situation to be snipered? He literally encased himself in a circle of bodyguards and didn't stop moving until he was inside his ride. Come on, Shamara, think back. We plotted a sniper run on this dude for four weeks back then and we confirmed that snipping him wasn't gonna work."

Kenyetta saw Shamara was grabbing at straws. "Tommy's got too many serious beefs to leave himself open for a hit like that. We'll be wasting valuable time trying to set-up another run like that and you know it, Shamara."

Shamara sighed as she stared at the wall. The more she thought about a sniper hit, the more it became obvious that it wouldn't work. They were right, they tried it already and Tommy wasn't stupid enough to put his guards down in public when he had crazy beefs coming from all directions. *Damn*, she couldn't see herself going there with Tommy and knew she might even do something to him impulsively and end up getting herself killed. There were a few other subliminal fears floating around in her head that was making her very uncomfortable. But, the more she looked at the idea of going out with Tommy, the more she had to admit this approach was the only logical one that stood a half ass chance of working. She sighed with indecisiveness. This was too much for her; she needed time to think about this. "Check this out. This ain't something I can make a decision right on the spot. I need some time to think about this. Maybe a couple of days, I'll figure out what I'm gonna do."

*   *   *   *

Tommy Bossett sat in front of his lawyer's desk, staring at Paul Winslow as if he was crazy. He had a document in his hand. "She's asking for half of my shit!?"

Paul's dark chocolate, clean-shaved facial expression displayed genuine concern. "That's what the divorce complaint is asking for. It's right there in black and white. There was no prenuptial agreement signed, so technically she can get it."

Tommy saw blood spots hovering before his eyes. He was so furious at the thought of this bitch Ashanta trying to straight rob him, he could see himself strangling her ass with his bare hands. Tommy flipped through the document and felt himself about to lose it. "If she even utters a fuckin' word about trying to take my son away, I'll—"

"There's no need for that Tommy. She agreed to allow you full custody of your son."

Tommy sighed with relief. His son was everything to him. Tommy was his ultimate love. Even the money and all his riches didn't hold as much value as him being able to watch his son grow into an adult. "That's a relief." He was glad Ashanta had enough sense to know he would have resulted to extreme measures if she had even attempted to take little Tommy away from him. It was good the bitch wasn't as crazy as she presented herself to be.

"There's a number of disturbing allegations in the complaint that we need to discuss, Tommy," Paul retrieved a notepad and pen. "I have twenty days to respond to this complaint or else we'll be in default, so we need to get right on this. At paragraph five of the complaint, your wife says you have engaged in dozens of adulterous acts over the course of the marriage, and that she has videotapes of some of these extra-curricula affairs. Is there any truth to those allegations? Before you respond, bear in mind that I can't defend you if I'm not forewarned, and don't feel embarrassed, since—"

"Embarrassed!?" Tommy wanted to laugh at Paul's last remark. "Listen Paul, ain't no shame in my game. When Ashanta married me, we both agreed this was basically a marriage of convenience, plan and simple. She was a gold digging, pretty little hoochie mama, I had big money, and I needed a wife to keep my public image right and to get myself into a lower tax bracket. She was getting what she wanted and I was getting what I wanted. Yeah, I didn't tell you all this, since it didn't matter back then. The bottom line is, Ashanta knew I was doin' me, and she agreed to it. Now that the little foul bitch done plugged into some new blue blood, she's ready to spread her wings."

"So, what are you saying? You have evidence that she's also engaging in adulterous acts?"

Tommy didn't have any evidence to prove Ashanta was fucking on the side, but he was certain he could uncover or even create some. "Yeah, I got evidence. Witnesses and the whole nine yards." He saw Paul write that down. Then, Tommy realized he would prefer to simply smoke this bitch. The thought of sending his killer bitches to blaze this tramp was growing by the seconds. After a moment of sensible thinking, he killed the thought because if something happened to her after she filed these divorce papers, it would be obvious who smoked her. He had to give it to her, she was smart enough to file her suit at a time when he least expected it, and at a time when she knew he wouldn't be able to touch that ass. She said she was spending a couple weeks down South with her family, and now he could see that she stepped out of the mansion with full intentions of never returning.

"There's another allegation I need some clarification on before I answer this compliant. At paragraph eight, she's alleging that you beat her several times. Is there any truth to these accusations?"

There was a whole lot of truth to those accusations, but it would be a cold day in hell before he would admit to them. "Hell no! I never laid a finger on her. If this is the truth, then tell her to produce evidence of these beatings." He knew there was no one on this planet that would testify that he had beaten her, since he had made sure he never left any scars or bruises on her and never argued or fought with her in the presence of others and especially his son. He felt this was a catch 22 situation because Ashanta was literally begging for those ass whippings. He wanted badly to reveal to Paul the fact that Ashanta was a freak for pain, she got her rocks off when she got slapped around, and displayed psychotic tendencies when she didn't get her way, but he knew revealing this would only complicate matters.

As Paul wrote several notes in his notepad, Tommy reflected back on the countless episodes of steamy hot sexual intercourse he had with Ashanta. He acknowledged that when it came to sex, if he didn't make it real rough, Ashanta would start a fight right there in bed and force him to beat her down. The first time he had sex with her, something told him to leave this crazy, sadomasochist bitch alone, but he couldn't resist her because he had a thing for beautiful high-risk and dangerous women with bangin' bodies. He never understood this crazy ass faddish of his, but it turned him on immensely when he embraced wild, exotic, seemingly untamable broads that would scare the average motherfucker into a frantic retreat. He guessed it was the mere challenge of it all that made it so appealing to him. This was why he found Shamara so amazingly attractive, and upon thinking about her, he felt his dick getting hard. On that note, he decided now that Ashanta was officially out of his life, he was going to make Shamara his new wifey, even if it killed him.

CHAPTER # 10

Shamara sat behind the reception counter at the dental office, typing in the daily treatment reports she received from Dr. Moore a few moments ago. Twice she typed in the wrong information and had to go back and edit the report. Her mind wasn't on her work, because it was on the issue dealing withTommy. Two days had gone by since Fashawn and Kenyetta suggested that she get close to Tommy so they could complete their mission and she still hadn't locked into a position.

Suddenly, Shamara looked up when she heard the jangling sound of the clinic door chimes activate and was surprised when she saw her Uncle Earl enter. The specks of gray in his head full of hair and in his beard and moustache seemed to multiply every month. She instantly saw he was no longer using his cane. Shamara rose to her feet and said, "Uncle Earl, what you doing here?"

"I stopped in to get my teeth cleaned," Uncle Earl propped one elbow on the counter as he gestured for Shamara to sit back down. Despite his sixty four years on this planet, and in spite of the heavy ripping and running he did in his youth, Earl looked damn good for his age. He knew he looked good, and most of all, had no problem letting people know he felt good despite his age. "So what's going on with you, Shamara? I see you haven't been down to the Church in quite a while, not even Sunday Services. What's the matter, you've totally given up on the Lord?"

Shamara sighed; she wanted to give him a piece of her mind, but couldn't. She'd always dreamed of telling her Uncle Earl off and could never do it, since she saw him as her father. Most of all she had deep respect for him even though she felt he didn't deserve it. After Tommy killed her mom and dad, he and his wife Tina raised her, and by all standards, since Uncle Earl was her father's older brother he technically and biologically was the closet to being her father. "Uncle Earl, please don't come in here gettin' on me about not going to Church." She knew the best way to shut him down was to throw some Bible quotes at him. "Even you said the good book says when God's children are ready to enter his house, he'll be there ready to embrace them with open arms, as long as their hearts are pure and their motives are just and righteous. I also remember another sermon of yours where you said God would prefer one true Christian over a hundred phonies. I told you when I come back to the church I'm going to be that one true Christian you be talkin' about all the time."

Uncle Earl smiled because she sure made his day when she said what she just said. The mere fact that she remembered his sermons was more than enough to please him, since it signified that what he'd said in the past was stuck in her mind. As long as it was there, there was always the chance that it would cultivate into something beautiful, like her coming on back to the church and doing God's work. He smiled wider and said, "Your aunt Tina told me to tell you, you better bring your butt on by for Sunday dinner soon." He loved his wife Tina, since she treated Shamara like she was a child that came straight from her own womb, and she was an advent follower of the word of Christ. "Can you squeeze me in for a teeth cleaning or what?"

"Of course, I can squeeze you in," Shamara rose to her feet. "As you can see today's a very slow day." She gestured at the waiting room that had only one patient, a middle aged black woman, who was reading one of those urban novels. "Let me tell Dr. Moore what time it is."

Shamara zipped down the hallway and returned two minutes later. "Uncle Earl, you good to go. Just take seat and he'll be with you in a few.

I know you wanna kick it with me, but I gotta knock this report out first, alright."

"Ah go on, girl. You know I ain't gone come in here and mess with you while you working." Uncle Earl took a seat and wondered if the Lord would punish him because he was lying through his teeth. He had full intentions of talking to Shamara until he couldn't talk any more. He also lied when he told her he was here solely to get his teeth cleaned. The real deal was he wanted to see her. He hadn't seen her in about a month and half and definitely missed talking to her. He also wanted to know how she was coming along with all that stuff she was up to. He'd been keeping heavy tabs on her and he just hoped and prayed to God that she was safe.

Shamara was about to get back into her report, but heard her cell phone ringing. She sighed as she snatched up her purse, searched inside of it, retrieved her phone, and talked. "What's up, talk to me."

"Hey, Shamara." Kenyetta said.

"What's up, man, what's happenin'?" Shamara said as she gave her back to her uncle and tried to keep her voice down.

"I got some good, bad news. I guess it depends on what you decided to do will determine whether it's either or."

Shamara sighed and said quickly, "I still ain't decide what I'm gonna do, Kenyetta and don't start rushing me."

"I'm not the one putting a rush on you. Actually, I think your man has already made that decision for you."

Shamara was confused beyond description. "My man!? Come on Kenyetta don't start with the mind games and shit—" She remembered Uncle Earl was nearby and struggle to keep it clean; she made it a habit to never curse in front of him, especially since he was an ordained minister. "What're you talking about Kenyetta!?"

"Tommy contacted me and told me to tell you he wants to see you tonight. He's got a special job for you. He wants to see you and only you. That was the gist of what he said. He wants to see you alone."

Shamara's heart started pounding and she didn't understand why her excitement mixed with terror was flaring up like this. She was about to spazz out and tell Kenyetta to call Tommy back and tell him that she wasn't going anywhere by herself, but she remembered Uncle Earl was sitting nearby. "Check this, I can't talk like I really want to right now—"

"What's the matter!? Your boss is standing there looking in your face?"

"Naw, my Uncle Earl is here."

"Yo', tell him I said what's up. I ain't see your uncle in ages." He saw this as the perfect opportunity to make it look good. "Tell him I said what's up."

"I'll tell him. But check this out. I'm calling an emergency meeting at our spot. Meet us there around eight o'clock."

"Tommy wants to see you at eight o'clock. If we gonna meet we gotta move it up to seven o'clock. That way we can talk and you can still make your appointment—"

"Who the fuck said—" She caught herself. "Who said I was going through with this!?"

"You ain't got no choice in the matter. Me and Fashawn voted that you gotta do it. We out voted you, and since we agreed to honor this voting policy, you've been out voted. I'll see y'all tonight at the spot. Make sure you dress appropriately. I'm assuming he wants to turn your meeting into a date, so dress with that in mind. Alright, peace." He hung up.

Shamara disconnected her cell phone and put it back in her purse. As she resumed preparing her report, she went into a mind churning daze, still unable to image herself dating the man that killed her family.

        *   *   *   *

Shamara sat in the back of the Limo asking herself how she could let them talk her into this. If it weren't for the fact she had agreed to a voting policy amongst themselves, she would have held firm to her position and forced them to find another way to deal with Tommy. She was dressed about two notches just above casual; not too formal and not too simple. The woman's black summer suit she wore gave her an executive look that still embraced urban roots. In the back waist area of her pants was her trusty old 9mm. Since she was apparently going to his mansion to probably go out on a date, it was only right that she test the waters to see how his security procedures worked under this situation with regard to her packing heat.

Sitting across from her was Malik and it was obvious he held the position as Tommy's personal gopher and middleman. He had picked her up at the Elizabeth restaurant they attended a few weeks back and now was transporting her to Tommy's mansion. Malik was sipping on a drink while listening to a Midnight Star slow jam, rocking his head to the beat. He was staring out the tinted window, gazing off into nowhere as the limo cruised down the New Jersey Turnpike. She noticed Malik apparently had a drinking problem, since every time she saw him he seemed to be drinking some kind of alcoholic beverage. He never appeared drunk or even tipsy, so she assumed he had built up an alcohol tolerance that enabled him to drink all day and still function.

When they pulled onto the grounds of Tommy's Rosell County mansion, Shamara gazed at the landscape and was even more amazed upon seeing this compound just before sunset. The last time she was here it was night, and although the features were noticeable, it was nothing like viewing this place with the aide of a little sunlight. She had to admit that this place was magnificent.

Moments later, Shamara exited the limo and headed towards the mansion. It came as not surprising when Kahmel and Kelvin slid out from behind the door with the metal detector wand and she received the answer to her inquiry. The gun issue was dead, even under these circumstances. They weren't playing when they said Tommy didn't allow anyone to carry a weapon in his presence.

After confiscating her nine, and waving the metal detector across her body, Kahmel said, "Tommy's waiting for you inside." Kahmel folded his arms across his chest and was wearing an evil grin. "Go ahead. You don't need an escort this time."

Shamara stared into his eyes and noticed just looking at him made her stomach turn. She opened the door, stepped inside and closed the door behind her. She saw Tommy standing near the gold trimmed spiral staircase, smiling while dressed in a brown and beige silk smoking jacket. She had to admit that he looked just like one of those rich white guys she saw in the movies. By her standards, he looked rather ridiculous, especially since she equated wearing such a garment with trying to be white. She guessed when folks had money of the likes of what Tommy was holding he had no choice but to wear such clothing, since it symbolized money, and money was something he obviously had plenty of. The next thing she noticed was the smell of French Lavender was replaced with a strawberry like aroma that was mixed with some unknown, exotic fragrance. Whatever it was, Shamara agreed it smelled damn good.

"Shamara, thanks for coming, sis," Tommy approached with his hand extended for a handshake. When Shamara shook his hand, he flipped her hand and kissed it. He saw this brought a smile to her face and he knew these hood girls didn't understand this sort of activity, but he was confident that she understood this was a way of telling her as clear as day that he was feelin' her. "Let me take your jacket."

As he eased Shamara's jacket off, Tommy savored the sight of her crazy shapely ass and that small waist of hers. *Goddamn, girl!* He could taste her already. Tommy spoke as he hung up the jacket on the nearby coat hanger. "I know you're wondering why I called you over here like this." He said as he headed towards the living room and she followed. "And I know you're probably thinking I'm trying to hit on you being that I'm kissing all on your hand and everything."

They entered the living room. Tommy gestured for her to sit down on the sofa and he sat next to her. "To be honest, it's a mixture of both business and non-business. Would you like something to drink?"

"I'll take whatever you're drinking," Shamara remembered that response from one of those TV shows and knew it was the best way to handle that, since she wasn't sure what rich people drank on a simple occasion like this one.

"Hey, Diana!" Tommy yelled and within seconds the heavyset lady from the other night appeared. "Let 'em get a bottle of Christal, please."

Shamara wasn't surprised he was flinging around a five hundred dollar bottle of champagne like it was all right. He definitely was holdin'.

After Diana left, Tommy picked up a remote control and said, "I hope you into oldies but goodies." He hit a button on the remote and Jody Watley's "I'm looking for a new love, baby" came through the speakers in various parts of the living room. The music was very low. It was at a speak easy level that instantly created a mood.

"I see you don't put much cut on it," Shamara said, forcing a smile onto her face, since it was obvious he was giving her a hint and a half.

Tommy smiled, "That's a good observation. I've always been considered the unadulterated type."

"Don't you got a wife?" Shamara said seriously. "Married men shouldn't be looking for a new love." She really wanted to burst his bubble point blank by telling him she wasn't interested, but she promised that when he came at her like this, she would play along.

"I'll be divorced by the end of next month. So, basically I'm about as free as a bird to go wherever else I chose to go. That marriage shit don't matter anyway, you know hat I'm sayin'; it's all game and it's all good. That's why I wanna get to know you, Shamara." Tommy inched closer to her. "I've always wanted a woman like you. From the moment I laid eyes on you and realized you were a hit woman, I knew I had to have you."

Shamara shook her head, realizing this dude was off the hook and said, "It doesn't scare you just a little knowing I'm a professional killer? Don't that make you pause just a little?"

Just as Tommy was about to answer the question, Diana entered with a tray of Christal and two champagne glasses. She sat the tray on the crystal coffee table and exited the living room

As Tommy poured the glass of Champagne, Shamara looked around and realized if she had a weapon she could blow his top off, but as far as escaping was concerned. That was another situation. The more she looked at the possible scenarios she realized this might not be as difficult as she assumed it would be.

Tommy handed Shamara a glass. He took a sip of his champagne as she sipped hers and said, "I didn't get where I'm at being scared of taking chances. I don't know how much you know about me . . ."

Shamara wanted to say, *you would be surprised how much I know about your foul black ass*, but instead she allowed him to continue.

" . . . I grew up in some of the roughest places in Brooklyn, like East New York, Brownsville, Bed-Stuy, Canarsie, East Flatbush, and I ran neck and neck with some of the most vicious street thugs to ever set foot on this planet. I been on this planet thirty five years and been putting work in from the moment I was able to walk. So, I know a whole lot about danger. I say this to say, after thirty five years on this planet, I've never had a thorough woman that was in the game and could hold down her own on the hard-core tip. Of course I came across a few ride or die hood rats that bust their gun and all, but they weren't professional killers." He looked into Shamara's eyes and said with clear sexual connotations. "I want to see how if feels to make a rare type of woman, my woman. A beautiful black woman, who's a professional killer, is about as rare as they can come. Not to mention, it would be a pleasant relief to know when we're out doing our thing, I don't have to worry about coming to your rescue at the first sign of drama. Hell, you'll be holdin' me down for a change."

Shamara giggled, because he was saying all the right things. She had to get close to him, and what he was saying was music to her ears because it was about to be on and poppin' in no time. She didn't want to say what she was about to say but she had to make sure she opened the door as wide as possible, so she could get this thing moving. "Well, you can imagine I'm just as motivated as you are. What sane woman wouldn't want to be wrapped in the arms of a rich, fine black man such as yourself." She allowed that to soak in and then said, "But, I still don't fully understand why you need a woman like me in your life."

Tommy smiled; he liked a woman that lacked a certain degree of cockiness. He massaged her leg, and when she didn't reject it, he knew he made a first base hit. "Shamara, my entire life I been that type of brother who always knew exactly what I wanted. And once my mind was made up about what I wanted I went out and got it."

He allowed that small bit of information to ferment inside her mind and after a moment he said excitedly as he sat his glass down on the table. "Hey, I wanna show you something that I know you're gonna just love." Tommy reached to the back waist of his pant and pulled out his golden 9mm. "Check this bad mufucka out." He held up the gun proudly, still admiring it despite having possession of it for years. "And it's real gold too, fourteen carat."

Shamara was not only surprised by the fact it was a real golden gun, but she was even more twisted by the fact he carried this thing around with him. *No good. This is no good at all.* Then, she started looking for a way to use this against him and suddenly realized she might be able to turn this into an opportunity if she could get possession of his gun and she went for it. "Can I see how it feels, lemme hold it?" She pretended to be in awe while drooling from the mouth.

"No disrespect, but I don't let anybody touch this piece. Call me superstitious, but I had my fortuneteller do a ritual on this piece, and she told me it would be bad luck to let anybody touch this weapon after she laced it up. She said if anyone else touches it, it'll break the good luck spell. I even keep this baby on me at all times. Wherever I go, you can bet my Golden 9 is ridin' along with me. So far it's provided me nothing but absolute good luck."

"Are you serious?" Shamara probed, hoping she heard him wrong. "You go everywhere with that gun!?"

"That's right. I even sleep with this bad boy." He thought about his statement, realizing it wasn't totally accurate. "Hold up, I gotta correct that. The only time I don't carry it is when I'm playing with my son;

that's probably the only time I don't carry it. Speaking of my son, I want you to meet him—"

"No, that's okay. He's probably playing or something. You don't have to disturb him on account of me."

"It's nothing. Little Tommy loves to be around fine women like you." He shouted. "Diana!"

Shamara sighed angrily. The last thing she needed was to start developing an attachment to the kid of the person she was striving to murder. Her heart wasn't built for this shit and it terrified her. She wanted to run out of the house before it was too late.

Diana entered and Tommy said, "Bring Little Tommy in here for me."

A moment later, little Tommy entered and smiled when he saw Shamara. He went to his father and said, "Is this gonna be my new mommy?"

Tommy laughed. "Man, you sure know how to read signals, don't you?"

Little Tommy went to Shamara moved her arms propped on her knees and found himself a seat on her lap.

Shamara was blown away by this act of affection as Tommy laughed joyously. That little voice inside of her head was telling her that this mission was rapidly falling apart. She loved children and her heart couldn't take this as she embraced Tommy Jr's little body, not having to pretend to be smiling, since she truly enjoyed the presence of children. In that moment, she realized she had to find another way to deal with this mission because there was no way she could continue at this pace, while in this state of mind.

CHAPTER # 11

Shamara sat with a plate of French gourmet food in front of her as Tommy sat across from her eating and talking. They were inside an elegant restaurant in Teaneck New Jersey, and everyone inside this place was dressed to the maximum formal degree, wearing classy suits and gowns made solely for expensive occasions. At the table next to the one where she and Tommy sat, was Kahmel and Caddy. Although the two were eating, Shamara saw they both kept their eyes peeled. Near the bar was Kelvin who was a very convincing decoy and a camouflaged set of eyes for the crew.

Shamara was definitely learning because if she hadn't known Tommy, she wouldn't have known Kelvin was even a part of Tommy's bodyguard team. Even outside she noticed Kahmel had two additional bodyguards roaming the area looking for anything out of the norm, and they all communicated with each other on their cell phones, hitting each other up whenever they needed to pass on important information. There was no doubt she had to commend Tommy on his well-organized security force.

But, the issue that fucked up her head the most was Tommy would not allow her to carry her own weapon. Kahmel had even waved his metal detector across her body to make sure she wasn't carrying heat, and she wanted to blow up on him because it was a clear indication that he thought she was lying when she told him she wouldn't carrying her weapon along with them to dinner. When Shamara asked Tommy why he didn't want her to carry her heater, he said, "This is our night out, Shamara. I want you to relax, and not feel like you're in the field, or at work. Plus, I got a miniature army who I pay very well to do what they

111

do. Let them bodyguard us." She wanted to debate him on this issue, but thought better of it, knowing it would create unnecessary suspicion.

As Shamara chewed the green beans, she sighed frustratedly because it was looking like a hit on Tommy wasn't going to happen no time soon. He was even digging his heels into their relationship as if he was about to hurl himself into it full force. He had taken her shopping and bought her the gown she was currently wearing; he paid a thousand dollars for it like it was nothing. When he hinted at either buying or giving her one of his luxury cars, she immediately had to shut him down, because he was moving way too fast for her. It had only been a week since their first date, and already he was showering her in expensive gifts. She was trying daily to keep her mind right by bringing up all the horrible memories of her past, but she hated to admit that she was enjoying Tommy's company and Tommy Jr wasn't making this situation any better.

"So when are you gonna tell me all about yourself, Shamara?" Tommy said as he finished off the last of his meal. "You said you would do that soon. I think this is about as soon as we can get. I mean look at it, I don't know much about you. I know you're twenty five years old; you're the most gorgeous contract killer I have ever seen in my life and that's the full extent of what I know of you."

Shamara swallowed the mouthful of parsley-broiled fish, took a sip of her white wine and said, "I got a boring ass life that's why I didn't wanna go into it." She had rehearsed what she would say, which was the main reason she put him off. He had caught her completely off guard when he started prying. "I'm a high school drop out, I had an alcoholic father that used to abuse me, but did teach me how to shoot a gun when I was seven; I went to prison for burglary and when I got out I teamed up with my home girl Fashawn who was a sergeant in the military, we got together and decided to become contract killers. We figured the fastest way to make some real money was to get down with an occupation where there's not much competition." She paused for a moment. "Oh, I almost forgot, I was born and raised in the Bronx." Kenyetta had helped get the area right since he was from the Bronx. "My stomping grounds were over on 141ᵗʰ Street and Willis Avenue, right there in Patterson Projects."

"Yeah, I got some peeps in those Projects. I know you know I was into the rap game, right?" He saw her nod her head. "I dropped an album back in the nineties; a piece called 'More Power to the People'. I had a rap style like Public Enemy, KRS1, and Poor Righteous Teachers mixed together with a touch of NWA, and my man Diamond Dee helped me lay down the tracks to most of those cuts on that album. He was from those Projects. You know him?"

Shamara smiled inwardly, because Kenyetta said Tommy would mention this name. "Yeah, I know Diamond Dee; he used to play mad music in the parks, at house parties and Community Center Jams. Shit, back in the day, Diamond was the man with that D-jaying shit. Couldn't nobody touch him on the wheels of steel. He's a short light skinned dude with a missing tooth."

"Yeap! That's Diamond." Tommy smiled, truly appreciating this walk down memory lane. He loved reminiscing about his rapping and D-jaying days. "Yo', he was straight off the chain when it came to making them beats."

"It was fucked up he died so young."

"Word up." Tommy's voice displayed genuine pain. "I can imagine where Diamond would be today if he didn't catch a bad one." He shook his head, remembering when he first heard Diamond got hit up in a drug deal that had gone bad. He fought like hell to stay alive and he was in the hospital for a whole week, but the five bullets were just too much for him. "He'd probably be the badest beat maker in the whole industry."

There was a moment of silence as Tommy and Shamara sipped on their wine.

Tommy sat his glass down and said, "Listen, tomorrow you and me are going to get us some blood tests. We're gonna put our cards on the table, before we get it on—"

"Hold up," Shamara couldn't believe he took it there and she definitely couldn't take it any longer. This nigga was talking about fuckin' her, she realized, and it was clear he was on some real bold shit at that. "I want to move a lot slower than this, Tommy."

"Don't tell me you one of those females that's scared of an HIV test!?" Tommy locked eyes with hers. Any woman afraid of an HIV test had something to hide, and therefore might even have the monster and was trying to lace him up with it. "In this day and age, any sane person will put their cards on the table before they get their hearts all locked up into a relationship, just to find out later they got some damaged goods, or maybe even got themselves twisted up with a death sentence hovering over their heads. That ain't happenin' to me." He shook his head meaningfully with a deep thought expression on his face to place clear emphasis on this last remark. "Uh hum, not me."

Shamara wanted to spazz out. *The nerve of this mufucka!* Her emotions became impulsively defensive.

There was a moment of silence as Tommy took a long sip of his wine.

Tommy saw Shamara's tensed response and he immediately started wondering if he should pull back. "I ain't trying to cram this gettin' tested issue down your throat, but health conscious folks usually love folks that are on their toes with issues like this."

After a moment of contemplating the situation, Shamara realized she was overreacting with the implications of fucking up this mission, and with this rationale surging through her mind, she quickly calmed herself down. When she saw the attitude on Tommy's face, she repeatedly told herself that it wasn't a surprise he was telling her it was time to fuck, because she obviously knew this was going to happen. Fashawn and Kenyetta knew at some point she was going to have to fuck him, and if she didn't, this relationship (and therefore this mission) would die. That was a simple, basic, inevitable fact.

Shamara sighed and said with a sensuous smile, "Be easy, Tommy. I'm not scared of an HIV test. I'm HIV negative, believe me, and I'm negative on all STDs. So you wanna do this tomorrow, you wanna put our heath cards on the table, so we both can know where we stand. Hey, let's do it. And for the record, it's a pleasure to see a brother got enough intelligence to know exactly what he's getting himself into before diving into things." The way she expressed her last remark she made certain it contained heavy sexual overtones. She hoped this would get him back on track, and defuse any suspicion caused by her hesitant response.

With a smile Tommy said. "I'm tellin' you, Shamara, I'm feeling you, girl. With this relationship, we both'll get something out of this. I ain't into telling women I love 'em and all that corny shit, 'cause if I love someone I show it through my actions, not words, but for some odd reason I feel we gonna go there with this relationship . . ."

As Tommy rattled on with a smile on his utterly handsome face, and then he started explaining to her how he only made special women in his life put their health status on the table, Shamara sighed knowing she had prevented this situation from spiraling out of control. That relief suddenly transformed into dread because now she knew this inevitable sexually intimate event was literally moments away and it scared her.

The source of her fright had nothing to do with the sexual act itself. She didn't believe there was a dick in the world big enough to scare her. In the subconscious regions of her mind, there was a powerful intuition that was moving about and it was clear that she was actually scared of having sex with Tommy because she was afraid that she was going to like it.

*   *   *   *

As the days progressed, so did Shamara's confusion and frustration. The following day after Tommy cracked on her about taking a blood test, they went to Tommy's personal doctor, had blood drawn, and both hers and Tommy's tests came back negative of all STDs. Just when she thought he was going to invite her to his mansion so they could get it on, Tommy did just opposite; he didn't call her for two days and to her surprise she felt the urge to call him. Meanwhile, Fashawn was beating her in the head assuming she had fucked up this mission somehow, and accused her of causing something to make Tommy not call her for two days. Shamara also noticed Fashawn was becoming insanely aggressive, extremely irritable, and almost psychotic with everything dealing what she called "the mission." Shamara started wondering if Fashawn's mental state had something to do with the meetings she was having with those military people.

On the third day, Shamara got a call from Tommy on her cell phone. He wanted to come pick her up the following morning and take her with him to a place he claimed was a surprise. Since the following day was a Sunday, she couldn't instantly figure out where he wanted to take her and impatiently asked, "Where are you taking me, Tommy?"

"I thought I just said it was a surprise!?" Tommy shot back. "Just be easy, Shamara, you're going to love it, believe me. Just make sure you dress in your Sunday's best."

When they hung up, Shamara called Fashawn and Kenyetta and informed them of the news. Since Tommy was under the impression that Shamara lived in Newark, and they had anticipated that there would come a time when Tommy would want to pick up Shamara at her doorstep, they had rented an apartment near their hideout but on the other side of town, exclusively for this purpose. Shamara didn't like the idea that she had to spend a night in their Newark secondary hideout apartment, since the place didn't have the same luxuries as their main hideout. In any event, she was able to endure the lack of amenities by imagining the moment she would get her revenge.

The following morning, when she heard the limo horn at about nine o'clock, Shamara raced out of the apartment dressed in a casual slack suit, and didn't know if this outfit would do the trick, but for all intents and purposes it was going to do whether Tommy liked it or not. As she approached the Limo, she saw Todd Banks, Tommy's personal limo driver, had the door held open for her, while Kahmel, Cabby, and two other unknown men were standing near the three jeeps, apparently providing Tommy with his standard bodyguard services.

When Shamara slid inside the limo and saw Tommy dressed in a suit and his son was also neatly dressed in a similar elegant suit, an image of where they were going instantly jumped into her mind, and she refused to believe this first mental impression. Her mind refused to believe Tommy was taking it there. After little Tommy gave her a kiss on the cheek, while big Tommy gave her a wet-one with tongues briefly flapping about, and the limo was in motion, Shamara started hoping and praying they weren't on their way to the only place most black folks went on Sunday mornings. It was bad enough Tommy was messing up her mind with all this affection, Little Tommy was embracing her with too much love, and now he was bringing her to the house of God, while her mind was saturated with sin. She wished she could find a way to turn off her conscience, but no matter how hard she tried to force a wave of blood curdling bitterness into her heart, she noticed it wouldn't stay for long once other issues came into play.

As they crossed the Brooklyn Bridge, heading towards the streets of Brooklyn, Shamara's heart pounded in her chest with nervousness because they were coming too close to her roots, and since Tommy continued to refuse to tell her exactly where he was taking her, she still couldn't firmly lock into a specific situation. Despite the plentiful small talk the three engaged in during the ride, Shamara was able to conceal her edginess with expert precision.

About ten minutes later they pulled up in front of the famous House of the Lord Church ran by Reverend Hebert Daughtery, located at 415 Atlantic Avenue, in downtown Brooklyn.

As Todd opened the limo door, Shamara said to Tommy, "I see you full of surprises. I would've never thought you were a man interested in the Church."

"As far as surprises go," Tommy said as he ushered his son out of the limo first. "You ain't seen nothing yet." He gestured for Shamara to exit next.

A few minutes later, Shamara, Tommy and Little Tommy were sitting in the front row of the Church listening to Reverend Daughtery give his sermon. The theme of his fiery sermon was forgiveness in conjunction with a message that black folks must learn how to work together, despite their conflicts, and to not allow petty emotions, such as hate, jealousy, envy and lust to become their greatest enemy. When the service was over, and after Tommy talked to about dozen big wigs, his entourage was on its way back to New Jersey. They stopped at a restaurant in Camden for a quick brunch and were on their way to Tommy's mansion by twelve o'clock.

Shamara entered the mansion, knowing it was going down today, since Tommy had given her a thousand and one hints he was ready to get his grove on. After Diana took control of Tommy Jr., Tommy escorted Shamara to his bedroom for the first time.

When Shamara stepped foot through the threshold of this room, she was blown away. This place literally looked like a palace right out of an Ancient Egyptian movie script. There were even Egyptian style pillars in strategic locations, the floor was made of shinny marble, and the huge double King size bed was huge enough to hold four couples. On the far side of the room she saw he had a Jacuzzi and next to this warm water pool was a Terrace leading to a magical looking garden that could've qualified as a storybook garden. The delicate and delicious smelling air fresher filled the room with a sweet, exotic aroma that was unfamiliar to her nose. This room was unbelievable; it made her feel as though she had walked through a time portal, and landed in the royal palace of King Tut. There was no way to conceal her awe.

Tommy came up behind her and gently wrapped his arms around her waist as his body caressed hers. He kissed her neck and said softly, "When you told me you wanted to go to Egypt one day so you could see how black folks lived back in the day, I figured I'd give you a little taste of that dream before I actually take you there on the real tip." He noticed she was so soft, and as he rubbed his crotch area against her ass he noticed her softness was universal.

Shamara felt her breathing accelerating as she felt his man-hood poking her backside. "This is totally off the hook." She had to move; she approached the pillars and touched them. Just looking at all this made her pussy moist with wanting. As she approached the bed and touched it,

Tommy embraced her, spun her around and began kissing her with a gentleness that wreaked her callus covered shield that she promised she would put up and keep up. Shamara decided to go with it. She might as well enjoy this once in a lifetime opportunity, Shamara concluded as she allowed herself to be guided down onto the bed.

When her body touched the mattress, it felt like she had just laid upon a cloud; the mattress swallowed up her body weight and it felt like she had sunk down into the feather filled mattress seven inches. She didn't know how to describe what she was feeling as she laid on this mattress; this had to be some kind of new, space age mattress because she'd never experienced this type of sinking sensation before. She literally felt like she was floating, almost like lying upon on a waterbed mattress, but far more fluid.

As Tommy slowly peeled off her clothing, savoring every moment like he was going to make this a moment she would never forget, Shamara forced all her bad memories out of her mind. With a small struggle she blocked out everything in that moment, and allowed her wild side to take control. She sat up and started unfastening Tommy's shirt as he pulled her blouse off. She saw his mouth watered with lust when her bra came off and her youthful, perky breasts jingled with succulent life.

Then, he laid her down, unfastened her pants, pulled them off with one smooth jerk, and went straight for her panties. Shamara felt her juices free flowing to life the second Tommy slid her tong style under panties off. Without hesitation he undressed, and immediately embraced her, kissing while fondling her.

About three minutes of this torturous teasing, Shamara was ready for some action. She was breathing hard with intense wanting, her pussy was dripping wet, and her mind was wild with a craving to be penetrated that was driving her insane. She was throwing herself at him, but Tommy kept kissing, fondling, and making her hotter and hotter; wetter and wetter. This went on for what seemed like forever.

Then, suddenly, she saw Tommy started kissing her breasts; moments later he went down to her stomach and his hot kisses continued easing slowly downtown. Shamara was about to scream with explosive ecstasy as his kisses went down, down, and down, until . . . *Oh, yes, he took it there. Oh, god, this is wonderful*, she thought as Tommy sucked, slurped, and tongued kissed her down there in ways she'd never had any other man do before. She cocked her legs up high in the air and a nut exploded from her like the spray from an aerosol can. She screamed in ecstasy as her toes, fingers, ears, ass cheeks, and even her eyes curled up with sheer euphoric pleasure. It felt like a week's worth of stress dissipated from her body with the release of this one nut. Even the sound of Tommy sucking up her juices seemed to make the nut that much more pleasurable.

With a glazed covering on his face, Shamara saw Tommy crawled up to her and started kissing her and she went with it. *What the hell*, she thought, it was her love juices anyway. When he entered her, a blast of rapture surged through her body, and the pleasure provoking sensations started up again. As he gentle pumped inside of her, she realized he was handling her as if there was a genuine care and concern for her. She'd been fucked before as well as experienced what it felt like to have a man make love to her. What Tommy was doing to her was making deep, passionate love that came straight from the heart and her heart was reacting.

With every thrust of his manhood, as he was hit internal parts of her insides that was sending rapid signals through out her body, Shamara felt herself falling. She was falling too fast and there was no way to stop it. Then, she exploded, and with expert coordination, Tommy worked on her gee spot just when she started screaming and it made her want to cry out with tears of delight because this felt too good to be true.

When she stopped convulsing with elation, and saw Tommy was still going strong, she knew she should have listened to her first mind. This powerful intuition told her not to go here with Tommy, because it was obvious he had a dick game that was way off the chart. When she realized what was happening to her heart, soul, and inner most being, she tried to pull up those memories of her mom and dad being shot, but the images of Tommy Jr. and the realization of how good this sex was, along with all the money that surrounded her shoved the images back. By the time she felt her second nut rolling in, and Tommy was still pounding and sweating away, she decided to stop fighting the inevitable and with this decision treading across the delicate regions of her mind, she let herself go.

CHAPTER # 12

As the days turned into weeks, and the weeks into months, Shamara was having the time of her life with Tommy. By the time two months after their first sexual encounter came and went, Tommy had showered her in incalculable gifts of all types, which included taking her on a couple of weekend boat cruises, a trip to the Bahamas, and one to the Virgin Islands, and each time he laid hands on her in a sexual manner she grew another yard further from her mission, and ten steps closer to doing exactly what she fought not to do. And the strangest thing was that the sex seemed to get better with each time they took it there.

To make matters worse, Shamara found out that Tommy was a down low humanitarian; he was donating money to all sorts of black causes, and never sought praise for the good deeds he had done. He was especially serious about doing things for kids, and this was an attribute that really proved to her that Tommy apparently was not the same person he was fifteen years ago. When she found out the main reason Tommy knocked off Ray Ray was because he had told Ray Ray to stop using kids to sell his drugs and Ray Ray ignored this warning, Shamara knew Tommy was sincere about his concern for kids. This moved her so deeply she could actually see herself having a baby by a man with this sort of mentality.

However, Shamara became alarmed one day when she sat daydreaming at work as she looked inside of herself introspectively and realized she couldn't deny the fact that the closer she drew to Tommy the more she realized he was the dream man she had been looking for. Every time this crossed her mind she thought she was going crazy and would start beating up herself for becoming weak and unfocussed, but instantly realized she had no control over the way her heart was reacting.

Shortly after that, she had finally allowed Tommy to buy her a luxury car; a baby blue Lexus. Tommy insisted that she should get a Mercedes, but she thought a Benz parked in the lot of the hideout in Newark would attract too much attention. Plus, she'd always wanted a Lexus after that time she saw one parked in front of her Uncle Earl's Church during one of his Sunday services. After she got the Lexus, she realized the Lexus was just as troublesome as a Mercedes, since it was just as expensive as the Benz. The way they solved that problem she decided to park the Lexus in a commercial parking garage a mile away. Tommy had even asked her to move in with him at the mansion, and although the temptation was strong, she had to decline that offer, because she was already growing deeply attached to Tommy Jr., and an attempt to move in would have completely destroyed all semblances of her trying to carry on with the mission.

Shamara could see as clear as day that Fashawn was furious and was seconds from blowing a gasket, since anybody could see she was procrastinating. When Shamara roll up at Fashawn's job with the Lexus, it didn't surprised Shamara when Fashawn cursed and ranted for a whole half hour, beefing a mile a minute about her slipping and losing focus of the mission. Shamara noticed her knit picking attitude had reached a point that made her honestly sensed some hatin' seeping into the picture. Shamara detected this was the case when she allowed Fashawn to sport the Lexus, and she had instantly toned down all the crying, complaining and accusing.

Shamara shut up Fashawn some more when she started giving her some of the money she was getting from Tommy, but that didn't last long because it was clear that Fashawn was far more concerned with taking Tommy's head than spending his money. She couldn't completely be bought, and was now accusing Shamara of deliberately not working hard enough to find a way to get beyond Tommy's security.

Kenyetta, on the other hand, was almost as uptight as Fashawn; he seemed more pissed off because they hadn't been offered any hits lately; since the weekly pay for just being on Tommy's teams wasn't enough for what Kenyetta was trying to do with this money (trying to start his own business), and when he confronted Malik with this problem, he simply said that the well was dried up for now, and that the first time anybody got out of line they would be the first to know about it. But, on the down low, Kenyetta knew this was all bullshit; he knew Tommy was fucking Shamara on the regular, and since he used to go out with Shamara (and wouldn't mind having her again) he knew their sudden lack of work had nothing to do with "the well running dry" and had everything to do with the fun Tommy was having between Shamara's legs. He could image Tommy feeling awkward sending a woman he had feelings for out into the field to put in work, even though she had a track record for putting that kind of work in. He now regretted he agreed to let Shamara do her thing with Tommy.

By the time December crept in, while sprinkles of snowflakes blanketed the landscape, and Shamara was still holding firm to her excuse that she couldn't get any closer to pulling off a clean hit, Fashawn and Kenyetta decided it was time they put their foot down and called an emergency meeting.

As Shamara cruised down the roadway of the Holland Tunnel, she sensed this was going to be a real hot meeting. She bobbed her head to the new Mary J. Blige song, as she smoked her Newport cigarette, while conjuring up another excuse to hit them in the head with. It was amazing how she no longer had the drive to kill Tommy anymore, and it was even crazier when she realized she couldn't imagine living without the loving he was laying on her. Shamara shook her head in an attempt to snap herself out of this way of thinking, and inwardly told herself she was bugging the fuck out. This creep killed her mom and dad and it was obvious she had to do what she had to do. She couldn't let him get away with what he had done, even if he was trying to make amends for all the foul shit he'd done by donating money to worthy causes.

But what about forgiveness? Shamara heard that voice in the back of her head inquired and she forced it to go sit down and shut up. This little back and forth ritual went on daily inside her mind, and she knew if a psychiatrist knew what was going on in her head, she was certain she would be deemed schizoid; one minute she was madly in love with Tommy, and the next minute she was plotting to kill him. Some days one emotional flare up was stronger than the other, while on other days she would bounce back and forth between the two to such a point that she would become mentally fatigued and would simply give in, bowing to the inward battle so as not to burn out any brain circuitry.

But, the memory that touched her real deep, so deep it scratched the bone, was the time when she was chilling at the mansion, watching an old Denzel Washington movie on Tommy's eighty inch TV screen. It was a week day evening at about eight o'clock, and Tommy Jr. came in the room, and asked her to help him with his homework. What followed would stay with her for the rest of her life.

Tommy Jr. said with his wonderful smile, looking like a perfect combination of his mom and dad, "Shamara, can you help me?" He had a notebook, a textbook and a pencil in his hands. "This stuff got me all messed up."

Shamara smiled as she pulled him over and sat him down next to her. "Let's see what's the deal."

Tommy Jr. flipped the pages of his biology book to the back of the second chapter to the list of questions he had to answer and said. "The teacher told us to find out this stuff, but it ain't nowhere in the chapter." He shoved the books into Shamara's lap.

Shamara read all five of the questions and wanted to laugh at Tommy Jr. because he was trying to get slick on her; he was trying to get her to do the work for him. It was clear after reading the questions that if he had read the chapter it would be obvious he could answer these questions. The different types of matter, the parts of an atom, etc., were basic biology information. She decided to get him to do his homework and try to make it fun in the process. "So how can we do this? Let's turn to the beginning of the chapter and take a look at all this good, juicy stuff."

Tommy Jr. smiled as he eased closer to Shamara; he loved the way she smelled; her perfume was real nice and he hoped his dad married her.

"Let's read this stuff together." Shamara sensed Tommy's tension in response to her suggestion, and so she moved even closer to him while placing her arm around his shoulder, caressing his little back as she read the first sentence. When she was finished, she said. "Now let me see you read the next one."

The two went back and forth, reading a sentence each, until they had read the first half of the chapter. In between the reading exchange (especially whenever the answers to the five questions came up) Shamara made jokes about the material with hopes that Tommy Jr. would remember the information later.

"Now, let's see if we can figure this stuff out," Shamara flipped to the questions at the back of the chapter. She read the first question out loud. "What are the three states of matter?"

Tommy excitedly blurred out the answer. "Solid, liquid and gas!"

"There you go!" Shamara gave him a playful rub on the back. "See, that wasn't hard, was it? Now, I bet you can answer the rest of them."

Tommy stopped in mid-motion as if something very heavy was on his mind; he turned his head, began staring into Shamara's eyes, and said, "When are you gonna come move in with us? My daddy said he asked you. My real mommy never did stuff like what you do with me, Shamara. Please, come and stay here. You know my daddy likes you a whole lot!"

Shamara sighed and shifted in her seat uncomfortably. She was at a lost for words; her conscience was ripping her insides to shreds because not only was she not going to move in, but she was actually planning to kill the child's only true parent, and the thought of all this was eating her up alive. When she stared into Tommy Jr's innocent eyes, her heart crumbled into pieces. With a smooth voice that tactically concealed her emotional struggle, Shamara said, "I can't do that right now, Tommy—"

"Why!?" Tommy Jr. said forcefully, making no effort to conceal his devastation and his refusal to take no for an answer. "I love you like a mommy, Shamara, and my daddy likes you too, believe me. He be doing things that he never do with all his other girlfriends. He even said you are special and he wanna marry you."

Shamara saw it was best to simply drop this discussion immediately while her heart was still beating. "I'll tell you what I'll do. Let me think about it for a couple days and I'll get back to you." Shamara shifted the topic before he could continue beefing. "Look at this question! This one is way easier than the last one . . .

Shamara exited from the daydream, realizing when this ordeal was over she was going to be an emotional wreck. She snuffed out her cigarette as the car was approaching the Holland Tunnel exit. When the car exited, she saw the sun was completely gone and was replaced with the dark bluish glow of the evening skies that still held reminisces of the sun's embrace. She looked at her rearview mirror and saw Fashawn was still perfectly on her trail. With the money they were receiving from Tommy to be on standby, Fashawn bought herself a used Cherokee Jeep, and it was clear that the vehicle fitted her rugged and adventurous personality to a tee.

Twenty minutes later, they pulled up into the driveway of their Newark house, and saw Kenyetta was already waiting as usual. Shamara and Fashawn parked their vehicles and entered the house. After they got comfortable, they dove into the meeting. Kenyetta was the first to set it off.

"You know why we having this meeting, Shamara?" Kenyetta said with a brotherly tone.

"Yeah, I know why we here," Shamara leaned back on the sofa comfortably. "But, it don't matter how much you beat me in the head about my so-called being unfocussed, it ain't gonna change the fact I can't kill this creep and get away. I'm still looking for the right way to pull it off. I told you I'm working on a couple of possibilities. I'll have something solid soon."

Fashawn was about to fly off the handle and start cursing, but had promised herself she was going to be easy. She took a deep breath and said. "Shamara, it's been over four months you been dating this nigga. You been on cruises with this cat, he took you on two trips to the Islands, and y'all been painting the town red like two love birds in heat. Not to mention, he's taken you to parties, Broadway shows, and even to church." With serious sarcasm in her tone she looked at Kenyetta while shaking her head in utter disbelief and said, "You believe this shit, Kenyetta!? The motherfucker takes her to church damn near every Sunday!? The bottom line, Shamara, I refuse to believe after all this hanging out, you still haven't found a way to push this chump's wig back and get away with it. You been confronted with a hundred scenarios and there's no way you can honestly tell us there wasn't at least one opportunity to blaze this fool."

"We know what time it is, Shamara," Kenyetta said, knowing he was about to pick a nerve. "That mufucka got your ass dick whipped, and now you—"

"Get the fuck outta here!" Shamara shot back with clear venom. "That motherfucker killed my family and that's—"

"Stop frontin'!" Fashawn hated head games and been waiting to check her on this issue. "The minute that nigga hit it, you been parading around here, smiling, and making every fuckin' excuse under the sun not to step to your business. It's clear as day you really don't want to take it there and it's the dick. It might be a little bit of the money too. I know you, Shamara. I can tell when a dude got your nose open. I know when you're procrastinating and that's exactly what you're doing. Procrastinating!" Fashawn sat next to her. "I'm even more surprised because we thought you were stronger than this."

"Word up!" Kenyetta chimed in. "If we had known you would let this dude get all inside your mind like this we would've never pushed you into going about it this way."

There was a moment of silence.

Shamara was on an emotional tidal wave. She was swaying up, down, to the left, and to the right. Her heart was twisted with a degree of confusion that made her want to scream to everyone to leave her the fuck alone. When her eyes started getting misty upon realizing she was betraying her mom and dad's memory because she was definitely sleeping with the enemy, she knew she had to do something to change the course she was currently on. She had to find a way to get herself back on track, get refocused back on the reason for going down this road, and get her mind right in order to take this thing where it was supposed to be going, especially since her life long friends were correct with their observations. She was dick whipped, money whipped, and she was becoming a sure enough sucker for love. She sighed violently and said, "Y'all right." She threw up both her hands with dramatic emphasis. "I--I don't know how the fuck I let my heart get all caught up in this shit."

Kenyetta and Fashawn both nodded their heads at the same time as though a collective realization instantly grabbed them. They gave each other relief-laden glances.

"There you go, girl," Fashawn massaged Shamara's shoulder. "Now, we're getting somewhere here." Even though she empathized with her best friend, she still couldn't believe the dick was that good. Just thinking about it made her want to take a crack at that thing to see if it was really all that. "By acknowledging that there's a problem, now we can work on the solution."

"Yeah," Kenyetta added. "You can't fix a problem until you recognize there is one."

"I think what we need to do first is find a way to reprogram you, girl." Fashawn's military mind started recalling the tactics she remembered the Corps used to control the minds of its soldiers. The hypnosis experiment she underwent crossed her mind, but she knew this particular approach was out of the question, since she knew nothing about hypnotizing a person. She decided to go with a simpler tactic, consisting of isolating the issue and showing the person it was a terrible way to go about doing whatever it was the person was doing. "We need to talk about what's making you feel this way about this creep, despite knowing he killed your mom and dad."

Shamara was surprised she suddenly felt a ping of embarrassment coming to life. The feeling perplexed her because Fashawn and Kenyetta were like family and vowed to be open with each other. It didn't take long for her to realize she was feeling this way because she now concluded that her emotional shift was stupid. It had to be outright stupid to allow her feelings to cause her to become emotionally attached to the man that killed her family. In fact, it was more than stupid. *This is sheer fuckin' madness*, she insisted inwardly.

Her mind shifted again and it started looking at what was going on underneath the surface of these issues. She couldn't lie to her. There were other issues going on here besides the dick being good and she decided to let them know what also played a part in causing her to act like this. "My pulling back like this ain't just about the sex. I—I knew I was going to run into problems when I laid eyes on his son, little Tommy." She stared off into the oblivion, while shaking her head. "I--I felt I was going to mess up that kid for life if I took his daddy away from him. The same way Tommy fucked me up and I—I just—" Her emotions were battering her mental facilities.

Ah shit, Fashawn thought as she and Kenyetta gave each other a momentary nervous eye exchange. Fashawn knew this was like treading a minefield as she lit up a Newport cigarette. There was no way of knowing where to step, since a bomb could ignite at any moment, no matter how lightly the step was taken. Convincing someone to hurt a child was no small feat for a person that had some degree of morals, principles and integrity and Fashawn immediately started digging into her bag of tricks. "Shamara, this is not about the kid. It's about justice and balancing that scale when someone upsets the balance."

Kenyetta knew this was going to take a tag team effort so he slid in the first chance he got. "When Tommy gunned down your family with

132

you standing right there he didn't give a fuck about you. Actually, it's a surprise he didn't put a few slugs in you. You don't owe him shit, Shamara. Why should he be afforded the courtesy of shielding his family from the same pain that he caused you and others to feel?"

"Some people can change," Shamara said, still refusing to give up her position. "And I know a lot of people make mistakes. Some people make bigger mistakes than others. I—I—don't understand what the fuck I'm feeling right now, 'cause I do wanna make his ass suffer for killing my family, but I don't wanna hurt little Tommy." She also wanted to point out that she was immensely enjoying Tommy's company, and especially his money, but that would only complicate matters. "I was trying to come up with another way to serve justice on this motherfucker—"

"There ain't no other way!" Fashawn interjected as if she was about to explode. "An eye for and eye is the only real justice in this case." She sighed and forced herself to relax. The thought of not being able to complete this mission was making her feel like the walls were closing in on her. "Shamara, think back to that time when I got home from overseas. Girl, you were a fuckin' wreak, moping around with a nasty ass attitude, blaming everybody for your situation. You had just got out of prison and shit was rough to say the least. Remember when you looked inside of yourself, and I told you to find that one thing that you felt turned your life into the living hell that it turned out to be and you said, the day your mom and dad died was the day your life became that hell? You remember that don't you?"

Shamara sighed as she shifted in her seat.

Fashawn continued. "And when I asked you how you think you could fix that problem and you said, if you could just make Tommy pay for what he did to your mom and dad, you would be able to live out the rest of your life in peace." She saw Shamara was deep in thought. "Answer me. Do you remember that?"

"Yes," Shamara said with a slight attitude, seconds from putting up her guards, but held herself in check because what Fashawn was saying was the truth. "You know I remember it."

"And I told you right then and there," Fashawn blew out a cloud of smoke. "I would hold you down if you wanted to free yourself from this brutal hold that this unresolved issue had on your life. You said if you could find a way to smoke Tommy you would be able to clear your mind, and the minute we decided to go for it, your whole life lit up with joy. You became a whole new person just knowing that justice was finally going to be served."

"That ain't no bullshit," Kenyetta said. "When we was growing up, Shamara, I saw what that incident did to you. It was a vicious scar that's been lingering and festering for all these years; eating away at her mind; killing you slowly, and now you got the opportunity to finally straighten out this drama that's the root of your life-long pain and suffering, and now you're gonna throw it all away?"

"Listen, Shamara," Fashawn said. "I invested a whole year showing you how to shoot guns and shit. You know I hate wasting my time. But, then again, it ain't about me, it's about you, your mom and your dad. Your family was bad cool with me and I'm not feeling this nigga is getting away with murder. To cut straight to the chase, you need to put your emotions in your pocket and let's complete what we started."

"I agree," Kenyetta said. "The kid will get over it. I hate to be so blunt about it, but if every murderer could get off just by throwing his kid into the equation, there wouldn't be any balance in the world. Your mom and dad are probably turning in their grave, knowing they died in vain. They were doing the right thing when they stood up to those drug dealers.

It's crazy! This cat got off without serving a day in jail. He's lived his life without one day of punishment." His anger resonated in his body language. "He's gotta go, Shamara. He killed your family and now it's time for him to pay the piper."

Shamara bowed her head into the palms of her hands, massaging the temple region of her head to relieve the stress and built up tension. She felt like she was bolted down inside the chair of a horrific amazement park ride and was screaming to get off, but couldn't budge. Her mind was bouncing back and forth once again and she simply didn't know which way to go. Everything Fashawn and Kenyetta said was the truth. Tommy was the source of most of her pain, suffering and misfortune. The lost of her family had put her in a self-destructive frame of mind and everything that followed was a course of action initiated by Tommy when he did what he did. There was no doubt he should pay for what he did, but that voice in her head wouldn't let her lock firmly into that position anymore.

Shamara looked up from her hands, and did the only thing she could do at the moment. "Listen y'all, I need a minute to myself. I need to think about this." When she saw they both were about to explode, she became firmer with her position. "I said, I need some fuckin' time to think about this shit!"

CHAPTER # 13

Two days later, Shamara sat in the back of Tommy's limousine with a glass of Christal in her hand. Tommy sat next to her and also had a glass of champagne in his hand. He was smiling and rocking his head to the Nas CD. Shamara was dressed in a silk suit and matching soft sole shoes with her hair done up into a bun. Her natural beauty was turned up full blast this evening and was inconsistent with what was going on inside of her. There was going to be some folks that were very upset with her. That much was for sure.

"Now, this cat Nas," Tommy said. "He's one of the badest rappers on the scene."

"He's alright," Shamara said. "In my opinion I think Jay-Z's got them all beat."

"Naw, mama, Jay-Z is good, but Nas got a style that's the epitome of what a modern day rapper should be about. He can go gansta if he wants, while at the same time he can hit it up on some conscious shit that's straight superb! After all that's said and done, he can even touch the pop charts on some mainstream shit, if he want to. The brother is on target and versatile like a mufucka."

"I see you feelin' Nas," Shamara sipped her champagne. "But on the DL I think you feelin' Nas like that because he got a similar style like yours when you was spittin'." She couldn't help but listen to Tommy's album, "More Power to the People", since he had crates full of that one album scattered all over his mansion, and after checking it out she had to admit that it wasn't that bad either, even though she never heard any of the cuts before.

Tommy smiled. He loved when folks remembered his album. "That's why I'm feelin' you so much, Shamara, you got an eye like a mufuckin' hawk. No wonder you so good with them tracks. It takes a good eye to be a good contract killer. I did a little damage myself back in the day. I know I'm on some mister softy shit nowadays, trying to help folks get right, and keepin' the game clean and all, but don't sleep now. I had, and still do, got a wicked gun game." He pulled his Golden 9 from the back waist of his pant to give his final comment its appropriate emphasis.

Shamara wanted to tell him she was well aware of that fact, but figured he'll find out soon enough that his distant pass of busting his gun was finally going to caught up with him.

*   *   *   *

Fashawn was behind the wheel of a black Nissan Maxima, cruising down highway ninety five heading North and was moving at fifty five miles per hour, well within the speed limit. The glare coming from the headlights of the oncoming cars in the southbound lanes was irritating her eyes, causing her to squint constantly. The doctor said there could be side effects that might interfere with her vision, and she figured this was the reason the headlights of the cars were annoying her so much.

Fashawn was, however, quite happy that Shamara had finally came to her senses. That last situation was a close call, she realized. It was only right that Tommy get his, and to allow him to wiggle his bitch ass out of meeting his maker, after all the hell he inflicted on Shamara, solely because he would leave a son behind, just wasn't sufficient enough reason to let him off the hook as far as she was concerned.

Fashawn was dressed in her black ninja fatigues and had a small arsenal in the trunk of the car. In the waist of her pants was her 9mm and it was merely a reach away. It felt good knowing they were finally about to put the clamps on this mission. According to Shamara, she convinced Tommy to spend a weekend up at his ranch like home he had in

Connecticut. The plan was simple. She would get Tommy drunk and kill him. However, the part Fashawn loved most was that she had to step to the bodyguards like a super ninja, and silently knock them out of the box, so they could implement a perfect escape.

She'd been itching for some action and felt her condition worsening with each week she couldn't relieve herself. But, all that was coming to an end tonight. Then, she wondered, what was she going to do about her craving after they knocked Tommy out of the picture? There was no doubt what she was doing was like therapy for her. The thought of actually becoming a hit woman for one of those crime organizations definitely crossed her mind. She quickly shoved this thought to the back of her mind and started focusing on this mission. The thunderous words of her commanding officer boomed inside her mind, "Sergeant, Corcino, a good Marine always focuses on the mission at hand, not on missions to come!"

Fashawn looked at her watch. It was ten to eleven o'clock. *Tommy's limo should almost be there*, she confirmed inwardly. She rocked back and forth in her seat; she couldn't wait to unleash the hell on Tommy's punk ass crew.

*   *   *   *

Shamara and Tommy entered the Stanford Connecticut house as Kahmel, Cabby and four other men lead the way. Three of the men immediately went to the back rooms to make sure everything was in order.

Kahmel approached Shamara with his metal detector wand and said, "Come on, Shamara, you know the drill."

"She's good," Tommy said, realizing Kahmel was getting crazy with all this paranoid super precautious bullshit he'd been locked into so tightly that he wouldn't even bend for his own momma. "You just

138

checked her before she got in the damn Limo. If she was good then she's good now." He embraced Shamara in front of his crew.

Shamara smiled as she kissed Tommy, while cutting her eyes at Kahmel as if to say I'm more important than you. She saw Kahmel rolled his eyes at her like a little bitch. Her smile grew even wider because she knew the fireworks were going down tonight and he was going to be a part of the show in an unfortunate way.

"Alright," Kahmel said as he headed for the door with his team on his heels. "I'll set up a perimeter. Once I get shit right I'll be in the room down the hall." Kahmel exited the house.

Tommy went straight to the liquor, wine and champagne cabinet and started pouring drinks.

Meanwhile, Shamara found the remote control and hit the "on" button to the stereo system and a Nas song came on. She and Tommy had been here once before and she was already familiar with this location, including the outer layout of the grounds, information she had given to Fashawn as they planned this hit. Shamara suddenly felt a wave of anxiety surging through her as she took a seat on the sofa. *This is it.* She was about to finally close this long chapter in her life and acquire the much-needed closure on this matter.

Her heart started pounding like it always did just before a hit. She hadn't done a hit in so long it felt like she was starting that whole anxiety trip all over again. Tommy gave her a glass of champagne and she drank it down fast, even though she was already tipsy from the drinks they consumed on the way here.

"Wow, baby girl," Tommy said. "Take it easy. We got the whole weekend. Ain't no need to rush this thing. You know I'm gonna treat you right tonight. We don't need liquor to take us there, so you ain't gotta drink so fast."

Shamara poured herself another glass and made a note to herself to slow it down before she put him on point that she was nervous. But, the minute her lips touched the glass, she was tempted to gulp it. She needed to get her head right for this job, she realized, because there was just too much shit working on her conscience. It seemed the closer she got to the point of stepping to her business, her heart and mind started talking, and she didn't like what it was saying.

About an hour later, Shamara saw she had far more than a buzz. She suddenly realized she had better not get drunk, since she still had to make sure they escaped from this place. Fashawn warned her to take it real easy on the drinks, and now she suddenly realized she may have had one too many. *Ah fuck*, she cursed inward as she got up to go to the bathroom and felt the room spin violently, and her legs wobbled uncontrollably. *Oh, goddamn!* She mumbled as she entered the bathroom and sat on the toilet.

When she finished her business, she looked at herself in the mirror and then looked at her watch. It was after one o'clock. It was time. She looked around frantically and noticed she left her purse in the living room. She was about to panic, because she had to hit Fashawn on her cell phone and tell her she was ready to start the show.

Shamara calmed down, and decided to just go out there, get her purse, and come back to the bathroom. If Tommy asked what she was doing she'd tell him she had to freshen up and forgot her bag. She stumbled out of the bathroom, snatched her purse and was surprised Tommy said nothing. He was all into an old rap song by Big Daddy Kane.

Shamara rushed into the bathroom, retrieved the cell phone, hit the re-dial button, and when Fashawn picked up she said, "I'm ready. Let's do it." She disconnected the call, stuffed her cell phone back into the purse, and now it was time to retrieved her heater. Shamara pulled her pants down, squatted, activated her pussy muscles, and the one-shot pen gun slid from her insides. The pen gun was soaked in pussy juice as she put it in her purse.

Shamara stood by the door breathing hard with excitement. Her mind was swirling with alcohol, but it wasn't in an altered enough state for her not to realize what she was about to do. Her heart was talking to her again and all the distracting mental images were bombarding her mind with intense fury. Even the voices in her head that judged her wouldn't shut up. She closed her eyes, cleared her mind, saw the bullets tearing at her mom and dad, and the image moved her into a mind frame of action.

She exited the bathroom knowing that within the next twenty minutes the shit was not only going to hit the fan, but was going to hit any and everything that was connected to Tommy's world.

*   *   *   *

Fashawn felt alive as she moved through the thick underbrush on the outskirts of Tommy's Sanford home, carrying a duffle bag with all her goodies inside. The house was up ahead, and she was on cloud nine since Shamara just called her and hit her with those magic words that basically said, "It's on!" She was dressed in all black with a black knit hat and leather gloves, *just like a ninja*, she thought. Earlier, with a set of infrared night vision binoculars she'd watched the four bodyguards along with Kahmel and Cabby moving about the location. She also saw there was a much smaller house, like a shack or something next to the main house, and she detected the bodyguards were using it as a place to take a break and warm themselves up. The January climate wasn't fiercely cold, since global warming was making it clear it was here to stay, but nonetheless, it was cold enough to require that the weather not be underestimated.

141

Fashawn decided this was going to be a sneak, hit, sneak, and hit again attack as she moved towards a thick cluster of bushes, found a perfect position that permitted her to see both the main house and the shack and began assembling her sharpshooter's rifle.

        *   *   *   *

Shamara took charge the moment she came out of the bathroom. She sat her purse down on the coffee table in reaching distance, and started kissing Tommy, insisting with her body language that she was ready to take it there as Tommy hit the remote and put on Teddy Pendergrass's "Turn off The lights."

Tommy almost never failed to respond when a woman gave him signals that it was time to tap that thang and he went with the flow, kissing and fondling Shamara in his usual fashion. Tommy suddenly noticed something wasn't right. Shamara's body was tense. She even seemed nervous. He stopped and said, "Hey, baby girl, you alright? Your body feels tense, Shamara."

Shamara was about to panic. "I'm good, Tommy. Come on, baby, I'm ready to do this." It was clear that she was losing control of the situation. Now she had to resort to extreme measures. *Ah shit*, he's about to take it somewhere else, she realized as she reached up and started tongue-kissing Tommy while pulling down her pants. She knew this would get his mind back on track.

She slid her panties down as well and laid down on the sofa with her legs cocked open, displaying her womanhood in its most explicit form. She saw the smile on Tommy's face that announced he was back on track and without further a due he went to work. He started munching down on Shamara's luscious goodies. Shamara's eyes rolled up into her head, and instantly dreaded the fact that she was going to deeply miss this part of the relationship, because Tommy had a vicious pussy eating game, and earned the title of being the best ever. She doubted if there was anyone who could do it the way Tommy did it and this began to disturb her. She quickly shifted her thoughts, but the mind-boggling pleasure was just too much. She felt herself about to hit her point of no return and tried to fight it, because Fashawn said the show would begin about twenty minutes after she got the call.

The sexual pleasure was so good it caused her lose track of the time, she noticed. She struggled to hold back the nut, even scooting away from Tommy's tongue, but he chased her across the sofa, increasing his sucking and slurping like a mad man, and finally it was just too much for her and she let her juices flow while throwing her body at him. The slurping and sucking sounds drove her wild as she hollered in ecstasy.

       *   *   *   *

Fashawn was in position and was getting nervous because she hadn't anticipated that the bodyguards wouldn't be in place. With the rifle's scope planted to her right eye, she scrolled her aim across the area, searching for the bodyguards to move pass the damn window. All fuckin' night they were moving pass the damn window, and the minute she was ready to start the fuckin' show, now all of a sudden nobody was moving near the fuckin' window, she cursed inwardly. She also realized she was way off schedule.

Just when she was about to abandon this tactic, get her handgun, rush over to the shack, kicked the door opened, and put it on the bodyguards, one of them came right in position.

ZIP!

The bullet shot through the barrel of the rifle and the silencer device, and Fashawn saw the man's head jerked violently. She didn't see the blood cloud, but knew this was because of the fact it was night and her visibility from this location was poor, to say the least.

Just as she suspected, Fashawn saw another bodyguard burst out of the shack, apparently on his way to the big house to warn the others. Fashawn took aim and pushed his wig back just as the scream shot from his mouth. She flipped her aim back to the windows of the shack and wanted to shout with glory when she saw one of the bodyguards stupidly peeking over the windowsill with the top of his head completely exposed. Fashawn immediately obliged him.

ZIP!

This time she noticed droplets of blood had splattered about the area when his head exploded from the 30.06 bullet.

In accordance with the plan, Fashawn frantically pulled the rifle from its stand and disassembled the weapon with the speed of a sheer specialist. It was time to get closer in order to make sure Shamara got away.

*   *   *   *

Moments earlier, Shamara was savoring every second of Tommy's tongue and when he tried to get up, apparently ready to penetrate her, Shamara grabbed his head with both hands and held him down there. She still hadn't gotten the signal and knew she needed just a few more minutes. She instantly wondered what the fuck was taking Fashawn so long to start this damn show as Tommy obeyed her wishes and continued doing his thing with her pleasure factory. As if Fashawn was in her head, she heard the signal go off when Kahmel rushed out of the backroom and raced through the back door.

Tommy got up off of Shamara and went to the window to see what was going on.

Shamara frantically grabbed her purse retrieved the pen gun, slid her pants on, dunked her feet into her slip on soft sole shoes, stood and took aim. As she watched him peering out the window to see what the fuck was going on, her mind started doing what she told it not to do; don't think about any of the good times she had with Tommy and Tommy Jr., and especially don't reminisce about what she was going to miss once she took it there with Tommy. With a head-shaking struggle, Shamara flung these invading thoughts to the back of her mind and said to Tommy's back, "Tommy." Everything was going in slow motion it seemed. She moved closer to Tommy to make sure she didn't miss.

When Shamara saw Tommy turn around and he saw the gun, she detected more of a hurting response than one of surprise. Instantly, she saw him go for his Golden 9 and she hit the button on the pen gun.

BANG!

The partially loud explosion ignited as Tommy convulsed while grabbing his stomach with both hands. Shamara ran, caught Tommy in the face with a sniff right and immediately took possession of his Golden 9 when he hit the floor.

"Shamara, what the fuck is this!?" Tommy cringed with wide-eyed shock as he frantically crawled towards the room in the back.

Just as Shamara took aim with the Golden 9, the door slammed open. She spun the gun in the direction of the newcomer.

BOOM! BOOM!

She pumped off two shots into one of the new bodyguard's chest as Tommy scrambled towards the backroom. Shamara spun the gun in Tommy's direction and fired two shots as Tommy bolted down the hall with bullets ricocheting.

"Tommy!" Kahmel screamed as he reentered the back door of the house. "It's a hit! It's a hit!"

Shamara heard Kahmel coming and knew it was time to break out. She knew Kahmel carried a compact Uzi with him and changed her mind about tangling with him. She raced towards the door, leaped over the bodyguard sprawled out in the doorway and realized she may have blown this mission. She was supposed to shoot Tommy, get his Golden 9, and empty the clip in him. The pen gun was to temporarily immobilize him, and that part of the plan worked out perfectly, but she was certain she didn't hit him with any of the bullets from the Golden 9.

As Shamara's leg's pumped as she headed for the getaway car, she noticed the crisp night air brushing across her face woke her up from the dream like state she was in. She ran towards the designated location she and Fashawn had planned to meet up, realizing with dread that the stomach bullet might not have been enough to complete the job.

When she thought of what she just threw away, and what the consequences would be if Tommy lived, she realized she should have took the chance by going with her first mind, and that was to shoot Tommy in the head first, even if head shots were difficult to pull off when compared to shots aimed at center mass.

CHAPTER # 14

"What the fuck you mean you not sure he's dead!?" Fashawn shouted from behind the steering wheel of her Nissan that was heading southbound. She looked at Shamara and saw she was visibly distraught. "Did you follow the plan!?"

"Yeah, I followed the plan."

Fashawn slammed her hand on the steering wheel. "Why you lied to me when you said everything was good?! We could've gone back and finished him."

Shamara felt two inches small and was speechless. Suddenly, she started crying and didn't understand why her emotions were going crazy.

Fashawn looked over and her anger grew ten-folds. "Girl, what the hell are you crying about!? I hope it's 'cause you're upset you missed an opportunity to smoke this nigga and not anything else."

Shamara sucked up her tears and was getting ready to go in hard on Fashawn. "Why you so fuckin' bitter about every god damn thing, Fashawn!? You act like a heartless bitch with everything! Here it is we running around here killing motherfuckers and you acting like this shit ain't supposed to affect a person. I ain't been in the fuckin' military like you, killing people everyday and shit. This is some real emotional shit for me. I probably killed this nigga, and now Tommy Jr. is gonna be all fucked up when he finds out. What the fuck, I can't cry knowing how that kid is gonna feel when he gets the news!?" This was partially the reason she was crying; there were other reasons she wouldn't dare discuss, mentally or otherwise.

Fashawn held on to that comment for a minute as she allowed the information to soak into her mind. Maybe this mission wasn't a complete disaster; maybe that one bullet did kill this chump. "The way you talking now; it's like you think you killed him or something. And for your information, this ain't gonna be no game if Tommy lives, Shamara. Even if your heart is still bleeding for him, if he lives you can bet one thing for sure; his heart won't be bleeding for you." She pulled her cell phone and tossed it to Shamara. "Call Kenyetta and tell him back-up plan B is in affect."

Shamara took the phone and punched in the number, realizing it was better to be safe than sorry, since there was still the chance Tommy wasn't dead. "Hey, Kenyetta . . . Yeah, we alright, both of us. I'm calling to tell you Back-up Plan B is in motion . . . I'm not sure . . . We'll meet you at the back-up crib, alright. Peace, big bro." She hung up.

There was a moment of silence as Fashawn lit up a Newport.

"I don't want to upset you, Shamara" Fashawn said as she blew out a cloud of smoke. "But, I hope you ready to take this thing wherever it's gotta go. You know me; I'm honored to do whatever it is we gotta do to end this shit with Tommy, even if we gotta turn our newly discovered skills of killing people professionally full force on everything Tommy loves; I'm with whatever. I just think you need to find a way to harden her heart a whole lot more, because even if you did kill Tommy, he's got a crew that loved him and they might not be willing to let it ride so easy. I know we hooked this thing up to where they don't got a clue where we live, but in the real world things don't always go according to plan, as you discovered tonight."

Shamara reached over, retrieved the pack of cigarettes and lit up a Newport, realizing for the first time that once she took this route she had opened a Pandora's Box because now everyone who loved Tommy had suddenly become her enemies. But, that voice in her head was telling her she fucked up royally because Tommy wasn't dead, and since he wasn't dead he was going to come up for her with everything thing he had, and once he found her the only thing moving would be flying bullets.

*   *   *   *

Tommy laid in the Sanford County hospital bed, looking at the news report on the TV up on the wall, still in a state of shock. His mind refused to believe Shamara did this to him. However, he was extremely grateful the stomach wound wasn't fatal. Not only was it a non-fatal wound, but he also noticed the bullet had stuck him on the side just above his hipbone, and didn't even injury any vital organs. According to the doctor, the small caliber bullet severed a small part of his small intestine as it entered and exited his body. He'd undergone an hour surgery and would be released within the next three days.

Suddenly, Kahmel entered along with Slick and Dubar, a hard-nosed brother with a cut across his mouth that made him look like he had a permanent smile.

Tommy sat up in bed, feeling embarrassed because he was shot by a woman that he swore up and down was his number one girl. He even told Kahmel that he was coming close to saying he loved Shamara. "So what's up with Caddy and the others?"

Kahmel sighed as his pain and fury sparked back up and said, "They all dead. Everyone that was shot, with the exception of you, died. None of them made it."

Tommy felt a rage boiling in his stomach. He couldn't believe Shamara did this to him and his crew, after the way he treated her. He instantly realized he was slipping because she had his nose totally open.

"Just so we're all on the same page," Kahmel said. "Popo stepped to me and Dave and we told them it was a bunch of masked men. They said they were coming back to talk to you, Tommy. I figured you oughta know what we told them, so our stories are consistent."

149

"That's good," Tommy said, realizing this shit was going to stir up another wave of problems. "Now, you know they're gonna be fuckin' with us for a good minute behind this shit, so keep this in mind when you start steppin' to shit. I guess we're lucky this shit didn't hit the papers, probably because the news reporters didn't catch on to this, at least not yet." He sighed and said, "So who's behind this shit?"

"This shit got us all fucked up, Tommy," Kahmel said with genuine bewilderment. "From what we getting from the streets, nobody's owning up to this hit."

"What the fuck's up with Skeeter?" Tommy didn't want to hear no shit like this and his anger was about to display itself with full vengeance. "This is the kind long range, elaborate contract hit a nigga like him might try to pull off."

Kahmel shook his head no with enthusiasm. "It ain't Skeeter. Our inside man is too close to Skeeter not to know he was about to hit us like this." He also wanted to inform Tommy that he was giving Skeeter more credit than he deserved, since this cat was still thinking like a petty street corner thug, catch up in all that flashy shit, but instead, he stayed focused on the issue at hand. "Believe me, Tommy, it ain't Skeeter. Neither is it the Dominicans. Even our eyes in that crew said they had nothing to do with this. We're still working on the Columbians and the Italians, but you probably know as well as I do, they ain't got no reason to come at us like this, especially since they got an invested interest in making sure you stay in the game."

"Me and my team checked out those apartments in Newark," Dubar said with a raspy voice that sounded like he was suffering from throat cancer. "Both of those places look like they were temporary; like they had them as decoy cribs or something. I ain't go in real deep yet, but by tomorrow, I'll find out who's name is on the lease, but I can almost bet you it'll be a bogus name. We'll check into it anyway."

Slick spoke when he sensed Dubar was finished, "We've checked every crew in the nearby hoods, and from the way it looks, they ain't have shit to do with these broads or Kenyetta. At first we thought it was a backlash from the Ray-Ray and Gangsta hits, but they peeps wasn't feelin' them like that anyway, and they ain't holdin' enough cheddar to pay for such a sophisticated super long range hit like this."

Tommy knew this was definitely a long range hit. Whoever was behind this shit, had sent these bitches at him, tricked him into believing they were simply trying to make some money, and once they were close to him they would kill him, or maybe someone got to them after they got close to him; either way, there had to be somebody big behind this hit and he had full intentions of finding out who it was. "I'll be outta here in two days. I don't want anybody to do anything to Malik until I get out of here. I just want you to watch him. He brought them to me, so as it stands, he's the one who would know what's going on."

Tommy drew in a deep breath at the thought of what he was planning to do to Malik if he didn't tell him what he wanted to know. It touched his heart deeply because he and Malik went back many years, and made a lot of money together. Despite all that, if he violated, he would be treated like all other violators. "Alright, check this Kahmel. Keep hittin' the streets. Focus on those two bitches and Kenyetta; somebody's gotta know something about them. When you get a lock on them don't do nothing to them. I wanna be the one to do the deed."

Tommy stopped in mid thought. He was about to tell him to make sure if he found them to get his Golden 9 back, but the mere fact Shamara was able to disarm him, made him feel extremely inadequate and utterly incompetent. With a struggle he swallowed his proud and said, "And make sure when you catch them, get my shit back to me."

Kahmel squinted his eyes, since Tommy never told him she took something from. "What you talking about? Get what back?"

Tommy gave Kahmel the look of death and said, "My piece. The bitch got my Golden 9. No matter what you do, get my shit back."

*   *   *   *

Two days later, in a second floor apartment at 364 Jefferson Avenue between Throop and Tompkins Avenue in the Bed-Stuy section of Brooklyn, Shamara, Fashawn and Kenyetta sat in a neatly kept living room talking. Shamara and Fashawn sat on the sofa, while Kenyetta sat in an armchair drinking a bottle of grape juice.

"That sounds good," Kenyetta said. "But it's not realistic, Fashawn. Tommy is gonna have super security everywhere he goes. It sounds good to believe it's wise to step to him while he's steppin' to us, but the reality is that we ain't built to go against an army of mufuckin' killers. Remember, before we got inside his organization, we tried to hit him twice and couldn't do it. After what just happened, it's gonna be a hundred times harder to get near this dude. When we missed him . . . we blew it."

Shamara felt real bad. There was no doubt she let the team down. She was the reason they were sitting here trying to find a way to kill Tommy before he killed them. "If you ask me, I say we lay low; let some time go by, and then take a hit at him again when he puts his guards down. He's too charged up right now to even think about trying to touch him."

Fashawn sighed with frustration. "We better start thinking about what's gonna happen when he starts tracking our black asses." Fashawn sucked on the cigarette between her fingers and blew out a cloud of

152

smoke. "With the money he's got, he's gonna hire some top notch hitters to look for us. This is why I say instead of running and hiding we should just go on and bring this shit to a head." She really wanted to beat up on Shamara again, but realized she did more than enough badgering already. "I don't like that felling of having to look over my shoulder every damn place I go and every time I step foot out of my house."

Kenyetta shook his head almost to symbolize just how much he felt Fashawn's analogy was pathetic. "Let me spell this out another way." He thought careful about what he was about to say and said. "If we come anywhere near this fool, and anyone recognizes us, we're gonna have at least a hundred gunslingers trying to take our heads off. I tried to reach out to my man Malik, but he ain't trying to vibe with me, even after I told him I knew nothing about what happened with Tommy and y'all. I was fishing for information and he kept trying to get me to meet him at the pool hall in Jersey City. This nigga is already trying to pull us into the open so they can kill us. Tommy's a big wig in Jersey and you can bet there's a ghetto APB out on all of us. If we step foot in any Hood in that town, somebody's gonna recognize us, and he'll send out an army in seconds. Listen, call me what you want, but I'm taking what I got out of all this and relocating, and I strongly suggest y'all do the same; at least for a year or two. It's about damn time y'all get out of that old broken down, fucked up as Canarsie."

Shamara and Fashawn looked at each as if to say that's not going to happen.

Kenyetta saw that little eye exchange and knew what that was all about. "So, y'all still stuck on that living in Canarsie shit forever, even after all this drama?"

"That's our home," Shamara said. "We were born and raised there and probably will die in Canarsie. And what's your beef? You hate Canarsie that much?"

"I don't totally hate Canarsie," Kenyetta countered. "I just don't have a whole lot of good memories connected to that place. The best memories I have of Canarsie are with you guys. Everything else, I wish I could reach down into my memory bank and pull all that shit out of my mind and hurl it into a fuckin' trash can."

"Come on, man." Fashawn said. "It wasn't that bad." She knew Kenyetta's father was a drunk, but she didn't think he was that brutal.

"Like most families in the Hood," Kenyetta sighed as he held the bottle up to his lips. "My family was experts at hiding all the dirt and foul shit they were doing to fellow family members." He let that hang in the air for a moment as he drank some more grape juice and decided to get the discussion back on track. "The bottom line is, even though Tommy and his peeps think we from New Jersey, and don't got a clue where we're really from, if Tommy hires a few big time investigators, which I'm sure is exactly what he's gonna do, it won't be long before he comes knocking on our doors." He locked eyes with them to place some importance on his remark. "He can come knocking on my old door all he wants, but you can bet he won't find me there, and as of this minute, I ain't leaving no more tracks. And I suggest you do the same."

"Well, like we said," Shamara said point blankly. "We're staying in Canarsie. We covered our tracks and I believe they won't find us. It's a chance we gotta take." She saw Fashawn nod her head. "I agree with you on the issue of not stepping to Tommy right now. That would be suicide." She saw Fashawn screw up her face. "He's not only on full alert, but I can almost guarantee you he's gonna do everything in his power to get this baby back."

Shamara pulled the Golden 9 from the back waist of her pants, savoring the sight, weight and explicit beauty of this real gold weapon. Shamara smiled as the hypnotic power of the gun took center stage of the meeting. She saw Fashawn was almost drooling from the mouth.

"I gotta hold this thing again," Fashawn said excitedly as she took hold of the gun, reacting almost as if she was experiencing an organism just by holding it.

"Well, one thing for sure," Kenyetta said nonchalantly. "At least you'll never go broke with that thing. You can get some serious gees for that mufucka that could keep you straight for a good little minute."

Shamara said with excitement in her voice, "How much you think I could get for a gun like this?"

"It's hard to say," Kenyetta said, suddenly sounding like a college professional. "There's a lot things you have to take into consideration. Like the actually weight and carat of the gold first off. But, a fair estimate of cost, I would say, you could get at least a hundred grand, give or take."

"Damn," Shamara said, wishing he had given a larger number. "That's about as much as we was getting for a job and half."

"Just let me know when you ready to get rid of it," Kenyetta sipped his juice. "I got this Polish cat that can get off anything."

Shamara looked at Kenyetta like he was insane. "I ain't selling this piece. A gun like this is something you hold on to. Plus, we made enough money from fuckin' with Tommy to hold us for some years as long as we live within our means."

"Now that we on the topic of money," Fashawn said to Shamara. "Don't think we forgot what you told us."

Shamara was genuine confused. "What I told y'all?"

"You said when you got the money after you sold that Lexus, you was gonna break me and Kenyetta off a few dollars."

"That's right," Kenyetta had sincerely forgotten she had said that. "Now that the cash flow is on hold, I need every dime I got coming to me."

"I got y'all," Shamara took the gun from Fashawn and put it back in the back waist of her pants. "So, we all agree we gonna lay low?"

"That's what I vote for," Kenyetta said as she chugged down the remainder of the grape juice. "Since that's a two against one vote, its law. The lay lows have it."

Shamara looked over at Fashawn and saw she was hot under the collar. Fashawn's excessive aggression was making her nervous and now she had a solid idea of what was the source of this behavior. She was tempted to put Fashawn on blast in front of Kenyetta and force her to explain the prescription bottle of medication she found with Fashawn's name on it. She looked up the name, Phenothiazine Chlorpromazine, found out it was an antipsychotic drug used to treat people with severe psychiatric problems. Shamara felt this was something Fashawn should've shared with her and Kenyetta on her own. After contemplating Fashawn's likely response—she might take it totally the wrong way—and because right now they didn't need any dissension amongst them, Shamara decided to sweep the issue under the rug, not even confront her one-on-one, at least for the time being.

CHAPTER # 15

Tommy exited the hospital; he moved slowly with a limp and a cane and a colistic bag attached to his stomach, promising to hit the scene like Hurricane Katrina. As he limped towards the white Ranger Rover Jeep—the limo was going to be put on hold, since he was officially in war mode now—Tommy had only one thing on his mind and that was finding Shamara, Fashawn and Kenyetta and crucifying them.

Todd held the passenger door open as Tommy slid inside the Jeep.

Minutes later, the Jeep was cruising down the road with five other vehicles following the Range Rover, each one possessing several of Tommy's best hitters. Tommy's mind started wandering as she sat staring out of the passenger window. He needed to know why Shamara did this to him; he inwardly asked this question once again, a question he asked himself nearly ten thousand times since he received the gut shot. He had subconsciously known all along that this had nothing to do with a contract hit coming from another crew, but he had to send his team out into the field to make sure and they confirmed what he suspected all along.

As Tommy watched the Connecticut roadway scroll pass his vision, in a daydream state of mind, he realized he still had feelings for Shamara. Even after the bitch shot him, he still felt something for her. He thought he was losing his goddamn mind but he couldn't lie to himself and pretend there wasn't something still lingering in his heart that made him feel for Shamara.

Something was obviously going on underneath it all, he knew for certain, because he knew Shamara felt something for him. If she was faking it all along, then she was the most deceptive person he'd ever met. In any event, his instincts, his observations, and most of all, his heart was

157

telling him Shamara did this to him not of her own volition. His mind recaptured the moment before she shot him, and her nervousness and tension was a signal she really didn't want to do what she did.

He also recalled the way she looked him in the eyes just before she fired the pen gun. There was a pleading like expression that was telling him she didn't want to do it, almost like she was telling him sorry with her eyes. He now realized if he had just talked to her instead of reaching for his weapon, she might not have taken it there. *She probably wouldn't have fired the shot if I had just talked to her instead of reaching!*

Then, he reexamined the moment when she got his Golden 9 and shot Reggie when he busted into the room with a gun in his hand; he now realized she had no choice but to shoot Reggie, since he had a weapon and it was a genuine kill or be killed situation.

And the Coup de Grace fact that wouldn't let Tommy's mind experience any peace was the fact that if she really wanted to shoot him she easily could have hit him with a bullet from the Golden 9 as he crawled to the back of the house. Those bullets missed him by a mile. He could still recall squinting his eyes and tensing up every muscle in his body as he moved towards the back of the house, anticipating the bullets tearing through his completely exposed back, but it never happened. At first he thought he was just plan lucky, but now that he was dissecting it all, putting everything under a microscope, he had to acknowledge these significant and indisputable facts.

Tommy sighed violently and with a jaw clinching mental shift, he hurled this thinking out of his mind, and replaced it with a treacherous form of thinking he used to be an expert at commanding and harboring. He started reactivating his super grime, hate filled thug mentality that he had put under wraps many years ago. He had vowed once he made the transition, he would never go back to that trifling way of thinking, but

Shamara had shot him—something no one ever did despite decades in the game—she disrespected him, stole his prize possession, violated him, humiliated him, and literally slapped him in the face in front of all his peeps when all he was guilty of was showing this bitch mad love, and unfortunately, the lying dogs could no longer lay still. The sleeping giant from within had been awaken with that one gut shot, and all those responsible for unleashing what he put on a leash years ago would play dearly. The old Tommy Gun was now back and about to wreck utter havoc. Even if she did pull her blows, she still crossed the line and would have to pay the consequences.

His first stop was to pay is homie Malik a visit. He wasn't even going to make a stop home first or even start his treatment consisting of bed-rest in conjunction with a whole regiment of medications. All that could wait until after he personally sat down with Malik and picked his mind. He even told Malik not to visit him at the hospital. When he stepped to Malik, it had to be when he was in shape enough to appreciate the wrath that was striving to get out. Although Malik was his homie, he once got this crazy vibe that Malik was creeping with his ex-wife Ashanta when she was his wife, and couldn't seem to get that incident out of his mind or system. They say women had this sixth sense like power and could detect when their men were creeping just by watching their reactions, facial expressions when confronted with the truth, and especially their sudden change in behavior, but what folks didn't realize was that some men also had this heighten sense of perception.

Several times Malik and Ashanta had one of those "eye moments" and one time their reckless eyeballing was almost too blatant for Tommy to miss it. The only thing that saved Malik from meeting his maker was the results of Kahmel and Caddy's investigation, which according to them, indicated nothing was going on between the two. But, with this current situation, he could no longer pretend not to know Malik had been hatin' on him ever since he blew up on the OG tip. Tommy was flattered when he saw his homie hating, but now that this hatin', jealous, envious ass motherfucker was bringing people into his organization who was trying to kill him, all those little ego stroking games were over.

About two hours later, Tommy and his entourage pulled up in front of Malik's two family house in Camden New Jersey, and Kahmel went and got Malik. Five minutes later, Malik approached Tommy's white Jeep.

With a smile Malik said, "Tommy, I'm glad you out man. I've been working like hell trying to track them mufuckas." He propped both hands on the door of the Jeep. "I definitely need to talk to you."

"That's why I'm here," Tommy said with a sincere looking smile. "Get in. I called a full meeting. I need everybody on deck, so we can get this plan rolling."

As Malik got in the backseat of the Jeep, his instincts suddenly told him something wasn't right. He slammed the door shut behind him and the Jeep took off. He knew it was a rarity when Tommy came personally to someone's doorstep and his heart started pounding. Then, he realized, Tommy just got shot. It was obvious he was about to go on a vicious mission, and with this in mind, Malik realized he was probably over-reacting. He told himself he was bugging to think Tommy would flip on him over something he had no control over. Malik also told himself he was apparently becoming defensive because he knew he was the one who brought Kenyetta, Shamara and Fashawn to this organization. Despite these reassuring mental talks, Malik couldn't get his mind to stop assuming this was the last ride of his life.

Twenty minutes later, Tommy sat in the back room of a warehouse he owned that was used to store huge shipments of drugs, stolen cars, and others underworld items that were about to hit the streets of New Jersey, New York, and even Connecticut. Sitting across from him was Malik and standing near the door were Kahmel and Slick.

Tommy sat silently just watching Malik, hoping this little trick would make Malik uncomfortable enough to just confess and get it over with.

Malik was sweating bullets. Even though he truly believed he had nothing to worry about, he knew in this line of work the truth never really meant much at difficult times in this one. He tried to ride out the infamous silent head game tactic, but it was just too much, and he gave in. "Tommy, man, you know I had no idea them mufuckas were about to do us dirty. That nigga Kenyetta, if he was down with this shit, played me. You know I would never betray you, Tommy. And let's keep it real; if I was down with this shit, I damn sure wouldn't take the chance of hanging around waiting for you to come trying to find out what's going on, I would've—"

"The fact that you mention that tells me you had time to think about all this." Tommy said smoothly. "Maybe that's all part of it. Make a mufucka think everything's gravy by doing just the opposite of what a guilty mufucka would do. Of all people, Malik, you know I know all the diversion tricks in the mufuckin' book."

There was a moment of silence.

"Tommy, man," Malik said, almost with a whining tone. "This is crazy bro. I want those mufuckas just as bad as you because—"

"How the fuck you want them as bad as me when I'm the one who got shot, nigga!?"

"Well, maybe not as bad as you, Tommy, but I want these mufuckas, since they played me! They used me to get inside our operation. I'm--I—Then again--The more I look at all the facts I can't help but to find it--" He sighed with frustration and confusion, because nothing was adding up. "It just don't make sense for them to get at us like this. Maybe somebody recently got to them, after they got in—I don't know, but I do know, we need to find these niggas and murder them real slowly."

Tommy liked the way Malik said the last part of his comment; it had a strong touch of wickedness to it, almost fiendish. Despite his good acting technique, Tommy still refused to accept his story. "So, where are they? You brought them in now tell us where the fuck are they?"

Malik was literally stuck. Immediately after he got word of the shooting, he had personally gone out to their crib in Newark and saw it was a decoy. He'd been making phone calls all week, and once he got in touch with Kenyetta, he did everything in his power to convince Kenyetta to meet him at various places with absolutely no good results. "Tommy, the minute I heard about this shit I been on it. I made mad phone calls, I went to both cribs, I hit the streets—"

"Where the fuck do they hang out!?" Tommy said, realizing that Shamara had kept her background somewhat vague even with him. "You brought them in and you better be able to tell me something. And it better be a whole lot more than you working on it."

Malik bowed his head, wondering should he beg Tommy not to kill him, because it wasn't hard to tell that the shit was about to hit the fan. "Tommy, I don't know where they're at—What about Shamara, you was hit that, didn't she tell you where she can be found—" He saw Tommy's eyes beam with anger. "A few more days, I can find them--I promise you, I'll find them. I'll invest everyday of my—"

"The same way you promised me I won't be disappointed if I bring them in as personal hitters for this team!? Is it the same kinda promise, Malik?"

Malik couldn't answer that question. Looking like a child who just upset an abusive parent, Malik sat there looking silly and pathetic. He wanted to lash out, because it was obvious Tommy was fucking with his head, making him feel weak and inadequate; he wanted to tell Tommy to kiss his ass and suck his dick, but that would only guarantee him a one-way ticket to an early grave. His anger was boiling by the seconds.

Malik stared into Tommy's eyes as his carefully concealed hate vibrated his very being. He felt it in his heart that this was the end of the road and it scared him. Despite his fear, he realized at least he could say he got his shit off on Tommy when he laid crazy dick to his trifling ass wife, Ashanta; he fucked her repeatedly just to prove to himself that Tommy's shit wasn't as tight as he thought it was. The urge to tell Tommy he fucked his wife was strong; if Tommy heard this right now his whole world would be shattered, and this would be an excellent way to hurt this niggas, but Malik knew that would guarantee his death. Even though he knew subconsciously that he was wasting his time, he had to try to talk his way of this! He firmly believed that Tommy should know he didn't bring them into this operation knowing they were going to kill him. When he realized Tommy could be the real closed minded type at times like this, his rage was growing to an uncontrollable level. He hated when Tommy beat him in the head when he made simple mistakes; shit, he was only human.

"So are you gonna answer my mufuckin' question or am I gonna have to get on some real serious—"

"No! No, it ain't the same fuckin' promise!" Malik shouted and instantly realized he let the stress of the moment make him unconsciously lash out. He instantly saw he crossed the line; his tone was totally disrespectfully and filled with frustration. He wished he could take it back, but it was too late. "Listen, Tommy, I'm sorry for that outburst, bro, but this shit got my mind all twisted—"

Tommy pulled a 9mm from the inner breast holster. *Well, he blew it*, Tommy thought; he was just about to give him a shot, and like most people, they always had a way of being their own worst enemy. Tommy waved the gun as he spoke. "Now, would I be wrong," He took aim at Malik's left kneecap. "If I—"

BANG!

The bullet ripped through its target as Malik screamed with lung shattering force. The pain was so excruciating it forced him out of the chair and onto the floor. He was clutching his knee with a face ridden with sheer agony.

Malik's eyes were wild with terror. "Please, Tommy, we go back too far for it to go down like this, man! Remember all the shit I did for you when you was in the rap game! I was the one who put you—"

BANG!

Tommy fired another shot into Malik's other leg, but in the thigh area.

Malik unleashed another ear torturous shriek. He was now crying since he didn't want to die. Now he wished he had run, like his girl Diana told him to do.

"You got one last chance to make it out of this shit alive, Malik," Tommy said, still sitting comfortably in his chair, waving the gun as if he was bored out of his mind. "Tell us exactly where we can find them? You answer that question and you live."

"Please, if I knew I would tell you! Just give me a minute and I can find them—"

"Wrong answer!" Tommy rose to his feet, took aim and held his finger down on the trigger.

BANG! BANG! BANG!

The rapidly fired bullets pounded Malik's chest with gruesome force.

Tommy stared down at Mailk's body as he noticed that feeling slowly returning and not to his surprise, it felt nothing like it used to. In fact, he noticed it made his stomach turn.

*   *   *   *

An hour later, Tommy's white Range Rover pulled to a stop in front of his mansion. Tommy Jr. burst from the front door screaming with delight as Tommy got out of the Jeep with a loving smile.

"Daddy! Daddy!" Tommy Jr. bolted towards his father with both arms extended.

Tommy braced himself for the impact with his son, not caring if the embrace was going to hurt like hell when his son collided with his bullet wound. He caught his son as he jumped into his arms. He sighed inwardly from the pain.

"Daddy, they said you was in the hospital." Tommy Jr. said. "What happened, daddy? What happened to you?"

Tommy carried his son towards the mansion. "We'll talk about that real soon. But right now I wanna know have you been driving Diana crazy!?"

"No, I was good, right, Aunty Diana." Tommy Jr. grinned deviously.

Diana laughed as she held the door open as the two entered. "Boy, you oughta be ashamed of yourself to ask me something like that when we all know how bad your behind is."

Five minutes later, Tommy sat with his son sitting next to him. He'd been rehearsing how he was going to break the news that his "new mommy" wasn't going to be his "new mommy" anymore since she was

165

the one who put his daddy in the hospital, and now that it was time to share the news with his son, Tommy noticed not only was his tongue tied, but so was his thoughts.

"I heard uncle Kahmel said you got shot." Tommy Jr's eyes grew wide with excitement; the looked was almost one of admiration. "Where did you get shot daddy?"

He reached over and riffled his son's head. "What I tell you about eavesdropping on people's conversations." He decided the best way to handle this was to give it to him in the raw, especially since there was no way of hiding the fact that Shamara wasn't going to return to this mansion. "Listen, Tommy, I got shot in the stomach, and—"

"Can I see it!?" Tommy Jr. said as serious as the 1980s crack epidemic. "Did it hurt?"

"I'll let you see it later and yeah it hurt." He paused as he struggled to come right out with it. This felt awkward because he'd been filling his son's head with talk about Shamara moving in soon and now it just felt crazy trying to explain that she shot him. Since he had no idea why she shot him it made it even more awkward and he definitely didn't want to lie to his son.

"Daddy, why did Shamara shoot you?" Tommy Jr. said softly.

Tommy was beyond shocked.

Tommy Jr. continued with his usual rapid-fire questions. "I thought Shamara is gonna be my new mommy? I thought she liked you daddy? Why did she shoot you? You ain't gonna shoot her back are you, daddy?"

Tommy was about to explode with fury. He was seconds from calling Diana and Kahmel in here and give them the third degree for running their fuckin' mouths while his son was in the midst. Then, he slowed himself down when he remembered Tommy Jr. was notorious for snooping around the mansion, hiding and creeping around, while eavesdropping on every conversation that came anywhere near the interior of the mansion. Then, another thing hit him. What else does his son know? What other conversations he heard that he shouldn't have heard? Did he ever hear him talking about the business? The thought of him knowing of all the illicit shit he was doing brought a chill down his spine. The last thing he wanted was his son to follow in his footsteps, and whether he knew it or not, he was doing all this so his only son didn't have to take the same route in order to live a good life.

Tommy Jr. became insistent when he saw his father daydreaming. "Why did she shoot you, daddy?"

Tommy sighed and told him the absolute truth. "I don't know. I honestly don't know why?"

CHAPTER # 16

BANG! BANG! BANG! . . .

The bullets battered the bull's eye paper target.

Shamara and Fashawn were target practicing and had their 9mms carefully aimed with ear muffs on. The makeshift, windowless shooting gallery in Fashawn's basement was well lit with thick padding covering every square inch of the subterranean room. Even the door leading up to the ground floor had three inch padding covering it.

After Shamara finished empting the clip, she took her earmuffs off. She saw Fashawn do the same. As Shamara closely examined her target several feet away, she said. "My shooting is getting as good as yours. Look at that there! Out of eighteen shots, I hit the bull's-eye ten times." She scrutinized Fashawn's target and smiled. "I'm one up on you, girl."

Fashawn loved to do things to help build Shamara's confidence. Plus, they were here to get Shamara's spirits up. All week long she'd be moping around like she was losing her mind or something. "Girl, don't even get gassed up 'cause your gun game is gettin' tight. Let's bust off a few more clips."

They reloaded their weapons, changed the bull's-eye targets and each fired their next eighteen shots at the target. Again, Shamara beat Fashawn out by one bull's-eye hit. Shamara was elated with happiness, and was so hyped up to the point she started bragged and joking with Fashawn about she was going to take her title soon enough. She kept this boastful attitude up until they went another round and Fashawn hit the bull's-eye every time she fired a shot. Shamara missed the bull's-eye five times out of her eighteen shots and it suddenly became clear to her that Fashawn was messing with her when she was letting her win earlier.

With a smile, Fashawn said sarcastically, "Damn, girl, will you look at that? I must've got real lucky that time, didn't I? I'm telling you, I just don't know how in the world I managed to hit that damn bull's-eye all eighteen times like that." She winked her eye at Shamara with a knowing expression.

Shamara wanted to dig off into Fashawn with some foul words for playing head games with her. She hated when Fashawn let her win unfairly. She sucked her teeth and said, "Luck my ass, Fashawn. Girl, that ain't right; I like to win straight up. "

Fashawn laughed. "But you gotta admit Shamara, your shit is tight." She moved to the other side of the room, retrieved the broom and started sweeping up the bullet casings scattered all over the floor. "I hope this helped clear up your mind a little bit. You gotta be easy with all that stress. You walking around here like you all depressed and shit."

Shamara grabbed the dustpan to assist with the clean up. "I'm not feelin' all this looking over my shoulder every minute of the day, wondering if Tommy's gonna creep up and start busting shots at me." There were more issues that were eating at her; like her urge to call little Tommy Jr. and apologize to him, and the fact that she was missing all that hanging out she'd been doing with Tommy, and not to mention all that good sex. A chill ran down her spine just remembering how good the sex felt. But, it was obvious she couldn't share any of this with Fashawn without making her think she'd completely lost her mind.

After Fashawn swept the pile of expended bullet shells into the dustpan, Shamara dumped them into the trashcan.

"That's exactly why I was saying we should step to our business," Fashawn sat the broom back where she got it while Shamara did the same with the dustpan. "We should find a way to get this shit over with." She headed towards the door, opened it and began ascending the stairs.

169

"Living with drama like this up in the air ain't good for your health. Stress is the root of damn near all diseases if you don't know." She stepped through the basement stairwell and stopped when Shamara stepped through. "I got this army buddy of mine who's got his own private investigation company and he said he'll give me a real nice hook up." She saw Shamara folded her arms, listening intently. "I'm gonna hire him and send him out to keep an eye on Tommy's bitch ass, so if he—"

"I thought we agreed to lay low?" Shamara's hands shot down to her hips as if her attitude was about to flare up. "What if these people you hiring—"

"I'm not keeping myself in the dark," Fashawn said and allowed her hands to shoot onto her hips as if she was teasing Shamara in Simon says fashion. "It's about the stupidest thing we can do to ourselves. I sat and closely looked at what we about to do and my years of military training is telling me this was suicide. This could be the biggest mistake of our lives. Just look at this scenario. Wouldn't it be wiser to at least know what Tommy's up to, so if he does get close to us, at least we can see the shit coming?"

Shamara's pessimistic thought process stopped in mid-motion. She was about to fight Fashawn on this issue like a wild animal protecting its cub. But, then, she closely looked at what Fashawn was saying and realized it made a lot of senses. It was crazy to keep themselves in the dark when they really didn't have to. She was definitely right for believing it was safer to know if Tommy got too close to them; that way they could see it coming and could avoid being the victim of a sneak attack. Even if they per se couldn't get close enough to Tommy to finish him off, maybe Fashawn's military people could keep tabs on him.

Shamara started nodding her head as a smile crept on her face. "When you're right you're right. If we got a heads up on what Tommy's up to it could help. But how are your army friends gonna get close enough to know what Tommy's up to? I thought we all agreed that Tommy's whole world is gonna be impenetrable now that he just got shot?"

"Don't worry, these cats got ways of doing shit, and they got hook ups and inside connections that are literally off the chart, girl. Their model is that if you got the money they can do whatever it is you want done."

Shamara didn't like the talk of spending money, since they no longer had big money coming in and these dudes sounded crazy expensive. She did a quick calculation of her stash and realized she wasn't kicking out nothing. "Listen, Fashawn, since it's your idea, the money's coming out of your pocket."

"That's cool with me," Fashawn smiled, since she was glad Shamara was willing to go along with the program and finally saw the light without the need of a long drawn out debate. She was also content because she knew it was just a matter of time before she would have them back in action once again. The thought of shooting Tommy and his crew made her stomach bubble with excitement and deep wanting.

Suddenly, the phone rang.

Fashawn went to get it; the phone was a few feet away in the living room. She snatched up the receiver. "Hello?"

"How you doing, Fashawn," Minister Earl Reid (Shamara's uncle Earl) said. "I need to ask you a few more things about all these new developments. It slipped my mind during our last discussion--"

"Not now," Fashawn cut her eyes at Shamara and saw she was apparently listening. "I'm busy right now. I got company . . . My home girl, Shamara and me are hanging out."

"Oh, I see. Alright, give me a call when you get a chance. It's very important I talk to you, Fashawn. Some issues came up and I need a few more details before I can make any moves. God bless you." He hung up the phone.

Fashawn sat the receiver back into its cradle.

"You didn't have to kill your business because of me. Who was that?"

"It was James. He wanted me to—ah--you know how James is," Fashawn was unable to quickly think of a plausible excuse, since all this caught her off guard. "He wanted me to help him install a heater for some people in Long Island. I told him I'm hanging out with my peeps." She headed for the refrigerator to get something to drink and to get away from Shamara before she started asking more questions.

As she opened the refrigerator and grabbed the carton of orange juice, Fashawn felt her anxiety stirring up. *What in the hell is the Minister talking about, "some issues came up?"* She hated it when she had to wait to find out important stuff like this. *Damn it!*

            *   *   *   *

Tommy sat in the VIP balcony section in the Oasis nightclub in East Orange surrounded by his most loyal workers; among the group were none other than Kahmel, Dubar, and Slick, his three closest. The other six men were workers from various areas of his organization, and were pulled from their regular assignments in order to focus on this all out man-hunt, or should we say, woman hunt. In the background, a hard-hitting Wu Tang song was livening up the atmosphere, and with a non-alcoholic drink in his hand, Tommy stared down into the dancing crowd below through the heavily tinted Plexiglas window and noticed his mind was wandering again.

He didn't know what this bitch did to him. He was literally craving for this broad. He'd come to the conclusion two days ago that she had put some kind of spell on him, or maybe it was because she had his gun, and was laying some kind of curse on him through the gun. The more he thought about it the more he realized all this shit was sounding crazy. But the one thing that he couldn't deny was he wanted to see her again, fuck her, taste her juices and embrace her. Shamara was even in his dreams and their dream sex was literally off the fuckin' chain! He had went to his fortune teller and told her about the situation with his golden gun and she even hinted that this could be the source of his discomfort and "inner turmoil" as she so eloquently put it.

Tommy shook loose of the daydream and decided to bring this meeting to order. He had called his top lieutenants here to discuss what they found and to determine where they were going. "Alright, alright y'all, let's get this shit poppin'."

All the lieutenants pulled up chairs and sat in a circle with Tommy at the head.

"So what happened with that Lexus, Dubar?" Tommy inquired with his right leg folded over the other.

"Yeah, I checked it out. It was her, Shamara Fox, and it's definitely the car. I looked at the sales records and the address she used was the Newark address. It's a dead-end."

Every time Tommy heard her last name it made him furious. Shamara Fox. With a last name like "Fox" he should've saw it coming, he realized as he forced his attention back to the matter at hand. "How about you, Slick, what's up with Patterson projects, anybody know her?"

"I talked to damn near all the old timers, and every one of them claimed they never even heard of her. I showed them the flicks of her and not one person out there said they ever saw her out there."

"Damn it!" Tommy said without concealing his clear frustration. "There's gotta be something we're overlooking; something we're missing. There's a connection here. If we can figure it out we'll know what this shit is all about and how to track them down. They came at us hard and money had nothing to do with it." That was obvious, since Shamara had dozens of opportunities to steal money from him when she was spending nights at his mansion.

Kahmel said, "Try to think back to all your old beefs; could be an old time enemy trying to get some get back. The way this shit went down, it's gotta be personal."

Tommy looked at Kahmel as though he was totally insane. "Try to remember all the beefs I had in my life time!? Nigga is you crazy!?" He started laughing and the whole room blew up with laughter. After a long moment of laughter, he said, "That'll be like trying to figure out the exact number of times I bust a nut, including jerking off, blow jobs, and getting trim. Man, I been grinding since I was twelve years old." As the laughter re-ignited, he thought about Kahmel's comment seriously and for the first time it felt like he came across something that made sense. This shooting may have something to do with one of his pass, long distance beefs. Whether he liked it or not, he was going to have to sit down and try to remember every single old time beef he'd ever had and see if he could come up with some answers.

Kahmel drank the rest of his drink and said, "Not to take us from the main issue here, but what's up with your birthday party next month? I just got word that P-Diddy is gonna show up if you still having that piece."

"Man, you damn right, I'm having that party. This bitch ain't fucked up the program like that. And we gonna do it up some kinda crazy. We gonna rent the whole top floor of Caesar's Palace in Atlantic City and have naked bitches everywhere. Especially the ones with the super humongous, rhinoceros asses!" he saw his team's mouths were watering already. "Sorry for y'all, 'cause you guys are gonna be working that night, since security is gonna have be real tight." When he saw they quickly shrugged it off, he decided to let them get their shit off now. "With that said, tonight's on me. Drinks, pussy, anything you want just put it on the tab."

As his team got up and exited the VIP room with the exception of Kahmel, Tommy's thoughts were running amuck. He saw Kahmel approaching; he sat next to him. Tommy said, "You know something, Kahmel, I think it's time you go talk to Walter Green; we might as well pull out the big guns and get this over with—"

"I say it's too earlier for him. Give us a little more time. Why spend all that money when we might be able to solve this shit on our own. And I remember we said we would use him only for the craziest situations. This ain't the type of situation I see as all out crazy."

Tommy stared off into the crowd below once again and said, "Well, I guess that's my decision to make, since it's my money."

*   *   *   *

Fashawn Corcino was on a mobile ladder checking the top shelves to see how many hardware items had been sold since the last time she had done a storage inventory report last week; she was currently up to the boxes of all-purpose rubber hoses. As she wrote down her notes in her notepad, Fashawn heard someone enter the stock area and she assumed it was one of her fellow employees until she noticed the hard sole shoes approaching.

When she turned her head, Fashawn saw the two men in suits, heading towards her. Upon closer observation, he saw it was Lieutenant McNamara. He was a white man with a body builder's physique, black short cut hair, and was clean-shaved. The other man was a red-bone black man with green eyes and was a complete stranger. The two men stopped at the base of the ladder. Staring down, Fashawn saw them staring up with conceited grins.

"Sergeant Corcino," Lieutenant McNamara said. "Come on down, we need to talk."

With a surge of rage heating up her blood to a boil, Fashawn stepped downward. She had told these mufuckas to never come to her fuckin' job. When her feet touched the floor she said, "With all due respect, Lieutenant, I thought we agreed no showing up at my job like this?"

"Well, Doctor Richards suggested it might be a good idea to do a surprise spot check to make sure our super soldier is behaving." Lieutenant McNamara moved around Fashawn as if she was standing in formation at a drill line up, undergoing a uniform inspection.

Fashawn looked over towards the entrance of the stock room to see if any of her co-workers were anywhere around or in hearing distance.

"Don't worry," The other man said. "We told them not come back here until we're finished talking to you. By the way, my name is Lieutenant Lockhart."

Fashawn's breathing became intense with fury, but she forced herself to speak easy. "What are you trying to do, get me fired? Why the fuck you barging in here, scaring up my co-workers, making everybody all uncomfortable?"

"Everyone knows you were in the service Corcino," Lieutenant McNamara said. "You got this job on the strength of your being in the

176

service. And, in any event, I'm sure you'll figure out a way to clean up any difficulties our visit may cause; give them any old excuse as to why the military is checking up on you from time to time. I mean, really, if it's that much of a pain in the ass we can fix that for you. Of course, it's up to you, you can let us transfer you to Leavenworth, that way we can have people come right to your cell, or you can bare with us doing little spot checks from time to time to make sure your treatment is coming along." He smiled. "Now, I'm going to ask you a serious question and I'm giving you a direct order to give me an honest answer." He looked over at Lieutenant Lockhart for dramatic effect. "Sergeant Corcino, have you been killing people? Have you finally gotten that faddish of yours under control?"

Fashawn felt her eyes become watery with anger and she was glad she didn't have a weapon on her because she probably would have used it. She wanted to tell them both to go fuck themselves. The urge to pick up the near by Monkey wrench on the shelf next to her and commence to bashing both of their brains in was even stronger. They were the ones who created her, made her who she was today. They fucked her mind up completely; they turned her into a desensitized killing machine, and when she did what they trained her to do, and did it according to her commanding officer's explicit instructions, they then turned around and made it look like she was some kind of crazy, psycho soldier with a faddish for killing, when all she did was follow instructions. It was true, she enjoyed the thrill of it all, but it was them that caused her to like it. They trained her to like it; they programmed her to be the best, and when she did her job to the utmost degree, they didn't like what she had to offer.

These sons of bitches don't know what the fuck they wanted! Fashawn drew in a deep breath and said, "No, I haven't killed anyone.

177

And I'm doing quite well with my therapy." She felt a compelling urge to rub their nerves, since they obviously knew what really went down in the town of Yusufiyah, about twelve miles southwest of Baghdad when she "took her mission instructions literally" as the Pentagon had put it in the records of her "honorable discharge"; an event she still hadn't figured out how her commanding officer was able to pull off and assumed it was because his ass would have fried if she fried so no one could fry. "So how's Colonel Richter holding up? How is his treatment coming along? I mean if it weren't for him, I would probably still be in the field? Did he ever tell you about that time when we laid siege to that small town over in—"

"Sergeant!" Lieutenant McNamara said frantically; he was seconds from blowing up.

The two Lieutenants looked at each other, knowing neither one could speak about such a thing, since that incident was deemed classified.

Lieutenant McNamara looked around nervously. "You better watch yourself, Corcino! That incident is classified and if you are playing one of your little sick head games with us, then you better check yourself real fast soldier. And yes, you are under our command until you complete this therapy. And I promise you, if you slip up, even once, I will have your ass in the slammer before you can complete the word boot camp."

With a smile, Fashawn shouted, "Sir, yes sir!" As she saluted the two and started climbing back up the ladder, she said, "Boot camp is two words sir, not one. Check the dictionary. A high-ranking officer such as yourself should have a firm handle on the English language, sir. I wonder what General Wilkins will think about that, sir."

As the two walked away, Fashawn realized she would have to be on her toes 100% from here on. She never thought they would send officers to do spot checks on her, especially one who she had beef with while she was on active duty. This shit was serious, very serious, and it was apparent somebody was up to something.

CHAPTER # 17

Shamara exited the Dental office looking around for any suspicious cars or anything out of the norm. When she saw everything was copastatic she preceded to her car down the block. She received a call from Fashawn to come to her crib immediately when she got off work; she claimed she had some good news coming from her investigator, who'd been on the job for two weeks. She also made clear that she couldn't discuss it over the phone.

As Shamara opened the door to her ride, Shamara felt the February wind cutting through her goose down ski jacket. She got in the ride, hit the ignition and drove away. He turned on the radio and Hot 97 was doing their thing on the Hot five at five. LL Cool J was dominating the number three spot and Shamara rocked her head to the beat.

Outwardly she looked like she was at peace, but internally there was a battle going on. A war was being waged and the conflicting emotions presented themselves in varying degrees. Shamara was also confused. There was love and hate in her blood at all times and these emotions would fluctuate back and forth whenever Tommy crossed her mind, which was a considerable portion of the day. She pulled to a stop at the intersection on Flatlands Avenue and East 98th Street and lit up a Newport. Whatever Fashawn had come across, Shamara was certain it was going to be the source of some more stress.

Twenty minutes later, Shamara was sitting in Fashawn's living room with a can of Pepsi in her hand, trying to determine if Fashawn was serious about what she was asking her to agree to. "This sounds like some mission impossible shit, Fashawn."

"His birthday ain't for a whole month," Fashawn was deterred to get this mission back on track and wasn't going to stop until she got her way.

"With a whole month to prepare we can hook up the perfect plan. My man, Georgio said he could get us inside Caesar's Palace. Once we get in, we can get right up on Tommy and put his lights out."

Shamara shook her head with heavy doubt. "You buggin', Fashawn. That's my word. You talking like we can just blaze a big time cat who got bodyguards all around him and then just walk out of that place without any opposition. What the fuck you think his bodyguards are gonna be doing while we shooting their boss?"

"Come on, Shamara, I got a plan for that! One of us'll dee-up on the bodyguards while the other steps to Tommy. That's obvious. I need you to get on board with me on this. Since we got a month to coordinate this hit, we're gonna have to do some legwork. We gotta case the place a few times, check out all the possible escape routes."

"Why you so obsessed with killing Tommy? It's like you making this more personal than I am and he's the one that killed my family. I'm telling you Fashawn you make me nervous some times when you get all crazy with these missions." She put special emphasis of the word "missions" as if the word had an awful taste in her mouth. She really wanted to force her to explain the medication she was taking and her visits to those army doctors, but decided it might be better to let her share that on her own. "This ain't the military, Fashawn, and I'm not trying to diss you or anything but you're not a soldier in the army anymore, and this is not some game to get off your rocks and thrills killing people—"

"Oh, so now I'm the fuckin' bad guy!" Fashawn was flaming with rage. "I stepped up to help you solve a fuckin' problem in your fuckin' life! I put my life on the line for you! Now I got some rich thug ass nigga looking to kill me, and because I'm taking this shit serious, I'm some kinda crazy bitch with a Jones for killing people!" She realized the truth sure did hurt. "Is that what the fuck you saying, Shamara?" She saw

181

Shamara could no longer look her in the eyes. "Tell me that's what it is 'cause, believe me, I'll pull back, and let you handle this shit by your damn self! What, you think Tommy's not gonna eventually find us!? You shot this nigga and humiliated him in front of his whole fuckin' squad, and this is an arrogant mufucka that's known to hold a grudge to the fuckin' grave. I don't know about you, but I'm not into the business of taking shit for granted. I value my life, what about you?"

Shamara wanted to lash out and engaged her in a tit for tat debate, but she wasn't up for it right now. In any event, she had to admit that Fashawn was correct on some of her points. "Fashawn, you know damn well I value my life, which is the reason I'm telling you walking up into Caesar's Palace while Tommy's having a birthday party would be a sure way of proving I don't value my life. Unless we got an airtight fuckin' plan, that's exactly what the fuck we'll be walking into. A death trap!"

Despite Shamara's initial decision to hold back asking Fashawn about her military issues, after hearing all this, she decided to change that position. "Since you think I'm attacking you, I need you to tell me a few things. I was hoping you would do it on your own, but apparently that's not gonna happen. What's up with that medication you been taking, and why are you hiding what's going on at those meetings you be having with those army people?"

Fashawn felt like a pin had just burst her balloon. *Medication!? How the fuck did she find out about the medication!?* Her mind was moving fast, searching for an excuse to convince Shamara that she wasn't crazy. "You know these creeps dump those medicines on people as a way to make money for those foul ass pharmaceutical companies. Nowadays if you sneeze wrong they wanna force you to take a pill. If you yawn when you're not supposed to they prescribe medications. Taking those meds was a part of my discharge agreement, but I don't be taking that shit. I take that medication only when I gotta go see these people, so if they force me to take a blood test they'll find the shit in my blood. As far as the visits with the army people, that's also just a part of the agreement for me to get out of the military with an honorable discharge. I agreed to two years supervision, kinda like parole; something you are fully aware of."

There was a moment of silence.

"I looked up that medication you're taking and it's some strong stuff, Fashawn. Now, before you get upset, please remember that I'm your best friend, girl. You can talk to me and you don't have to hide things from me. I got your back no matter what it is." She really wanted to say, "even if you are crazy as hell, I'll still hold you down" but she smiled instead.

Fashawn realized that wasn't so hard after all. "And I got your back too. That's why we need to find a way to bring some closure to this issue." Her mind was searching for a way to take the spotlight off of her and flip it on Shamara. Suddenly, a way to do it jumped in her mind. "If you holding back because you still got feeling for this chump, you better wake up and smell the reality. The dick might have been good, you still got feeling for the kid, and still fantasizing about how it could've been or how it could be, and all that other delusional shit, but the bottom line is that Tommy is looking for us. And when he finds us, we're dead."

Shamara thought about that comment and had to disagree. "I don't know about that, Fashawn. I don't wanna debate you, or go back and forth arguing about this, but have you ever stopped to think that forgiveness does exist in some people?" She saw Fashawn squint her eyes while twisting up her face to illustrate either her confusion or disagreement. "I mean, you're just assuming it was the dick, the kid, and the money that's causing me to hesitate. Have you ever stopped to think it just might be some forgiveness playing a part in all this?" She held the eye-to-eye contact for a moment and continued. "And has it ever crossed your mind that maybe Tommy also has it in his heart to forgive?"

Fashawn was about to panic. She saw the mission rapidly deteriorating; the words she spoke were a clear indication she was letting her heart cloud her judgment. "Wow! I know you ain't starting that shit again. Shamara, would you listen to yourself, girl? Tommy's a cold-blooded murderer. He's a drug dealer, a heartless thug with a body count bigger than a front-line infirmary soldier, and—oh, yeah, I forgot to mention this to you; he even killed is right hand man, Malik, probably because he brought us in. I know you got a good heart, Shamara, but when you shot Tommy . . . You turned this into a point of no return situation. You can't take it back and there's only one way to deal with this."

Shamara was about to debate her on the issues she just presented; point out all the surprisingly positive things she discovered about Tommy that made her realize he wasn't any of the things an outsider would naturally assume once they became aware that he was a part of the underworld. She sighed with dramatic force and decided to hold that thought for herself because Fashawn would never understand, nor was she trying to understand.

Then, another voice told Shamara to be very careful with her bleeding heart enthusiasm, as a wave of other thoughts came to the forefront of her mind, reminding her of just how foul and dangerous the average street thug could get once he had been disrespected in front of his crew. She knew there was nothing more deadly than a male ego flaring up, especially when it was a woman responsible for belittling him in the worst way.

Then, suddenly, Shamara remembered the several times when a few of her childhood friends lost their lives, because they thought an old beef was dead. The other person had strategically rocked them to sleep, and then murdered them when their backs were turned. The old street adage surfaced with the force of a nuclear explosion: "It's better to be judge by twelve than carried by six" and with this reality circulating inside her mind, Shamara realized she had better stop allowing her sensitive side to continue laying the groundwork that would probably lead to her demise.

Shamara sighed again as her position instantly shifted and said, "Maybe you're right, girl. You might be right. Maybe the jenny's out of the bottle and it can't go back in."

Fashawn smiled; she got her back on track. "We got two choices. Sit around waiting for him to find us, or we can get him before he gets us. You already know my position. Make a decision, Shamara, and I need it now so I can tell Georgio what to do about hooking us up as workers in Caesar's Palace."

Shamara saw Fashawn was truly a relentless person. She wasn't going to give up, no matter what she said, or what was up in the air. Shamara sighed and did what she always did before making a complicated decision, "I need some time to think about it."

*   *   *   *

Three weeks later, Tommy was in his exercise room lifting weights. He was lying under the two hundred pound barbells, bench-pressing the weight. Each time he pressed the weight up into the air, he hollered like a football player amped up with too much testosterone in his blood stream. Kahmel was at the head of the bench spotting Tommy, while Dubar sat at another bench a few feet away doing one arm curls. Two other brothers were working on the pulley machine.

Tommy came up for some air. He sat upright and was dripping sweat as he nodded to the table containing the bottle of sports drinks, and Kahmel went and retrieved a bottle. Tommy drank half the bottle in one swig. "I took your advice and tried to remember all the beefs I had. I focused on all the major ones, like shootings, stabbings, crazy beat downs, stolen girlfriends, cats who caught life bids for the sake of the team, and forgot that the game don't stop just 'cause a nigga on lockdown, you know, all that real funky shit that mufuckas hold grudges over and I'm convinced it can't any of them."

Tommy noticed his ego and pride wouldn't allow him to tell Kahmel that he had reached out to some of these people he had fucked around back in the day and made amends for his wrongs by hitting them off a few dollars. Once he started back going to church, he felt compelled to "cleanse his soul" after hearing some of the sermons. Even though Kahmel was open minded at times, he didn't want to appear as if he was getting too soft in the game. Weakness was like food in a famished area; if it was present in the midst of hungry people, it was going to be eaten. Also, everybody knew when fellow hustlers in the game saw weakness in other fellow hustlers it had a way of bringing out cutthroat tendencies in the same fashion as blood attracted sharks.

But what really made Tommy believe the hit on him had nothing to do with one of his old beefs, was because of the fact most of those people he had drama with didn't have the kind of money to pay for an elaborate contract hit such as the one he was a victim of.

Tommy drank the remaining portion of the drink and tried to shoot the bottle in the trashcan about two yards away and missed. "This birthday party is coming up real fast." He scooped up the dumbbells and started his one arm curl routine as he talked. "What's this I'm hearing

186

about the Palace won't let us lock down the top floors with our own security?"

"Naw, they didn't say that," Kahmel was drinking one of the sports drinking. "We can have our own security. What they're saying is that we gotta work in conjunction with their security. The reason I was making an issue out of it is because if that's in play we're gonna have to be extra careful moving like that. I don't trust anybody, but our own, and who knows what their security is all about. I don't know if they can be bought, or what."

"Did you offer to pay them to bend that policy for just that night?"

"Most definitely. They said it's non-negotiable. Some kinda company policy."

Tommy continued working his biceps as he thought about what was just said. Something was telling him that Shamara, Fashawn and Kenyetta were long gone. They had skipped town long ago, probably never to return. But, another vibe was telling him it wasn't over and that something was going to force Shamara back into his life either to finish the job, or she was going to come back because she couldn't resist him. He was certain he had her ass wide open. She was dick whipped and he had her heart on lock down. If he didn't he wouldn't be here to think about this, he was sure of it. He had enough women in his life to know when he broke her down both sexually and emotionally, and since he put his all into building the relationship with Shamara, he was certain she would never forget him and might even come back for more.

For all it was worth, Tommy had to admit that the feeling was mutual, since every woman he got with since the falling out with Shamara had turned out to be a bunch of empty fuck sessions that amounted to nothing but the flinging around of bodily fluids, and momentary orgasmic sensations. He fucked five women since then and not one of them interested him enough to want to call them back for another round. To describe them as hit and runs would be a gross understatement. In the end, he had to admit, he still wanted Shamara back in his life, even though she shot him, but couldn't dare express this to his team. They would think he'd completely lost his mind, and would dub him as being pussy whipped and a straight sucker for love, a jacket he would never permit to be placed on his reputation.

Tommy sat the weights down, rose to his feet, stretched his back and arms, and headed towards the squat rack. "Listen, run down the security set up from the top again." He fitted his body into the rack. "There's a part in there I'm not sure I heard you correctly." Tommy began doing squats.

"We're gonna have two floors to cover, the penthouse and the floor just below. Our security will focus on you. We'll let the Palace security handle all the other issues. You know our main guest, P-Diddy, is gonna have his own security and so will Jermain Dupree. I got it hooked up to where at all times we got four men on you. They'll be two floaters playing the crowd, listening and looking for any suspicious characters. Obviously, everybody'll be thoroughly checked for guns and weapons. Now, here's the part you might like. If there's a situation of any kind all entrances and exits will automatically shut down. Nobody can enter or leave the two floors once the alarm is activated. Whether it means anything, or has any importance, I don't know, but if anyone acts up, they'll be no way to escape . . . "

As Kahmel continued on with his presentation of the security for the upcoming birthday party, Tommy's mind locked in on the part about, no one being able to escape, and realized, what difference would it make once the person or persons completed what they came to do?

After scrutinizing this hook up more thoroughly, Tommy realized it didn't matter, since most folks wouldn't be stupid enough to step to someone while they were inside a place like the Caesar's Palace with hundreds of witnesses. Then, he made a note to start advertising his birthday party a little more aggressively with hopes that it touched the right ears, in particular, the ears of those who tried to kill him.

CHAPTER # 18

Tommy Bossett moved across the dance floor dressed in a black tuxedo with a beautiful woman on his arm. Cheryl Johnson was an up and raising super model and was dressed in a tight fitting gown that had gold glitter scattered all over it. Caesar's Palace was jammed packed with people similarly dressed as Tommy and Cheryl and the music banging through the Palace's sound system was inconsistent with the universal formal manner of dress, since Tupac Shakur was raping about Hail Mary, and all those on the dance floor were still rocking to the beat with street style dance moves, despite their hard sole shoes and high heels.

Tommy was scanning the faces as he headed towards the VIP booth where P-Diddy and Jermain Dupree sat waiting for him. Moving up Tommy's rear was Kahmel, and on both of his sides were Slick and Dubar. As they moved, partygoers waved, smiled and gave heart-felt acknowledgment to the man of the hour, and Tommy acknowledged. Although Tommy turned thirty six years old yesterday, March 4th, which was a Thursday, a one-day delay between the birthday and the party really didn't make much of a difference, being that Friday night was always considered the official party night.

Tommy sat and kicked it with his main guests as they drank champagne and enjoyed each other's company. Throughout the conversation, Tommy kept looking at the many faces moving about, and several times he had to scold myself inwardly because he realized he was wasting his time looking for the faces of people who would have to be completely insane to try to get at him during an event such as this one.

*　　　　*　　　　*　　　　*

Shamara sat at a table on the far side of the Palace floor, staring at Tommy in the VIP booth with P-Diddy and Jermain Dupree as the crowd was stepping to an R. Kelly tune instructing folks to step in the name of love. She had a glass of champagne in her hand and a bottle sitting on the table in front of her; she was utterly uncomfortable with the disguise she wore, and twice she had to rush to the bathroom to fix her goat-tee and matching thick eyebrows that constantly felt as if they were becoming unattached from her face.

Shamara was dressed in a black tuxedo and had once again transformed herself into a man. Fashawn was somewhere on the other side, and she also was dressed as a man. Underneath their suits were a miniature arsenal; they both had two silencer-equipped eighteen shot 9mm and were in possession of enough bullet clips to engage any group in an hour shoot-out if they thought it was a game. As she sipped the champagne, Shamara still didn't understand why she let Fashawn talk her into this shit.

Shamara had been closely watching the drop-dead gorgeous woman on Tommy's arm, and noticed she couldn't control her emotions. She was jealous, envious and she couldn't understand why she felt so infuriated to see that beautiful woman on Tommy's arm. He wasn't her man anymore. She was here to kill him. He probably wanted to kill her. Their relationship had been over ever since she shot him almost two months ago.

So why am I feeling this way!? She asked herself this simple question several times and didn't like the answers. She felt herself growing sick with confusion, indecisiveness and a bunch of other mental states that even she couldn't identify when she stared at Tommy while reflecting back on the good times she had with him. Every time the image of her mom and dad being shot by Tommy crossed her mind, she noticed it didn't have the same powerful affect as it once had, and she felt like she was betraying them as a result. She had to pull her mind back on track with a violent shake of the head.

Shamara decided to think about other things until the moment came for them to take it to the next level; she reflected back on how she and Fashawn got into this place, and realized they could be an excellent secret agent or spy team. They had entered the Palace at about five o'clock during the evening shift change and as Fashawn's army buddy, Georgio, had promised, no one had suspected they were not a part of the clean-up staff once they produced their fake employee ID.

Dressed in standard employee clean-up staff uniforms, Shamara and Fashawn were assigned to the penthouse area. With their personal bags containing their disguises, they stashed these bags in the ceiling inside a storage closet, an area where traffic was non-existent. After cleaning the numerous hotel rooms, along with three other women—one of them was a Mexican immigrant who couldn't speak a lick of English—and after their work shift was over, Shamara and Fashawn climbed up into the ceiling inside the storage closet where they had stashed their disguises and waited.

Shamara was going stir crazy sitting in that claustrophobic area for hours, and knew Fashawn had to be insane since she was taking it all in stride, acting as if she was enjoying every minute of it and was having the time of her life. Twice they heard the Palace's security staff moving about the area checking to make sure everything was secured for the upcoming party. When the party participants started entering, Fashawn and Shamara climbed down from the ceiling, put on their disguises, exited the storage closet, went to the men's room to make sure their costumes were good to go, and then merged with the crowd.

Shamara was pulled out of her daydream when she saw Fashawn heading towards the restroom. Fashawn gave her the eye signal that something was wrong, and Shamara felt her heart fluttered with anxiety. *What the hell went wrong!?* She was about to jump to her feet and follow, but quickly remembered they had devised a method of responding to their non-verbal communication, which consisted of never impulsively reacting.   Everything had to be nice and easy, so as not to draw an attention if they were being watched.   Since they knew Tommy had floaters that mingled with the crowd and they had already detected Slick, since they knew him already, they had to be extra precautious with the way they communicated with each other.   After waiting a minute, Shamara headed towards the restroom.

*   *   *   *

Tommy decided it was time to go to the gambling area and try his hand with Lady Luck. He drank the rest of the glass of champagne and said to his guests. "I don't know about y'all, but I'm in the mood to throw a little dice up in this piece."

Both P-Diddy and Jermain indicated they were cool and would remain where they were.

"Alright, I'll be back in a few." Tommy was about to leave and noticed Cheryl was following along. He stopped, "Cheryl, the gambling spot ain't for you, if you got a problem being around naked women."

Cheryl said as she sat back down, "I'll be here when you get back." She felt like God had answered her prayers because she'd been dying to get the chance to sit here with P-Diddy and Jermain Dupree without Tommy around, even if the two had dates with them. She was confident she could get a raise out of one of them, and would slip either one her number when the opportunity arose.

Tommy and his three closet bodyguards approached the other side of the palace, heading towards the gambling section. As Tommy drew closer he saw a short, slim man exiting the men's room, and for some strange reason, he felt odd when the man momentarily locked eyes with him. As he passed this dude, he felt the urge to look back, since those eyes had something in them. As fast as the speed of thought, and with the help of the alcohol, Tommy concluded he was too preoccupied with trivial issues and was causing his mind to see things that weren't there.

With this in mind, Tommy swept what he thought he saw under the rug within his subconscious mind and continued onward to the gambling area, not realizing that his instincts were correct. He had just locked eyes with the woman he'd been searching for.

      *   *   *   *

Shamara sat back down in her seat and was furious. Fashawn had told her that she had just found out that the exits and entrances in and out of these top two floors will shut down the minute an altercation jumped off. Georgio had just called her on her cell phone and had put her on point. Shamara had tried to convince Fashawn to abandon this whole mission, but she refused, and as she tried to persuade her Fashawn said, "We'll just have to resort to escape plan B! That's why we constructed that plan, to use it if we have to, remember!?" and then walked out of the bathroom without giving Shamara the chance to debate the issue.

That's when Shamara saw Tommy as she exited the bathroom moments later; she could've sworn her facial reaction had blown the mission, but he didn't notice the agitation in her eyes.

As Shamara nervously poured herself another glass of Champagne and drank it greedily, she realized she did not want to take part in escape plan B. That fuckin' plan was nothing short of sheer insanity, and most of all, it was downright suicidal. A million and one things could go wrong with that idiotic plan, and Shamara sensed that Fashawn was going to get her killed before the night was over.

      *   *   *   *

After playing several games of blackjack, Tommy lost damn near two thousand dollars, and reluctantly realized Lady Luck wasn't on his side tonight. The blackjack table was loaded with big time spenders, and a few well know millionaires. His friend, Richard Manicello, a Hollywood Producer, was winning everything moving, and it was obvious it was his night tonight.

The naked women that were serving drinks on golden platters were out of this world. They had the whole rainbow spectrum, black, white, yellow, red, brown, and all in between. Twice Kahmel stepped in front of one of the women that tried to suddenly get too close to Tommy, and he did it again when a light skinned sister approached.

"Damn, Kahmel!" Tommy said. "Can't you see this woman is harmless!? She's butt ass naked! You see any weapons on her!?" Tommy reached over and gave the light skinned sister with an ass big enough to fill three pairs of pants a huge church hug.

She whispered in Tommy's ear, "Can we get together when this is all over?"

Tommy pulled away from the embrace and stared shorty in the eyes, wondering if this big butt and a smile was worth it and said, "I'll let you know before the night's over. I gotta scope out a few more things first."

She smiled and walked away.

Tommy felt his dick about to get hard as he watched that perfect Hottentot ass shake, jingle, and switch. He turned and got back into the game.

Twenty minutes later, Tommy lost another thousand dollars and decided to call it quits.

"Yo', that's it for me," Tommy announced to the other players and stepped away from the table and headed towards the exit. He said to Kahmel, "Let's go check out this outdoor Terrace. Since it's costing me a small fortune, I might as well get a taste of everything this place has to offer before the night's over."

Tommy snatched up Cheryl who was running her mouth a mile a minute, and he sensed from P-Diddy and Jermain's expressions that they were glad he had came and got her. Tommy and the group headed for the Terrace.

*   *   *   *

Shamara's heart started pounding as she saw Tommy and his crew heading for the Terrace. It was show time! When she turned her head, Shamara saw Fashawn was already in motion, nonchalantly following them towards the Terrace. They had decided to set it off once he went outside on the huge Terrace in order to avoid hurting any innocent by-standers, and Shamara saw it was about to be on and poppin'.

Shamara rose to her feet and moved briskly towards the Terrace. She saw Tommy and his team enter the Terrace as she moved towards the Terrace while watching for the floaters they knew Tommy was notorious for utilizing at events like this. She thought she had detected one of them earlier, but upon further observation she knew he wasn't affiliated with Tommy's security staff by the reckless manner in which he was drinking.

Shamara entered the Terrace and the crisp late night air had a refreshing affect on her anxiety battered senses. But this didn't last long when she saw the Terrace had too many people out here. They couldn't start shooting with all these innocent people out here. She saw Fashawn already taking position behind a statute of a Bald Eagle. Shamara gave Fashawn the signal to be easy as she saw Tommy go towards the ledge looking over at the wonderful 43rd floor sight of Atlantic City. The lights that covered the horizon transmitted a breathtaking image of grandness and sheer inner city beauty.

Shamara was desperately looking for a way to get some of these people off this Terrace and she moved quickly the second an idea popped into her head. She approached the nearest couple who was sitting on one of the many huge square flower beds that also served as sitting instruments and whispered with a low manly voice, "If you're a part of the raffle, I hear they moved it up. It's about to start."

Shamara saw the couple scurried inside and she hastily did the same thing with four more couples. By the time she was about to approach the fifth couple, Shamara saw Fashawn was in the zone; her eyes had the look of death in them and she had just given her the point of no return signal. She also saw Fashawn had retrieved the two backpacks she had stashed inside the base of the statute.

Shamara raced over to the water sprinklers and pulled both of her 9mm. The plan was simple; she would get the first shot off, knock Tommy out while Fashawn would take down the bodyguards and cover the entrance. Shamara looked over at Tommy, then at Fashawn and took aim. As Tommy's back was in the sights of her carefully aimed 9mm, she suddenly noticed she couldn't take the first shot. She couldn't pull the trigger!

Shamara tried it again, took aim, and her finger was locked. When she nervously looked the other way and saw Kahmel looking around at everything in the vicinity, turning around as he examined the immediate area, she realized Kahmel was apparently going to see her once he faced her and Fashawn, and yet she still couldn't pull the trigger.

Fashawn was seconds from blowing a gasket due to the rage gripping her mind. *This bitch is getting emotional again!?* She realized as she also noticed Kahmel was about to look in their direction. She decided to end this shit once and for all. Fashawn took aim at Tommy's back and fired her weapon while holding down on the trigger. The silenced bullets were spitting from the barrel of her weapon with ferocious force and the first to be struck was Dubar, who had miraculously stepped right in the way of the bullet aimed at Tommy.

With her gun pointed, Shamara finally fired a shot upon noticing Fashawn had set it off and saw Tommy and his girlfriend had frantically ducked out of sight. She wasn't certain if Fashawn had hit him, but from the way he rushed for cover she was sure it didn't look like he was hit.

Then, she saw Kahmel take aim and shattered the whole night

BANG! BANG!

Kahmel's two shots aimed at Fashawn hiding behind the statute turned the entire event into sheer pandemonium. The partygoers inside and the few on the Terrace were screaming and running hysterically for cover, knocking each other down, while stampeding over anyone unfortunate enough to trip and fall as everybody sought safety.

Suddenly, a black man in a tan suit came barreling through the Terrace entrance, and Fashawn cut him down with a shot to his side.

At least they found out who the floater was, Shamara thought, and realized he definitely had them fooled because they had saw this man earlier and they would've never suspected he was the floater.

As the floater fell, the Palace security staff stopped in their tracks. They were about to rush outside onto the Terrace to respond to the situation until they saw the man in the tan suit collapse from an apparent gunshot. They instantly changed their mind about going out there.

Shamara knew they were now officially on the clock, and were working with mere minutes; there was not a second to be wasted if they intended to get away. She aimed both of her weapons and pumped off several shots at Kahmel and Slick as she ran towards Fashawn, who also fired shots to provide her with cover. She arrived next to Fashawn and instantly saw the rage seething from her facial expression.

"Put the chute on, hurry!" Fashawn tossed Shamara the parachute as she fired shots at the area where Tommy and his boys were located to prevent anyone from firing as Shamara put on her parachute.

Shamara fastened the buckles on the chute and was trembling as though she was experiencing an epileptic fit. She picked up her guns, and as Fashawn was putting on her parachute, a man with a gun rushed through the entrance of the Terrace, and Shamara instinctive fired at him, dropping him.

Once Fashawn's parachute was on she inserted fresh clips in her guns and said, "I think we missed him. Load up, hurry!"

Shamara frantically inserted fresh clips into her weapon as Kahmel and Slick periodically fired at them. The bullets ricocheted and hurled dust particles and pebbles everywhere as they pounded the statute and the wall behind them.

When Shamara was finished reloading, Fashawn said, "We gone finish this mufucka tonight. Let's go!" She took off before Shamara could protest.

Kahmel and Slick fired their weapons when they saw the two moved towards them as they hidden behind the huge square flowerbeds that also served as benches.

Knelling behind a flowerbed, Fashawn was forced to come to a stop upon realizing there was no way they could get any closer without being shot.

Suddenly, the faint sound of approaching police sirens appeared.

Shamara and Fashawn looked at each other and knew the show was over.

"You ready!?" Fashawn said with her eyes wide with delirium. The minute she saw Shamara nervously nodded her head. She reached inside her pocket, pulled out six huge candle-like instruments (smoke bombs), pulled the pins, and tossed them around the immediate area. She instantly rose to her feet with both guns spitting silenced bullets.

Shamara was supposed to run and jump off the roof first, but her legs locked up on her.

"Come on! Go!" Fashawn shouted as she paced her shots so as not to expend her clips. "We're working with seconds!" She fired two more shots and said, "I'll meet you down on ground." She took off running and leaped off the building.

Shamara heard that voice in her head shout, "it's now or never" while mental images of her returning to prison flashed across her third eye, which both galvanized her into action. Just as she ran the smoke bombs Fashawn tossed started exploding as huge clouds of thick gray smoke engulfed the area.

Shamara leaped off the ledge just as gunfire rang out.

BANG! BANG! . . .

Shamara felt the anger bullets whizzing pass her just as she saw the awesome forty three story drop. The adrenaline rush was literally mind numbing, causing her to nearly pass out from terror as she rapidly plummeted downward towards the concrete pavement feet first. The cold, violent winds lashing at her face made it hard to breathe or see clearly. One of the fake eyebrows dislodged itself from her face.

Within seconds, she saw Fashawn's parachute shot open, the cloth blossoming into a huge cap that instantly brought Fashawn to a stop in mid-air. Shamara was startled at how fast everything was moving. She'd never skydived before and Fashawn had forewarned her that everything would be based "on split second decisions." She was zipping down towards Fashawn's parachute so fast it was like she blinked and already she was about to hit it.

Just when she was seconds from colliding with the parachute, Shamara frantically pulled the ripcord. The chute shot from the backpack and she jerked to a stop that phased into a slow glide towards the street below. Shamara wanted to scream a shout of delight from the adrenaline surge but her stomach felt like it was stuck in her throat. She thought she was losing her mind, since she realized this skydiving shit wasn't that bad after all.

Fashawn landed and with military precision and had her backpack off in seconds, ready to flee.

Shamara landed seconds later, about several yards away from Fashawn, who as running towards her. She saw Fashawn kept looking up at the roof they just jumped from. As Shamara hastily unfastened the backpack she noticed a crowd already formulating even though it was three o'clock in the morning. Fashawn assisted her with taking off her parachute.

Within seconds, Shamara and Fashawn were running towards the motorcycle they had stashed about two blocks away. Moments later, they turned a street corner, saw the bike and raced for it. Just as they mounted the huge Harley Davidson, a police car turned the same street corner they had come from.

WOOP!! WOOP!

Fashawn hastily started the bike with Shamara sitting on the back seat. The bike rivved to life like an angry beast as the police car moved towards them with their lights now flashing. Fashawn gunned the bike full throttle, jettisoning the motorcycle down the street as the police gave chase.

CHAPTER # 19

Tommy Bossett entered the conference room in his mansion and took a seat at the head of the huge circular table. Kahmel sat next to him on his right hand side, while Slick sat on his left hand side. Tommy was in a state of rage mixed with so many other hostile emotions that he could barely think straight. Two days had gone by since the birthday party fiasco and his rage still hadn't subsided.

"Let's hear it," Tommy said to Kahmel.

"You were right," Kahmel said. "It was Shamara and Fashawn. I looked at the video surveillance tapes. I saw them enter Caesar's Palace posing as employees. They also appeared on the surveillance tapes on the penthouse floor. Once I saw them I didn't need to look any further. The two men they're looking for, I saw those surveillance tapes as well." He nodded his head enthusiastically. "Yeap, it's them. They did the same shit they did when they hit up Gangsta. They dressed up as men."

Tommy sat staring at the door across from him with a catatonic, blank, and emotionless expression. His thirst to kill was blindingly powerful. "Did they catch on to any of this? When you watched the surveillance tapes did the security guards detect Shamara and Fashawn might be the two shooters?"

"No, I made sure I navigated them away from thinking that. This is our beef and we're gonna deal with this. But, don't put too much hope in them not eventually finding out. They already know that the two gunmen had apparently hid inside and came out when the party started. Now that the police are making this a top priority investigation, there's no telling where all this is gonna go."

"There's one other place we know where this fucked up shit is taking us," Slick said with clear frustration. "They're fuckin' with our cash flow 'cause of these bitches. I got word from Rome that the police kicked in the door of the Newark warehouse and we lost fifteen brand spanking new rides. Just this morning they started fuckin' with our stash houses in Jersey City. Looking at all the newspaper articles on this shit I think this is only the beginning. They talking about this is a drug clan battle over turf, and all that bullshit. Now we gotta come up with a way to deal with this bullshit, Tommy, or they're gonna fuck up our ability to eat love love."

Tommy was boiling with something much stronger than rage. Just being reminded that the media was blowing this shit out of proportion, while the police were now investigating him and his organization stirred up all sorts of fierce emotions. All this undeserved drama was transforming him into a very dangerous man. The thought of finding and breaking the neck of that news reporter, Donald Breslin, who wrote those articles claiming the shooting was a drug gang war over turf when there was no evidence of any such thing was growing daily. Even though it was clear this was a failed contract hit on Tommy Bossett's life, they even acknowledged that, and it was clear he should be treated as the victim here, they instantly flipped the whole shit on him and now he was the bad guy. Fuck the fact that two of his friends were killed, while another one (Dubar) was currently in the hospital on critical with multiple gunshot wounds; fuck all that! The only thing they were interested in was how and why he was living large like this. *Them hatin' sons of bitches!*

Tommy sighed as he allowed his mind to get deeply enmeshed into the toxic mental aerobics situation he was locked in and he realized he anticipated this would happen. He'd always known they would eventually start investigating him one day, and now he hoped all the years of preparing for this day would all pay off. The good thing was that all his properties, investments, bank accounts, business holdings were all legit, thanks to his pass career in the music industry, his current involvement in music producing, and most of all, thanks to the good lawyers and accountants that were specialists in hiding and making illegal money legal.

Another major plus would be he made it a habit of making sure Uncle Sam technically owed him money, which he hoped would be enough to slow them down, since the Feds were bound to get involved, and it was just a matter of time before they would find out about the other spotlight that these bitches had placed on him. He was almost out of the woods with that last failed hit that transpired in Connecticut and the Sanford police were about to deem the case closed; they were seconds from concluding it was a blotched robbery, but with this second similar incident all hell was about to break loose, and that fuckin' reporter, Breslin, was bound to make the connection.

Tommy sat fully erect in his seat and said, "Did you get copies of those surveillance tapes?"

"Not yet," Kahmel said. "But I did crack for them. Don't worry about those tapes. The second in command of the security staff at Caesar's Palace is a friend of mine. We trained together at the same security personnel school and he said if push comes to shove, he'll take care of me under the table."

"Good," Tommy nodded his head with a crazy screw faced expression as he said to Kahmel. "I got one more thing I need you to do before you to start focusing on the street businesses. Get in touch with Walter Green. Tell him I got a straight mill. I want the top of the line service. I want it fast and I want it now. It's time we find these bitches and put an end to this shit right here and now!"

*   *   *   *

At about the same moment Tommy was engaged in a meeting with his two most loyal workers, Shamara was locked in an argument with Fashawn as they sat in Shamara's living room with the radio on Power 105, Hot 97's arch rival.

"No!" Shamara shouted as she sat with a cigarette between her fingers. "I'm not fuckin' with that anymore, Fashawn." She sucked on the Newport, savored the smoke in her lungs, and blew it out. "I let you talk me into that last shit and I'm done with it. That was it! After all the fucked up shit we just went through and still made it out of that shit alive, and in one piece, is God's way of telling us to stop this madness while we're ahead. We came way too close to getting caught this time, Fashawn."

A chill ran down Shamara's spine just remembering how they escaped that high-speed police chase on that motorcycle. Once the police car started chasing them, Fashawn had gunned the bike to speeds that made Shamara feel like the Harley was going to take flight and become airborne. Consistent with Fashawn's always ready for anything personality, she had made a dozen turns down sidewalks, through people's backyards, down alleyways, and then ditched the bike behind a factory where they had a van stashed (she still couldn't figure out how she was able to predict the need for this stashed van, but she did it). They got in the van and drove away. By the time the police found the bike, they were cruising down the New Jersey Turnpike arguing over how they had messed up this hit when it was so perfectly planned.

Fashawn tilted the can of ginger ale up to her mouth, drank, and then stared at Shamara, wishing she had come at her another way. It was apparent she wasn't going for the old disrespecting her mom and dad's legacy by letting them die in vain trick. She quickly pondered her options and went with the first thing that came into her head. "You know something, Shamara. You are a remarkable person. I knew something was wrong, and I wanted to believe you wouldn't deliberately walk us into a situation knowing you was straight lying."

"Lying!?" Shamara sat into a full attention stance. "What the fuck I lied about!?"

"Don't play stupid!" Fashawn sipped on the can of Ginger ale. "You were protecting that nigga! That's how—"

"Get the fuck out of here! Why you keep saying that!? You straight buggin', Fashawn. Why in the fuck would I protect a mufucka that killed my whole family and—"

"Because you allowed your heart to get caught up in this shit! That's fuckin' why! This game ass nigga laid that dick on you, let you play with his little junior, gave you a little taste of that rich living and the nigga got your whole fuckin' world turned upside down."

There was a heavy silence.

Shamara stared Fashawn down with an attitude. "You know something, Fashawn, I'm tired of your bullshit—"

"Tired of my bullshit!? Oh, so now this shit is all my fuckin' fault, huh? Since you wanna take it there, you a foul mufucka for going on these missions, knowing god damn well you didn't wanna kill this mufucka. The least you could do is be straight up with me. Look at what you did during this hit. You had a clear shot, wouldn't take it, and I was the one who had to set it off." Fashawn drank the last of the ginger ale and sat the can on the coffee table. "You did the same shit at his Connecticut crib. How is it that you keep missing this chump, while with all the others you came through with flying colors? It's almost like I'm wasting my time trying to help you get your mind right—"

"Stop fuckin' frontin'! Please, Fashawn. You was getting way more outta this shit than me. What, you think I can't see that you strung out on killing mufuckas? Oh, like I don't recognize the fact you pushing this shit like your life depended on it, and killing Tommy and his people is just an excuse. You doing it because it must be some kinda sick in the head, twisted ass therapy for you—"

"You calling me crazy!?" Fashawn shot to her feet with clenched fists. Her mind nearly snapped in half, and she was in full combat mode with deranged ridden wide eyes.

Shamara wasn't totally surprised Fashawn had finally lash-out at her like this. She snuffed out the cigarette in the ashtray. However, a wave of nervousness tugged at her inner workings, since everybody knew crazy people were known to even hurt loved ones while in a state of blind rage. She also felt a deep, proliferating hatred for the military people that did this to Fashawn. Prior to her tour in the army she wasn't like this. Of course she was a thrill seeker, highly adventurous, and didn't take shit from anybody, but she was nowhere like this. They turned her best friend into a fuckin' serial killer, almost like they programmed her, brained washed her, turned her on but either forgot, or didn't know how to turn her off.

Looking into Fashawn's eyes and at her bodily gestures, Shamara saw it was clear Fashawn was in a zone where she could do something she would regret later. Shamara knew she had to be the sensible one for the sake of them both and said softly, "I didn't mean to call you crazy, Fashawn. And the last thing I'm gonna do is let this come between our friendship. I don't see you as just my best friend; you're like a biological sister. I was an only child, and so were you, and we always been sisters and always will be."

Fashawn felt her mind fade back into a state of calm and she instantly realized what she had done or was about to do. She was going to attack her only friend!? *Oh, this is bad, real fuckin' bad*, Fashawn said to herself as she sat back down and started massaging her temples with her head bowed while breathing deeply. A wave of guilt grabbed her heart and that inner voice started unleashing a bombardment of reality checks. This shit definitely wasn't worth jeopardizing her life long friendship, even if keeping a mission percolating was crucial to her mental well being. The thought of not having a mission to look forward to was frightening, but losing Shamara was even more terrifying. Even more frightening was the thought of having to take that medication. Every time she consumed that stuff it turned her into a zombie and made her feel like she was dying slowly. Although she knew one of the side effects of not taking the meds was that she felt compelled to start working on a mission or her mind would snap in half, she felt she could deal with the missions as opposed to walking around like she was the victim of a liquid lobotomy.

Fashawn sighed and looked up into her friend's eyes and said, "I'm sorry for spazzing out like that, Shamara. I—I—I would never hurt you, girl. You the only family I got; you my sister for real." She wanted to tell Shamara what she wanted to hear; that she agreed with calling it quits with the hits, but the thought of not having a mission to work on made her feel like the walls were closing in on her. A hyperventilating sensation grew as the horrifying thought of all missions coming to a complete end gripped her mind. She stood up and gave into the compelling urge to pace.

Fashawn suddenly felt like she was trapped inside a coffin and was buried alive. The image of her banging on that buried coffin and couldn't get out was driving her further into a state of delirium. She couldn't move!! Fashawn felt like she was about to cry when she realized Shamara was done with the missions. It was written all over her face; it could be seen in her body movements and she said it straight out, *no more missions!*

Shamara saw the deep pain in Fashawn's expressions. She had to comfort her friend, but she also had to be firm; the last mission was the last. "Fashawn, don't be so hard on yourself, girl. You helped me try to straighten out my life and I'm forever grateful for what you did. But, I don't know what happened once I started vibing with this dude. I never mentioned it because I didn't think you would understand, but I think it's time I come clean. Dealing with Tommy was like it caused something to wake up inside me, and it ain't have shit to do with sex and money and all that trivial shit. I saw something in Tommy that made me realize that, even though this creep was a murderer, he had another side that was human, caring, and filled with compassion. It was—it was—it's hard to explain, but it made me see something inside myself. You believe this nigga goes to church and takes his son with him? He donates money to countless black causes, and I seen the checks, and record of donations to prove it. And I've talked to this dude, Fashawn, I got inside his head, and it may sound straight insane to say this, but the dude ain't as foul as people make him out to be. I know this shit sounds crazy, being that he murdered my family. But, what I'm really saying is that after I learned more about him, I felt the spirit of forgiveness controlling my actions. Another thing that helped he to reach that level of forgiveness is that Tommy had told me he used to work for some famous Brooklyn street thugs named Eternal and Remus; he said that these cats used to make him do things under the threat of killing his mother, his little brother and two sisters. I don't know if what he said was game, but since he didn't have any reason to lie to me when he told me this; in fact, he had a reason not to lie to me, since it painted him as being weak, I suspect it was the truth. Even though he didn't say it outright, that told me that he killed my family in order to save his. I didn't tell you all this before because after all the shit you did to help me do this, I just didn't feel right telling you this."

"You see, that's where you're wrong, Shamara." Fashawn suddenly realized it wasn't over, and another style of a mission was already in play. "We homies and you could've told me what time it was and I probably would've understood. But, let's look at the situation as it is now. Tommy might have been pressured to do what he did. But, after these two attempts on his life, he's coming for us whether we like it or not. He killed Malik, and when he finds us, we'll have to bang out with him, whether we like it or not."

"Maybe, maybe not," Shamara said. "If he knew why we did it, he might understand." She knew this was a long shot and it was almost idiotic to believe what she was suggesting, but she recalled a church sermon Reverend Daughtery gave on the issue of forgiveness and Tommy's response to it.

Fashawn looked at Shamara like she was crazy. "I love you, girl, but just because you're filled with all this forgiveness, don't mean his heart has the same ability to forgive. You shot him, remember that, and you tried it again. If there was some forgiveness left in his heart we killed that when we came at him repeatedly. In his mind it's a kill or be killed situation."

Shamara sighed because it was obvious Fashawn was right. She was tired of being on this merry go around and decided she was officially getting off of it. She felt she needed some serious guidance. She had the solution and figured she'd bring Fashawn along for the ride with hopes that it'll bring some peace to her turmoil-ridden life. "Listen, Fashawn, I'm going back to church. We both need Jesus in our lives. You need to come with me—"

Fashawn laughed. "Church!?" She laughed even harder. "I'm sorry, Shamara, I didn't mean to laugh like that at you." She toned down her laughter. "I hope you don't think because Tommy goes to church that this'll stop him from getting at you—"

"This ain't about Tommy. It's about me. It's about our souls. I scarred, tarnished, and contaminated my soul long enough with all this seeking revenge bullshit, and when it's all said and done, even if I did kill him, it won't bring back my family. I feel like I need to cleanse my soul after all the shit we just did. I think the church might help me find that peace of mind I've been searching so hard and so long for."

"Well, Shamara, we talked about this a hundred times before, and we both know the church is the biggest hustle in the hood. There's so many pimps in the pulpit, you couldn't begin to name, count or detect them." She wanted to give her a rude awakening about her Uncle Earl, but she figured she'd save that for another time. "Well, I'll say this, Shamara. If you feel the church can help you find some peace of mind, I respect that. For me, I'll find my peace of mind by getting ready to deal with Tommy, if and when he finds us. No disrespect, but I think black folks have been searching too long for help in the wrong places. I believe in that famous quote that says, 'the nearest place to find a helping hand is at the end of your own arm.'"

CHAPTER # 20

"Here's another run down of what I offer," Walter Green said as he walked along side Tommy as the two strolled along a weather worn pathway in a park. "For a million dollars it's only right I spell it out clearly in case you may have forgotten." Walter's neatly trimmed sandy brown hair, the matching thin moustache, his blue eyes, along with his medium built physique underneath his beige trench coat made him look like the typical Dick. However, his deep, authoritative voice gave hints at his true status in society; a special agent of the Federal Bureau of Investigations, AKA the FBI. In view of his physical appearance—he had straight shooter, and honesty written all over him—the last thing anyone would have thought was that he was a firm believer in the adage that everything has a price, even the services of one of the most sophisticated information gathering agencies in the world.

Tommy said with his gloved hands behind his back. "I really don't think that's necessary, Mr. Green. I was satisfied the last time we dealt. The main thing I need to know is that the million dollars on the table is secured, and if the services don't add up to the two million, you'll refund the difference." Tommy wanted to laugh at that one; he couldn't imagine this money hungry creep returning any money, even if the services cost one-tenth the cost. "I think I remember them well enough to know what can and can't be done."

"Fine," Walter Green said. "That precludes the formalities. Tell me how I can help you specifically."

"I need to find three people. Two black women and a man. I want to know where they're from, where they're currently at, where they grew up. In a nutshell, I want to know everything about them, even down to the foods they like."

212

"That shouldn't be very difficult, if you have a picture of them and enough information for me to pin them down to a certain area."

"I got more than that. I got videotapes of all of them."

Walter nodded his head approvingly. "That'll help tremendously. Here's what I need you to do. Give me everything you got on them. The tapes, names, last known addresses, anything you got that'll give me a place to start and I'll take a crack at it. It may take some time being that I have to squeeze these services into my official routine. Here's a brief run down of what's to come. First, I'll run a universal video transmission scan with our local main frame, match the faces to particular video feeds and then narrow it down to a specific area. If they have entered any areas with surveillance cameras of any kind within the last three years their images may have been recorded and stored. Once I get a handle on who they are, their back ground info, then we'll figure out where they are."

"You said this could take some time. About how much time are we talking about?"

Walter Green did a quick calculation and said, "If it's limited to a local search, I would say about two to four weeks. If it's a national search maybe two to three months. An International search, at least six months and better. If time is of the essence, I do have a special rates package that provides accelerated results, but it's really quite expensive. My advice to you; let's work with the standard services."

Tommy didn't like when people made decisions for him, and particularly hated when people assumed they knew what was best for him. In any event, he wanted to know how much the accelerated service cost for future reference. "Thanks for the advice, Mr. Green, but how much would the accelerated service cost? I might even consider using it if this thing turns into an international search."

"Whatever the initial cost is, double it."

Tommy felt an eye-raising jolt; giving this chump two million was definitely out of the question! "Yeah, now I see why you give that advice." Tommy stopped walking and faced Special Agent Green. "I'll send Kahmel over immediately with the tapes and the money. Obviously, I'm ready to get this thing rolling as soon as possible."

Special agent Green extended his hand and as Tommy shook it, he said, "I look forward to making you a satisfied customer once again."

        *   *   *   *

Three and a half weeks later, Tommy and Special Agent Green sat on a bench in the same park. Walter Green had a laptop computer in front of him with its lid flipped open, while Tommy sat next to him, looking at the screen. In light of the beautiful April weather, they were dressed accordingly, in spring jackets and basic casual attire.

Special agent Green typed in the information as he said, "I ran into a few bumps during this investigation, but everything worked itself out." He turned the laptop so Tommy could see it. "His real name is Kenyetta Jones. I was surprised he and the others used their actual first names, but altered their last. It was a very ingenuous trick because the first thing I assumed was that the entire name was bogus, which did throw he for a loop. I wasn't able to track him beyond the Bronx. About six months ago these are some of the stores he frequented on a daily basis, and it's fair to say at that time he lived in that area. I'm planning to continue the search, move it up to the next level. The only reason I'm calling you here is because I got firm confirmations with the other two and I figured there was no sense in making your wait unnecessarily. I'll put all the info I obtained on Mr. Jones on this disk."

Tommy's anxiety raced, and was ready to come right out and ask about Shamara Fox. She was the main issue here, but he maintained his patience.

Special agent Green flipped the laptop back and began typing. Seconds later, he turned the laptop back so Tommy could see the screen clearly. "This one here was a ball of fun tracking. Her name is Fashawn Corcino. Ex-military sergeant, discharged from the military about a year and half ago. She's one you need to be very careful with. The Pentagon is watching her very closely and the last thing you wanna do is cross their path. A personal word of advice, you might wanna pull back from this one, being that there's some kind of investigation with her in progress. This is highly classified shit here. This woman's case was so top secret I couldn't even retrieve the basic information on that investigation, since I needed a level five-security clearance, which I obviously can't get. She apparently lives in Brooklyn, Canarsie. I'll provide you with all the videotape recordings of the businesses she frequented as well."

Tommy was surprised she was so close to him. Brooklyn was technically right over the Hudson River.

Special agent Green flipped the laptop back, typed, and turned it back towards Tommy, "Her name is Shamara Reid. Did time in Bedford Hills for arm robbery, had several minor brushes with the law prior to that. She works in a dental office that has several surveillance cameras, so I was able to get plenty of good footage on her. She and the solider girl apparently live in the same area, Canarsie, and are close friends. There's a lot of footage of them shopping together, stuff like that . . . "

As Special agent Green went on and on about other aspects of his search, Tommy's mind was re-analyzing all the Brooklyn drama he was involved in back in the day and he started to see how this was connected to his past dealings in Canarsie. The manner in which they had terrorized that area was foul enough to make him suddenly feel a sensation of disgust. If he could dig up Eternal and Remus's bodies, and kill them again, he would do it with a smile. The level of their viciousness was legendary in that area and he now saw the consequences of rolling with such a crew were now haunting him. Then, something hit him, and he realized there was something else, he rudely cut into agent Green's dialogue, "Excuse me, what did you say Shamara's real last name was?"

Special agent Walter Green hit a button, looked at the screen and said, "Her last name is Reid."

"How's it spelled?"

"R-E-I-D. Reid."

Tommy couldn't believe what he just heard. He hoped his ears were playing tricks on him, but as realty set in it was obvious that was merely wishful thinking. He shook his head in disbelief. As the initial shock began to fade, he felt a blinding rage take its place and he realized it was time to do some serious house cleaning.

*   *   *   *

"I knew there had to be a connection," Tommy said to Kahmel and Slick as they sat in Tommy's living room with drinks in their hands. "The connection is that mufuckin' hit I did in Canarsie way back in the day. Shamara's the daughter of this couple Eternal and Remus pressured me into blazing. It was a hit right in front of the Church; done as a way to send a message that if they continued their community campaign to run out all the drug dealers, more bodies would drop everyday."

"So her whole agenda was to get revenge on you?" Kahmel shook his head disbelievingly, finding it hard to believe Shamara became a professional killer just to get close to Tommy, so she could push his wig back. "I know how powerful revenge is, but there's gotta be some other shit going on here."

"Knowing what motivated her is all good," Slick said as he flicked the cigarette ashes into the ashtray. "But in my opinion all that shit is

216

irrelevant right now. The only thing I wanna hear is how we gonna step to these mufuckas."

Tommy was in deep thought; he stared off into nowhere as his mind churned with a silent fury. "The plan is gonna be a simple one." He immediately knew there was going to have to be two plans; one that involved Minster Reid, and the other that dealt with Shamara, Fashawn and Kenyetta. He still couldn't believe Minister Reid, Shamara's uncle, let some shit like this go down. That nigga told him everything was forgiven, and even took his money as a way to "balance the scales of justice." He'd been giving Minister Reid money for years to help build his church under the premise that he was making amends for that shooting.

Tommy honestly wondered did Minister Reid know anything about this!? Certainly he would have to find out if this was the case, and then come up with a way to deal with the esteemed Minister if he found out he was trying to fuck him around. Suddenly, the thought of the consequences for killing a Minister touched the most intricate section of his mind and Tommy cringed at the level of sinfulness such a homicide would illustrate. He sighed with deep inner pain, confusion, and dread. Ever since he found out who Shamara really was the question of how he was going to step to everyone connected to this situation had been heavy on his mind. Despite the variety of ways to address this matter, there was one thing that was certain. The folks responsible for this shit were going to pay with their lives for what they had done.

Tommy pulled himself from the penetrating reverie and said, "I need y'all to get as many extra hands as you can find. If you can snatch anybody from the businesses without severely hurting the cash flow do it. The only thing I want done right now is to find out exactly where they live, figure out their routines, and if possible, sneak inside their cribs and

do some snooping around, but make sure you do nothing to anyone of
them. Basically, I want you to watch them real closely. That's it. I'll
repeat this again, so there's no misunderstanding the seriousness of what
I'm saying here. Do not touch anyone of them. That honor goes to me and
me alone."

CHAPTER # 21

Shamara was cruising down Pennsylvania Avenue nervously looking through her rearview mirror for the green car she could've sworn was following her. Dressed in a gray sweat suit, Shamara caressed the Golden 9 in her waist to make sure it was positioned correctly and noticed the mere touching of the weapon gave her a sense of security.

Shamara was on her way to the Evergreen Cemetery to visit her mom and dad's gravesite, and usually, this was a soothing moment, but because of the sudden increased feeling of being followed, her mind was somewhere else.

Shamara examined the cars in back of her very carefully and noticed the green car was gone. Her mind jumped back to the topic she had been grappling with since she and Fashawn had their last discussion. She was locked in a jihad within herself; a struggle she noticed she was losing terribly. She was bouncing back and forth with what she wanted to do. One minute she was going back to the church, then the next minute she wasn't. Also, her conscience was beating her up, while her guilt was counteracting her conscience; in the meantime, her anger due to the lost of her family was refusing to take a backseat. Every morning she arose from bed her mind felt like an utter mess. The only solution was to go to that one place where she often found guidance and that was to the gravesite of her family.

Twenty minutes later, Shamara approached the two tombstones with two colorful bouquets of flowers in her hands. She stared down and read the writing on her mother's headstone, even though she knew the information by heart:

"Shirley Reid   December 13 1962 – June 25, 1990
Here, lies a true Champion of God's Gift of Charity.

A woman who died in the name of helping others."

Then her view slid over to her father's headstone, which said:
"Wallace Reid   May 31, 1960 – June 25, 1990
A Great man who served the cause of God's
Gift of Charity, and gave his life for it."
Shamara laid a batch of flowers on each gravesite and did what she always did each time she visited this gravesite, twice a year. She first flashed back to the time when they both were alive. Vivid images of love filled moments coursed through her mind. The times when her mom would read the bible to her; the times when her father showed her how to ride her bike; the first day she went to public school and both mom and dad waved her on with smiles; the family picnics with Fashawn and her family; the church trips to Bear Mountain; the love, kisses, and intense moments of sheer affection that was so plentiful it was almost breathtaking. She noticed these memories brought a river of tears from underneath her eyes as always. Shamara wiped her face and told herself she had to be strong.

She came here for an answer, and knew if she asked it out loud, she would receive the answer. Her heart would let her know if she was correct and she let it ride.

"Mom and dad. I need to talk to y'all. I know I've done some bad things you guys wouldn't approve of, but I did it because it seemed right at the time. I—I thought it would make everything right, but now I see it hasn't! You guys gave your lives for what you believed in and I don't think I could ever be as brave as you two. Even when you received all those death threats from the drug dealers, warning you to stop your campaign to force the people of Canarsie to rise up against the drug dealers and you refused to back down. You were always my heroes, and that's why I did what I did because if y'all were brave enough to stand up to well known killers, murderers, and vicious people, the least I could do is be brave enough to make sure those responsible for killing you, didn't get away with murdering y'all, especially when the police could do nothing!"

With a grilled facial expression, Shamara's mind re-enacted that day with profound clarity. Shamara was ten going on eleven and remembered she was very happy that morning because she had won a Sunday school pop quiz about Baby Jesus, and received a little black doll of Jesus. As she and her family were about to leave the church, her mother said, "Shamara, you won because you are a gift from God" and kissed her on the forehead. Immediately after that her daddy scooped her up into his strong arms and kissed her on the cheek and said, "See what hard work can get you." He put her down and they exited the church. As they were moving down the stairs, Shamara remembered her father suddenly became alarmed and violently pushed her to the ground just as loud explosions were heard.

She saw both her parents do a violent dance of death as the machine gun bullets gnawed at their bodies with gruesome viciousness, mowing them down before they could even retreat back into the Church. With eyes wide with brain shattering terror, Shamara saw a young, brown skinned man hanging out of a parked car, and it was obvious he was the one who did it, since the violent strips of fire was leaping from the gun aimed at her mom and dad. After her mom and dad fell down on the church stairs, the car screamed away. That's when her hell on Earth began.

With a slight struggle, Shamara forced the flashback out of her mind as the constipated look on her face grew in leaps and bounds, and she continued, "I'm confused and I don't know what I should do. Mom, I

221

know you always said that whenever I'm in need of peace of mind that I should look to the church, but the church is so—so—" She felt awkward saying the church was so hypocritical, so she searched for a more respectful description. "So inconsistent. And you daddy, I remember you said that the answer to peace on all levels, be it external or internal, I could find the solution in the word of Jesus Christ. But--but I just don't know if that's—" She bowed her head; she had stopped going to church years ago, and vowed she would only go back when she felt she was ready to be a true Christian. "What I'm saying to you two, is that after all the terrible things I have done; I've shot and killed some bad people, just to find out that the man that killed you guys was forced to do it, and now my conscience won't allow me to kill him; can you please tell what I should do? Should I go back to the church knowing I'm a sinner of the first degree, a sinner that violated the First Commandment, or should I live my days out, walking around harboring all this bad energy mixed with guilt and regret?"

Shamara knew there wouldn't be a verbal response, but she was sure she would get an internal vibration; some kinda gut instinct that would be clear enough for her to read the signal, and gain the answer and the solution. She wiped her eyes and suddenly felt like someone was watching her. She rapidly blinked away the tears, because this feeling was real.

She swiftly turned around with her hand on the Golden 9 tucked in the front waist of her sweat pants and saw two black men looking down at a headstone about a hundred yards away. She instantly sighed with partial relief and realized she had to get herself under control. Lately, it seemed like she was scared of her own shadow.

Then, Shamara scrutinized the men very closely before assuming everything was safe and she felt her gut talking to her. There was something about the way they were dressed that just didn't sit right with her; it was like a cross between a thug and a business executive; sought of like they had big money. For some odd reason Tommy jumped inside of her head.

When one of the men nervously cut his eye at her and then the other one did the same moments later, Shamara decided she received the answer as to whether or not they were following her. Even if she was jumping to conclusions, she decided she wasn't taking any chances and would assume the worse.

As Shamara walked away from her parent's gravesite, she realized she received her mom and dad's answer. Inconspicuously, Shamara looked back at the two men and noticed they were still cutting their eyes at her.

*   *   *   *

Fashawn smiled behind the wheel of her Jeep as she cruised down Flatlands Avenue. She looked through the rearview mirror, saw the headlights and hoped it was who she thought it was. She had spoke with Shamara earlier; she had called her and was all upset about feeling like she was being followed.

Fashawn reached over and lit up a Newport. She had convinced Shamara that it was just her imagination, even though she had noticed two days ago that she was also being followed. At first she didn't know if it was the police or the military people fucking with her, so she decided to find out for sure. The last thing she needed was to coordinate a mission against people she technically view as the good guys, although some of them were worse than the drug dealers who she hated with an outlandish passion.

Yesterday, Fashawn received confirmation from Georgio, who followed the two black men in a black car as they followed her, and

Georgio was certain that these guys weren't law enforcement and definitely weren't connected to the military. When Fashawn heard that, she was beaming with joy, and wanted to thank God for blessing her with another mission because she was on the verge of losing control; she was very edgy constantly, since there was no mission brewing, and her subconscious mind knew this. She noticed it was an absolute prerequisite to her mental balance that she have a mission brewing and percolating or her anxiety would start making her a very difficulty person to be around.

The lack of a mission in progress had cost her the new boyfriend she was using to get her rocks off, and after two sexual encounters, Jakwan stopped calling her, and wouldn't return her calls. She figured this was due to her aggressively taking charge of most situations, and because she was a strong black woman, it was just too much for Jakwan. Not to mention, he felt intimidated by the fact he noticed she had lots of guns in her crib. Since she got off a few well-deserved organisms, two of which were worth remembering, it didn't matter anyway. She concluded that he served his purpose. *Fuck him!*

Fashawn blew out a cloud of smoke as she went over the steps involved in this current mission again inside her head, and knew it was airtight. The mere thought of her doing her thing on these mufuckas following her brought on a sensation of paradise.

She turned down East 108th street, and was now in Breauklene projects; the phase one location of this mission. She looked at her watch, saw it was almost midnight, and hoped it was late enough. Two seconds into wondering if the timing was right, she relaxed her mind because she was sure no one was roaming the streets at this time of night, with the exception of crack-heads and other drug addicts.

Then, another pestering thought invading her mind. *Who are these mufuckas!?* As usual, this one question flared up an onslaught of

224

countless other questions. *Why are they following us!? Why didn't they start shooting? Should I tell Shamara the truth that these people are following both of us!? Isn't it obvious this apparently has something to do with Tommy!? Or at least it has something to do with the things we did when we worked for Tommy!? What if it's someone planning to kill us because we killed one of their peeps!? Shouldn't we start thinking about making it harder for them to kill us, if they take it there!? What about Kenyetta, is he being followed!?*

Fashawn slammed on the breaks inside her head, and once again, told herself that if she started answering these questions it would be the equivalent of her ending all of these future missions. The thought of no more missions was just too much. In any event, she decided she was going to take care of it all, all by herself.

First, she was going to take care of these chumps following her, then she was going to contact Kenyetta and put him on point, and after that she was going to step to the one's messing with Shamara, and every time they brought in a new set of dudes to follow them around, she was going to turn each and everyone of them into a new mission.

Two minutes later, Fashawn turned into the housing project parking lot near the corner of Stanley Avenue, and found a parking space. As she took her sweet time parking the Jeep, she saw the black small car that was apparently following her cruise by; the tinted windowed car moved slowly, and she realized whoever these creeps were, weren't very good at following a target. She could definitely teach these fools a thing or two about coordinating a clandestine car pursuit.

After she parked, Fashawn grabbed the brown paper bag with her change of clothing, and took her time getting out the Jeep. Fashawn headed towards the 523 East 108th Street, and just as she suspected, the car had made a U-turn and had stupidly cruised by again but in the opposite direction. Fashawn continued on her way as if she didn't even notice the vehicle; she pulled out the master key, opened the door, and then entered the building.

Fashawn got on the elevator, went up to the top floor (seventh floor), proceeded up to the roof, changed her jacket to a brown one, put on a matching knit hat along with a set of wire frame glasses, opened the roof door with another master key, and tiptoed over the gravel to the railing to see exactly where her pursuers were located.

It took ten seconds to find them. They were parked on a 108th Street across from a FedEx factory. Fashawn closely examined the logistical set-up and within two minutes had devised the perfect plan. Since Breauklene project buildings were constructed with two buildings connected, and merely by crossing the roof, a person could come out the other side (the connecting building) Fashawn had chosen this area for this strategic reason.

Fashawn slid out of the connecting building, walked towards Williams Avenue, made a turn, cut through the back of the project buildings, came out on 108th Street several buildings down from the parked car and eased up behind the two men watching the building she had entered. With her hands tucked in the front of her jacket pocket, while caressing the silencer equipped 9mm, Fashawn strolled right up to the car . . .

SZK! SZK! SZK!

The first bullet shattered the passenger window while simultaneously splattering the brains of the passenger target. Her two other bullets struck the driver in the cheek and the forehead.

Fashawn looked at the nearby apartment windows to make sure everything was still in order, and when she determine no one heard the shattering glass, she opened the passenger door, retrieved the key from the ignition, opened the trunk, dragged the two men out of the car, and stuffed them in the trunk.

Fashawn then drove the black car to Canarsie pier about a mile away, with full intentions of dumping the car into the waters of Rockaway Bay, but as she pulled up to the entrance of the pier, she saw a rust colored sports car was parked in the pier, apparently some kids on some lover's lane bullshit she thought. She had done this lover's lane shit at this very same pier when she was young and knew this could be an all night wait if she didn't do something. After a minute she came up with an idea and went for it.

Fashawn got out the car and approached the sports car. She looked inside and saw the teens fuckin' up a storm, the chocolate colored guy had the caramel colored girl's legs cocked high in the air. Her knees were damn near touching her ears and he was drilling and pounding her with the good old long dick maneuver. Fashawn really didn't want to disturb this grove they had going, since she remembered how much fun it used to be, but she had business to take care of. She tapped on the window and saw the teens frantically jumped out of the fuck feast mode.

Fashawn flipped her wallet real fast, "NYPD, I need you to clear this area please." She saw the guy roll down his window with a confused expression that was mixed with a sense of recognition and frustration, and Fashawn instantly smelled the pungent smell of sex shoot out the car. "My name is Detective Matthew. I need you to—" She stopped in mid-sentence because she recognized this guy's face. It was the face of one of the teens that came to the hardware store on a constant basis.

Fashawn quickly shifted her whole game plan with the smoothness of a three card Monty con man's flick of the wrist. "Hah, I got cha, didn't I!? Man, what y'all doing out here fuckin' like this? Why don't you treat that girl like a lady and take her somewhere decent and respectable, like at a house, or a hotel?"

The pretty girl said, "See, I told you that's how we should do it."

The boy shot back, "Your mom's is home and so is mine."

Fashawn was becoming impatient. "Listen, it's damn near one o'clock in morning, you need to be home sleep, getting ready for school."

The boy sucked his teeth as he started the car. He gave Fashawn a screw face and pulled off.

Five minutes later, Fashawn had driven the car into the Bay and was walking down Rockaway Parkway, looking for a cab to take her back to the parking lot to pick up her ride, so that she could official call it a beautiful night.

*   *   *   *

At about the same moment Fashawn was about to drive the black car into Rockaway Bay, two of Tommy's most ruthless soldiers were hiding on the side of Kenyetta's nice, white picket fenced styled home on Durham North Carolina, waiting for him to pull up in front of his house. They had just received a call from their partners who were currently following Kenyetta from a club he either worked at or owned. They had been following him since yesterday and Tommy gave them the word earlier to "put his lights out."

Two minutes later, Kenyetta's custom-made candy red Nissan Maxima pulled into the driveway.

As Kenyetta killed the engine, he realized he was still furious over the fact that the new girl had the gall to get caught smoking weed and then had the fuckin' audacity to catch an attitude when he told her getting high on the job wasn't allowed. He still didn't understand why he didn't just fire the bitch on the spot.

As he gathered his folder and briefcase, Kenyetta guessed it was because that child had way too much ass to throw to the waste side. Kenyetta and his homie Carl Tillman had merged their money together and opened up a strip club. Although the money was up and down, at least he was fulfilling his life-long dream of owning his own business.

As Kenyetta stepped out of the car, he sensed something was wrong, and before he could turn he heard the rushing movement.

BANG! BANG!

Kenyetta jerked violently from the bullets tearing at his unsuspecting flesh. The first bullet hit him in the stomach and the other in his right hip. He fell to the pavement, already knowing what had happened. Somebody shot him, but for what!? He rolled onto his back as the searing hot pain shot through his body.

One of the men, who had a mouth full of gold teeth, rushed up to Kenyetta and said, "Tommy sends his regards, Kenyetta." Looking down into Kenyetta's terror filled eyes he said. "He told me to make sure I told you . . . have a nice trip." He took aim at Kenyetta's forehead.

BANG!

As the two men ran, Kenyetta's cell phone began to ring. It rang hard and long.

On the other end of the line Fashawn had the cell phone clamped to her ear. She was inside a cab on her way back to the project parking lot to pick up her ride; she figured it was only right that she call Kenyetta and at least put him on point. She knew she should've done this yesterday, but she had to first complete at least one mission; just in case she couldn't convince him not to go run his mouth to Shamara or Minister Reid.

After the phone rung almost two dozen times, Fashawn hung up wondering why Kenyetta wasn't answering his cell phone. She shrugged it off, assuming he was probably getting some trim and didn't want to be bothered. She decided to try it again tomorrow.

CHAPTER 22

"What's going on, Fashawn!?" Minister Reid said with genuine tears in his eyes. He stood in the back office of the Holy Family Church of the Lord; a Church he basically owned on Flatlands Avenue and Rockaway Parkway. "Do you think his death has anything to do with our mission!?"

Fashawn still couldn't fix her mind to believe Kenyetta was found dead this morning from multiple gunshot wounds. "Minister Reid, I honestly don't know." Her tears were dried up, since she'd cried hard and long upon hearing the news. The water was now replaced with blood in her eyes. Despite her rage, she still couldn't reveal that there was a good chance Tommy was behind his death. "But I can tell you that we covered our tracks according to the plan. I don't think it was Tommy that did it. He ain't on to us."

Minister Reid sat behind his desk, struggling to compose himself. "For God's sake I pray Kenyetta's death has nothing to do with this because . . ." He couldn't say that he wouldn't be able to live himself, since his ultimate fear was knowing he encouraged something that lead to the death of someone he watched grow from a child.

"It probably has something to do with the business he started down there. Those strip-clubs can get real crazy. They got all kinds of folks in the game that go to those clubs and things are known to turn violent." Fashawn felt self conscious of the fact she was lying about not suspecting something was in the air, but she knew Minister Reid, and if he thought Tommy was on to them, he might pull the plug on the mission. She wanted to say something, but she just couldn't do that.

Fashawn sat down in the chair in front of his maple oak desk. "If Kenyetta's death was Tommy's doing I think we would've got a hint of him being on to us by now. Even you said the last time you spoke to him everything was as it should be."

Minister Reid pulled the hanky from his back pocket, wiped the tears from his eyes and blew his nose. He put the hanky back, sighed as if he was back to himself and said, "When we started this mission I thought it would be a simple situation where we could just punish this murdering bastard and go about our lives." He looked at Fashawn suspiciously because he'd sensed a while back that she was pushing her own agenda. He was almost sure she was still up to something; he felt that Fashawn was dragging this thing out on purpose. "It seems like every week there's something new. First, there's no way to sniper this creep; then you gotta get inside his organization to do it; once you get inside then you can't complete the mission because he's too well protected; next thing I know you do a hit and still can't complete the job, then you crash his party and miss again. Fashawn, please, explain what is so complicated about completing this mission!? Tommy can't be that lucky!?"

Fashawn sighed and knew she wasn't going to tell him that some of it was do to her not taking an aggressive stance to remedy the situation, knowing it would drag this thing out. "Well, Minister Reid, if you want my honest opinion—"

"Yes, I want your honest opinion. That way we can look at the problem and address it and end this once and for all."

"I think when we decided to let Shamara be the one who killed this creep was the root of it all. She let her emotions get caught up in the mission and when it came time to step to her business, her conscience got in the way."

Minister Reid suspected this was the cause, but needed to hear it from Fashawn's mouth. He sighed loudly. "Now, you see why I felt it wasn't a good idea to let Shamara be the one to get close to him. I told y'all it had to be done without her getting intimate with him in any way. Shamara's the very sensitive type; you know this Fashawn. But, I'm still not gonna change my position that she had to be the one to do it. She needs this to make her whole again." He reflected back on how terrible it was for Shamara growing up knowing the murderer had gotten away with killing her family and a surge of rage grabbed his heart.

"Believe me," Fashawn said with a serious facial expression. "I was hoping and praying Tommy wanted to get with me. I would've happily gave him a run for his money. Tommy came onto Shamara; he was drooling all over her the minute he saw her and if we were going to infiltrate his organization, she had to do what she had to do. We really didn't have a choice in the matter."

Minister Reid leaned back in his chair and went into deep thought. After a moment he said, "I need to find out for certain if he's on to us. I don't know why, but I just feel like something's not right." He thought about giving Tommy a call and asking him for some money for the upcoming food drive, but he felt that might draw unwarranted suspicion.

After tossing around a myriad of possible ways to find out, Minister Reid decided it was time to get off this merry go round all together. For years he'd been ducking and dodging the reality of the situation; ignoring his heart and allowing himself to be bought. Although Tommy had approached him, claiming he wanted to make amends for what he had done, and insisted that he was forced to do the shooting, Earl's heart had become so harden after he saw the damage that that incident caused Shamara, he knew there was nothing Tommy could say or do to change the fact that in his mind the only appropriate justice would have to be his death. Even the Old Testament agreed with this analogy; an eye for and eye!

And considering the fact Tommy was still doing exactly what he was doing when he killed his brother and his wife, Earl was certain Tommy was just shooting game under his belt, since he was still an enemy of the people; selling drugs and exploiting poor, innocent and ignorant people. Now that he sensed that time was running out and Tommy would eventually find out he took part in these attempts on his life, he knew he had to stop talking, thinking and dreaming about settling the score and had to take some affirmative action. It was time to do what he should've done years ago. "Fashawn, how do you feel about ending this madness right here and now?"

Fashawn smiled with mixed emotions. "You talking about inviting him here?"

"Yeah, I think it's finally time to take it there. I always wanted to do it this way, but we all felt it would subject us all to a lifetime of danger if his friends started retaliating.   I'm just so sick and tired of it all! I should've done this years ago, the minute he killed my brother. The way things are going he's bound to catch on, so it's only right we get him before he finds out. He'll never suspect me, and once he's inside this church, I guess I'll have to stop being a coward and do what I should've done years ago." Although his fear of getting caught and going to prison was great, his fear of being killed or seeing Shamara and Fashawn killed was even greater. "I say we draw him to this church and end this madness. You can be positioned somewhere outside, so if things get out of hand you can have my back."

Fashawn smiled brilliantly. "Minister Reid, I would be more than delighted to have your back. You're right, maybe it's time we end this mission."

*   *   *   *

"Well ain't this about a bitch!?" Tommy said to Kahmel and Slick as he sat in a lounge chair in back of his mansion, about twenty feet away was the empty pool that had a pile of weather worn leaves and other debris inside of it. Kahmel and Slick were sitting across from him. "After all the money I hit that nigga off with and this is how he repays me!? You know, I made that Church of his what it is today." He shook his head at the level of ungratefulness Minister Reid was now displaying, and especially in light of the fact all the game he was talking when he told him he forgave him for killing his brother was apparently a fuckin' bold face lie.

Tommy had always sensed he could never totally trust Earl, but he thought that his being a man of the Church made it highly unlikely that he would lie like this. He definitely would've never imagined Earl would try to kill him. Tommy sighed loudly. "You ain't gonna believe this shit." He smiled, but it wasn't because he was happy. "Old bitch ass Minister Reid has finally got up enough nerve to step to me."

Kahmel squinted his eyes. "He stepped to you!? When was this!?"

"The nigga just called me and invited me over to see how my money's being spent. Out of all the times in the world, he suddenly decides it's time for me to come visit him, just when we find out his niece, who he raised, is trying to kill me, and I just happen to be the one that killed her mother and father. I can't believe this clown ass nigga! Now, I know for sure he's down with this shit. At first I was thinking it was just Shamara, seeking revenge. It's obvious he's trying to pull he into his church and then'll probably try to push my shit back." Tommy laughed while shaking his head in disbelief. He could already visualize the fun he was going to have murdering each and every one of them.

Kahmel screwed up his face as he said, "Come on, Tommy, this dude is old enough to be my grandfather. He's probably too old to hold a damn gun steady."

"Word up," Slick also couldn't see a man who was a part of the Church being built for any real drama. "How dangerous can this cat be, Tommy? What he gonna do, call the police on us?"

Tommy nodded his head, realizing their response was a natural one and said, "Back in the days this dude Earl did some serious gang bangin' and he had a lot of heart, so don't assume he's not capable of taking it there, just 'cause he's a minister. He used to run with the Black Spades and was nasty with that fifty-two shit. I grew up out there and heard a lot of war stories. He wasn't a slouch, believe me." He saw the doubt in their eyes instantly disappear. He restrained himself from revealing that this was one of the additional reasons he started hitting Earl off with money, since he felt out of respect it was only right that he try to do the right thing after what he did to his baby brother.

Tommy also knew that at the time of the shooting Earl had just became a pastor for the church, which was probably the only reason he didn't pick up a gun and retaliate. "But, despite all that, I will say this cat got a lot of heart coming at me like this. That alone is grounds to show this nigga what happens to folks that take my kindness for weakness." He paused as he started formulating a plan of attack. "We're going in tonight. We're gonna hit all three of them at the same time, if possible. At least we know they don't know we know what time it is. That definitely gives us the upper hand."

"Don't jump the gun, Tommy" Slick said with a cigarette between his fingers. "I still ain't heard from Jay and Spider. Something's up with this shit. It ain't like Jay to not answer his cell. The last time he hit me up, he said they were following Fashawn. I ain't trying to put no shit in the game, but maybe they got to them. If popo knocked them off I would've been the first person Jay called, so we know it ain't the police that got to them. Maybe they know what time it is and that's why they stepping to you like this."

Tommy realized this one piece of evidence changed the whole picture. He now had to assume they knew he was on to them. He sighed and said, "Looks like this is gonna be one of those all out bang outs. We gonna do one of those shock and awe type of hits. Roll up with an army, hit 'em with everything but the bathroom sink, and basically mash 'em the fuck out before they know what hit 'em. With the Minister, I'm stepping to him personally and we're gonna make sure he gets it while he's inside his precious Church."

"I'll pull as many cats as I can from everywhere." Kahmel said with excitement racing through his blood. "I would suggest we shut down a few spots and bring the wildest heads we got. . . .

As Kahmel explained the plan of action they would utilize tonight, Tommy couldn't help but think about Shamara and what he was going to do with her. He still couldn't understand why he felt bad knowing that he couldn't stop himself from doing to her what he felt he had to do and didn't like the way his heart was currently reacting.

*   *   *   *

Fashawn cruised pass her house looking for anything out of the norm. After what she did late last night, she knew she had to be extra precautious, and one of the tactics was to drive by her crib while checking out everything before entering. The coast looked clear and the next time she entered the block she parked and entered her apartment.

She fixed herself a Turkey and Swiss cheese hero, and just as she turned on the TV and sat down to relax, eat, watch TV, and get her mind cleared up for tonight's grand finale, there was a hard knock on the door.

237

Fashawn sprung to her feet with her gun in the ready. That was an authoritative knock and it had police written all over it. Her heart started beating in double time. Fashawn tiptoed to the door, peeked out the peephole and saw Lieutenant McNamara with Lieutenant Lockhart standing behind him.

"Come on open up, Corcino, we know you're in there."

Fashawn tiptoed to the sofa and stuffed the gun underneath the cushion. Just as she approached the door . . . .

CRASH! BOOM!

Suddenly, the door was batter-rammed off its hinges, and in stepped the Lieutenants along with five apparent soldiers who were dressed in civilian clothing.

Fashawn braced herself, since she was about to go off completely on these mufuckas! Her eyes twinkled with fury, but she fought to keep her anger under wraps.

Lieutenant McNamara approached Fashawn as three of the soldiers immediately started searching her house. "Sorry for stopping in like this, but unfortunately, Corcino, your release was been terminated."

The two remaining soldiers rushed over to Fashawn and got behind her.

Lieutenant McNamara continued, "Doctor Richards says he received the test results from your blood work." He shook his head with an evil smile. "Thought you could trick us, huh? According the results, you haven't been taking your medication as prescribed, Corcino."

Lieutenant Lockhart said, "The doc says there's clear and convincing evidence that you've been taking your meds hours before your visits, and apparently weren't taking it daily as you were supposed to. That's a first degree violation of your discharge agreement, punishable by termination of your—"

"We found something!" One of the soldiers shouted. "In the basement!"

"You mufuckas!" Fashawn rushed at McNamara, but the two soldiers pounced on her and took her to the ground. She felt her arms were roughly twisted behind her back and the handcuffs were placed on her. They yanked her back onto her feet.

"Oh, so you want to add more charges?" McNamara said with a wide-eyed expression. "How about we add striking an officer in the line of duty? That one'll surely get you Court Marshaled."

McNamara headed for the basement, went door stairs, and when she saw the shooting gallery, he sighed with delight. He knew they said payback was a bitch, but this was just too much. This was more than too good to be true, which made his mind wallow happily in the realty that Fashawn wasn't going to see the light of day for a very long time. It felt so good he laughed out loud.

CHAPTER 23

"Yo', the DTs snatched her up," Beverly Greene, Fashawn's next door neighbor, said to Shamara as they stood looking at Fashawn's crashed in door that was hanging on one hinge. "They took Faye out in handcuffs."

Shamara's mind couldn't take any more. *DTs!?* The sun had set about an hour ago and her mind was just as dark and dreary as the night skies. Her heart pounded in her chest as her mind was about to snap from the overload of bad events that were bombarding her all at once. When she got the news from Fashawn that Kenyetta was found dead this morning from multiple gunshots wounds, including one to the head, she cried for almost an hour and had to leave work. Now her best friend was just snatched up by some men, probably the police.

Shamara said to Beverly with a trembling voice. "How did they look, Beverly? How you know it was the police, did you hear them say they were the police?'

Beverly looked at Shamara like she was crazy. "Who the hell else would kick a mufucka's door off the damn hinges and drag a person out in cuffs?"

Suddenly, Andrew, a medium built black man, who lived four houses down and was styling a shiny baldhead, came up to Shamara and Beverly and said, "They wasn't the police. It was the U.S. Marines who snatched her up."

"How you know that?" Shamara said, realizing she couldn't remember this man's name, but knew it started with an "A." "Did you see them leave with her?"

"Yeah, I saw the cars they drove up in. The license plates were military and they had a cardboard sign in the window that said 'U.S. Marines'"

Shamara didn't know if this was good or bad, but at least she felt relieved Fashawn wasn't snatched up for something they were doing with respect to their dealings with Tommy. She concluded they probably were fucking with Fashawn because she violated the terms of her discharge; sort of like a parole violation. "Check this out, Beverly," she said as she reached into her pocket, pulled out her wallet, and then a web of money. "I need you to call the locksmith and get them to put a door back up." She piled off several bills, handed Beverly more than enough to cover the cost, and pay for her time. "Keep the change. I need you to keep an eye on her shit." She headed towards her car. "I'll be back later."

Beverly was about to protest until she saw the three one hundred dollar bills. She smiled and said as Shamara got in her car. "Don't worry, Shamara, I got this."

Shamara pulled away. Suddenly, the tears started back up. She didn't know why, but she could sense everything was about to go from bad to worse. Fashawn had told her that they had to go to her Uncle Earl's Church tonight and she was supposed to let her know what this shit was all about. She tried to force Fashawn to tell her what was going on the minute she mentioned it, but she insisted she would explain it all once she got to her crib. She could tell by Fashawn's voice that there was some shit going on that she wasn't privy of, and since she mentioned her Uncle Earl, she was now on her way to find out what he knew about what Fashawn was talking about.

Five minutes later, Shamara pulled up in front of the Church her uncle worked, realizing she was so worked up over what happened to Fashawn, she didn't even check to see if the brown car was still following her. She hastily looked around to see if she saw the car, but didn't detect it. She caressed the two 9mms (Tommy's Golden 9 and her own). She felt the five extra clips in her pockets and then exited the car, heading for the Church as her eyes watched all the cars moving about the streets.

Shamara entered the Church and saw her uncle sitting on the first step of the altar. She noticed the minute she entered, her Uncle Earl nervously jumped to attention. She saw him rise to his feet with a shocked expression upon noticing it was her. *Something is definitely wrong here.* "Uncle Earl, did you hear what happened?" She couldn't help crying just thinking about Kenyetta's death. She raised her arms for an embrace.

"I heard about, Kenyetta," Minister Reid embraced Shamara. "Yes, I heard they found him dead this morning."

"And they just snatched up Fashawn!"

"What!?" Uncle Earl pulled away from the embrace and looked her in the eyes with terror. "Who snatched up Fashawn!? What happen!?"

"I just came from her house. Her neighbors said some military people kicked her door down and took her out in cuffs." Shamara sat on the step and saw her Uncle was clearly in a state of distress as a result of hearing this news. "So what's going on Uncle Earl? Fashawn said she had to meet you here tonight. She also said there was some things that she was going to tell me. She said she was gonna explain it all once I got here. By the look on your face, it's obvious you know what time it is."

Minister Reid was on fire with fury. He had told Fashawn this was to be kept from Shamara. He was even more upset by the fact Fashawn wasn't going to be able to make sure she had his back. He looked at his watch, saw it was 7:35, and saw he had about another hour in a half before Tommy would show up.

242

Suddenly, Frank Johnson raced out from the back, not realizing Shamara was sitting on the step. "Minster Reid—" He saw Minister Reid waving him back.

Shamara saw her Uncle Earl's response, hastily turned her head and saw Frankie with the AK-47 in his hands. Her eyes nearly popped from their sockets.

Minister Reid shouted, "For Christ sakes, Frankie, I told you to look at what you're doing before you bring that thing out here."

"What the--!?" Shamara rose to her feet to get a clearer look at the weapon. "Uncle Earl, what's going on!?"

"Sorry, Minister Reid, I didn't see her. I just wanted to tell you, Rodney said he's on his way." Frank rushed back to where he came from.

Minister Reid sighed as he sat down on the step, causing Shamara to sit back down beside him and said, "Shamara, I hope your heart is open, your spirit is calm, and most of all, I pray that your mind is receptive to the bitterness of the truth, because what I'm going to tell you may upset you . . .

*   *   *   *

Meanwhile, Tommy sat in the passenger seat of the blue Ford Tahoe Jeep; Kahmel was behind the wheel. They were cruising down Flatbush Extension and had just got off the Manhattan Bridge. Behind the Jeep was a convey of five other assorted vehicles containing Tommy's thirteen man hit team, not including the two that were following Shamara, the other two that were watching the Church, and a new two man crew that was following Fashawn.

Suddenly, Tommy's cell phone rang and he retrieved it from the front pocket of his jacket. "Yeah, what's up?"

"It's me, T-Bone," He was sitting in a car about a block from Minister Earl's Church. Sitting next to him was Carlito, who had a set of binoculars to his eyes watching the Church. "We got some good news. We followed Shamara to the Church; she's inside."

Tommy smiled, realizing he could kill two birds with one stone. "That's good. Put the team in motion. Set 'em up around the Church, so you can see anything coming and going."

"I got all that in the smash," T-Bone said. "I got some more good news. I just kicked it with Gizmo and he said that some dudes snatched up that broad Fashawn. He ain't sure who it was, but they took her ass out of her crib in handcuffs. It's fair to say she's out of the picture."

Tommy smiled, "That's perfect." It didn't take a mind of the likes of Imhotep to know Fashawn was the strength of that team and without her there would be no serious resistance. "Okay, lay low. Don't do nothin' until you talk to me first. We'll be there in a few. Get in touch with all the others and remind them they better not do anything unless I give the call. Alright, I'll hit you when I'm on the set. Later." He disconnected phone.

Kahmel said, "Sound like good news. Come on and hit me with it."

"Shamara's in the Church and Fashawn is out the picture. Looks like the police snatched Fashawn up."

"It can't get any sweeter than that. With that army broad out the picture, they done off."

"Yeah, but don't think she's gettin' off. It's all good for now. We'll have to touch that ass at a later date." Tommy sighed as he turned on the radio and kept the volume low to just above a whisper. Mary J. Blige was announcing to the world, "Love is all we need." He started thinking hard about the situation with a smile on his face. It was clear that in light of the new developments this hit was going to be too easy to just walk in, shoot them and break out. He needed to make this thing more interesting. He needed to fuck with their heads in the same way they fucked with his.

With their strongest hitter out of the way, Tommy realized he could step to them in all sorts of fun ways, even psychologically. As Mary J. Blige's lyrics danced within his mind, an idea hit him. "I just came up with another way to step to these Negroes. Check this shit out and tell me what you think about this . . .

*   *   *   *

Fashawn sat in the corner of a padded cell, staring catatonically at the white padded door. She was dressed in a white gown and her mind was swirling crazily with the high-powered meds they had injected her with about ten minutes ago, but her inner most consciousness was fully intact. She was fighting the effects of the mind-altering drug with some success thanks to her prior training, but she suspected it was just a matter of time before she would succumb to its awesome power.

Her inner workings were too calm; this intense tranquility was interfering with what she had to do. She hated this feeling. This was the main reason she despised these meds; they made her feel like she was slowed down to a rate similar to being dead. She was inside a mental coffin, buried in the ground, and couldn't move.

Fashawn stood and started pacing, trying to walk the medication off. She felt like she was drunk. Instantly, hundreds of images were flashing across her mind. She stretched her arms and was glad they didn't put her in a straitjacket. At least she could move freely if the opportunity ever arose where she could make a move. But, it wasn't hard to figure out that they didn't have to put her in a physical straitjacket, because they had put one on her mind when they shot her up with the meds.

I gotta get out of here! She repeated this statement over and over inside her head, and each time this command registered in her mind she felt a pulsating power that was keeping her focused. *I gotta warn*

Shamara and Minister Reid that they're in danger, she concluded as she looked around the cell.

Despite the calming effects of the meds surging through her blood stream, it also was making her see things much more clearly. The clear analogy indicated she had fucked up royally when she failed to mention that Tommy was on to them. They all were being followed, which could mean only one thing. It seemed like each minute that slid by, this fact became clearer and clearer. *What the fuck was I thinking!? How the fuck could I not put them on point!?*

She felt the urge to cry when Kenyetta popped into her mind. *Look what the fuck you did!?* That voice shouted as the tears rolled from underneath her tears. *You killed him!?* She cried even harder as her knees gave out.

As she laid on the padded floor Fashawn heard that voice pounding at her heart. It was now telling her that if Shamara and Minister Reid were killed by Tommy, it would be her fault. They would lose their lives all because she wanted to keep her fuckin' missions going!

The images started flashing inside her mind as she laid on her back staring up at the ceiling. Then, the voices started talking and the violent sounds of the heavy artillery gunfire were heard.

Suddenly, Fashawn was back in Iraq. She was dressed in full combat attire with a standard issue M16A2. She tried to pull her third eye away from the view of this horrific event, but her mind was stuck. The meds ensured that this little walk down memory lane ran its course.

Fashawn and her platoon of about three-dozen troops (all under her command) were positioned on the outskirts of the town of Yusufiyah, about twelve miles southwest of Baghdad. They were gearing up for a covert raid to rescue four U.S. Marines who were captured by an insurgence group in possession of heavy artillery. Fashawn had her night

246

vision binoculars to her eyes, examining the four story building; the suspected holding facility of their kidnapped comrades. She was still riding high on her many successes, since she was making history. She was one of the first black female enlisted personnel to command troops involving direct ground combat, and to the surprise of all, she had scored higher than all other Marines in infantry tactics during her advanced training at Twentynine Palms, California. Also, when she attended the School of Infantry at Camp Lejeune, North Carolina, she came in third place in her graduating class.

Suddenly, Fashawn's communications device rattled to life and she answered it. "Sergeant Corcino here."

"This is Colonel Richter. I need to see you immediately, sergeant."

Fashawn jogged over to the makeshift command station. She saw the Colonel and headed towards him. When she arrived, Fashawn said, "Reporting as instructed, sir."

"I just received a new set of instructions, Corcino, coming straight from top command. You are to not only rescue our fellow Marines, engage enemy combatants, and level the building where the insurgents are holding our troops, but you are also instructed to clear this town of all insurgents. Use whatever means necessary to complete your mission." He knew he would not receive any bleeding heart responses about being too aggressive, or talks of Geneva Convention restrictions, and possible Amnesty International investigations from this sergeant, since Corcino was one of their most effective soldiers that did magnificent work in the field. She was a living testament of the success of their new mind control protocol; he beamed with pride. "If any enemy resistance is detected you are authorized to neutralize any facility harboring any combatants."

"Sir, yes, sir! Instructions noted. I'm on it, sir." Fashawn wanted to jump for joy as she jogged back to the launch location. After she saw how the insurgencies were mutilating her good friends on a regular basis, while kidnapping Marines with the intent of pressuring them into releasing their murderous comrades, she was dying to get some get back. Even though she had coordinated the neutralization of four small towns, killing countless people who looked like combatants, her thirst for "some get back" seemed as if it could not be quenched. The mind-boggling urge to punish these people was so powerful at times, she often wondered if she killed them all would this terrible mental itch ever stop. Thanks to her special training—a tutoring they claimed was a top-secret experiment—she knew she was the best of the best and she was showing and proving it with each and every mission they sent her on.

Fashawn arrived at the launch location and said excitedly, "Listen up everyone. We got new instructions. Basically," She shouted. "It's party time!"

The platoon cheered as if they were a bloodthirsty Germanic tribe about to converge on Rome.

Fashawn continued, "This is still a rescue and destroy mission. The only additives are that we are to cleanse the town of all insurgents while leveling the town in the progress, especially any facilities harboring those who engage us in anyway. Wally, I need you and your squad to focus on rescue efforts. The others and me will concentrate on the destroy aspects. Ready for action!?"

"Yeah!" The platoon collectively shouted.

Five minutes later, under cover of night, Fashawn lead her platoon towards the town. When they were within yards of the town enemy fire erupted and the bloodbath began. Two hours later, two of the four U.S. Marines were rescued—the other two were killed by what appeared to be friendly fire—and every single insurgent fighter was tracked down and slain with gruesome mercilessness. Several of the Marines had captured combatants and Fashawn personally neutralized them all with carefully executed headshots. Her special training was geared exclusively towards utter destruction and the mental tailoring protocol mandated that no hostages were allowed. Through brainwashing, when she heard the words "level the" or "neutralize" whatever, it meant one thing and one thing only: Complete and utter obliteration and no one was immune from the wrath of the greatest killing machine ever to sweep across the global.

Fashawn started coughing explosively, and the convulsive power of her lungs pushing out violent breaths of air, forced her from the reverie. It all came back to her like an explosion. She had to get out of this place. She had to find a way out of here! Shamara and Minister Reid were in great danger, a life-threatening situation caused by her. *I gotta get out of here!* She shouted over and over inwardly, and felt her willpower becoming as saturated with determination as it was when she was overseas.

Fashawn rolled onto her feet, and remembered some of the special training they had taught her. The lessons of how to control the crippling effects of mental altering substances were wiggling their way through all the layers of cobwebs within the subterranean regions of her mind. She'd never had the opportunity or the need to utilize such a tactic before, but now she was going to see if her top-secret training really worked.

As she wobbled to her feet, Fashawn suddenly realized this wasn't going to be as simple as she hoped it would be when saw her vision was now blurred and the drunken sensation had increased tremendously.

CHAPTER # 24

" . . . I always wanted to punish Tommy for what he did," Minister Reid said with his head partially bowed. The tone of his voice was meek and humble. "But I was locked into a mentality of forgiveness. All the years I watched what that incident had done to you and it was killing me with guilt, Shamara. We tried everything to help you; therapy, family talks, special Sunday school lessons, love and kisses, everything, but deep down I always knew if you could see this murderer receive his justice for what he did, that would be the cure to solve the inner turmoil that was haunting you."

Minister Reid sighed as though he was either collecting his thoughts or catching his breath, but was actually wondering if Shamara remembered the time when she was about twelve years old and had blamed him for not doing something to Tommy for killing her mom and dad. Since she was in a fit of rage at the time, he doubted she remembered.

Those words she uttered had cut so deep into him that they left a permanent scar. The temptation to speak about that incident was too strong not to mention it. "But, what really pushed me to this point, Shamara, was that time when you wanted those expensive shoes, and I couldn't buy them because of the financial problem the Church and we were in, and you were very upset. You said something that devastated me and I knew it was the truth."

Shamara instantly remembered it. *Oh, my God, I remember that.* Viewing it with an adult mind she could now see the affect those words would have on a person, especially a man who once grew up in the wild and tumble streets of Brooklyn. "I remember. I had blamed you for not doing something to Tommy because I was young and didn't understand.

I'm sorry I said those things." But, deep down inside, she sensed she wasn't totally wrong for feeling the way she did.

"There were other things that drove me to this; like the police dropping the case with that lame excuse about not having evidence; the people who saw the shooting and wouldn't come forth. When I reached inside of myself for an answer, I kept running into issues that made it harder for me to continue running from this. I even sought biblical guidance to stop this harsh thinking, and in fact, I found verse after verse that actually supported it. The most famous of them all; an eye of and eye!"

"So how did Fashawn become a part of all this?" She said. "And Kenyetta?"

Minister Reid sighed, realizing this was the reason he prayed Shamara would never find out. His conscious wasn't built for this. "When Fashawn came home from the service, she stopped by and we had a nice talk. You came up in our conversation and we both agreed that you were suffering. It was apparent you were in pain and still struggling over the death of your mom and dad, even after all these years. She actually suggested that something should be done about Tommy." He suddenly realized that Fashawn was a bit aggressive in her proposal. "And since I was already at the point of washing my hands on forgiving him, even though he was donating huge amounts of money to this Church under the premise that he was making amends for what he had done, it didn't take much for her to convince me to invest some money in getting this project off the ground."

Shamara was upset by the fact she was left in the dark; they all knew this was a plan sponsored by her Uncle and nobody told her. "This is foul, Uncle Earl. So basically I was manipulated—"

"No, Shamara, you know that's not true. You always wanted to punish him. I watched you grow up. I heard the pain in your heart daily and I saw how you became an emotionally sound person once you were striving towards punishing this creep for what he did. It was like watching a magic trick the way you lit up with life and vitality."

Shamara was shocked she was hearing her Uncle Earl talk like this. She still couldn't fathom her Uncle knowing she was roaming the streets posing as a contract killer, and especially couldn't believe he was promoting it. "This is—This is crazy, Uncle Earl!" Although it was an uncomfortable piece of information, she could understand it to some degree, because she always gave hints throughout her life that Tommy should get his justice and she became a whole new person once they set out to punish him. Then, her mind shifted to the situation at hand. "So this is why Fashawn was coming here? Tommy's on his way here?"

"Yeah, he doesn't know I'm about to put an end to this. I asked him to come here, so I could share with him what's the status of all the money he's donated. Actually, this was an idea we tossed around before we decided to hit him in New Jersey, but it was just too dangerous. If he had been shot in or around this Church, it could've lead to terrible consequences. But the more I think of it, the more I realize I should've done this a long time ago."

"Are you sure he doesn't know? I ask this because me and Fashawn were being followed for the last couple of days. The way things are going there's no telling what that's all about."

"And Fashawn knew this!?" Minister Reid felt the shock ripple through his body.

"Yeah, she knew this. We don't know for certain who it is, and we didn't want to jump to any conclusions."

Minister Reid reflected back on his phone conversation with Tommy and the tone and texture of his sudden happy go lucky attitude told him that he knew what time it was. "What the hell was Fashawn thinking!? If you guys are being followed, and now Kenyetta turns up dead, it's a strong chance it's Tommy behind this. You guys weren't involved in anything else besides what you were doing with Tommy, so I can't imagine it being anything else. Oh, Jesus Christ, this changes everything!"

As Shamara watched her Uncle in deep thought, she reflected back on her relationship with Tommy, and still believed she could end all this without the need for any further bloodshed. She wished she had done this the minute her heart started talking to her, and subconsciously she knew she was the cause of Kenyetta's death.

After all the delicate moments she spent with Tommy, and finally discovering his sensitive side, Shamara felt it in her bones she could talk him out of it, even after all the crazy shit she did. "Uncle Earl, listen to me." She drew in a lung full of air, let it out slowly and said, "We don't have to go this route. All of this violence might not be necessary. You might think I'm crazy for saying this, but I honestly believe I can talk Tommy out of all this without us shooting it out." She saw her uncle's eyes widen with sincere surprise. "When we infiltrated his organization, you know I had to get intimate with him. I know they told you all about it. Tommy told me things, and opened up his heart to me in ways that— that shocked me!"

Shamara couldn't believe she was doing this again. How could she be standing here justifying and making excuses for the murderer of her family!? "Besides the fact he said he was forced to commit that shooting, which I felt he was telling the truth, he tried to fix what he did wrong. You even said he was giving you money to make right what he did wrong. I—I even got close to his son, and all I'm saying right now; please give me a chance to see if I can talk him out of this before we jump to all the violence. If I explain to him what's going on, I can make him stop all this once and for—"

"Shamara, I understand your righteous heart. You've always had a unique goodness of character, which is why I tried hard to keep my involvement in this away from you, but what you're saying is not realistic. Tommy is a murderer; always has been and always will be. Don't you realize you made several attempts on his life? Knowing a person like Tommy, once you attempted to kill him, the only objective in his mind at this moment is to kill you before you get him. Even if he still has feeling for you he's not gonna chance it. Once you shot him, you killed the trust. Shamara, if you attempt to talk sense into him, he'll think it's a trick to make him put down his guards. You need to get that out of your head, and let's start preparing—"

Suddenly, Rodney Jones entered the church wearing an old olive green army field jacket and approached with a disturbed look on his face. He had gray hairs scattered through his goatee, and by the way he walked it was clear he was a throw back from days of the Black Panthers.

Impulsively, Shamara and Minister Reid reached for their weapons. Shamara was surprised once again when she saw her old gray haired Uncle reaching for his gun.

Rodney stopped in front of them and said with a confident voice, "There's two strange cars parked outside with men inside of 'em and they don't look too friendly. They're watching this here Church." He pulled a 9mm from his back waist. "I'm here to serve you as best I can Minister Reid. This is something we should've done with this Tommy son of a bit—" He looked up at the black Jesus on the cross. "Excuse me, my lord. "

Shamara and Minister Reid gave each other an unsteady look of readiness. They're expressions showed their severe uncertainty, since they both knew they weren't equipped to make it through this once Tommy rolled in and the fireworks ignited.

*   *   *   *

Fashawn heard the padded door open. She was lying curled up in a fetal position facing the door, pretending to be sound asleep. She knew she was being watched from the surveillance camera located near the ceiling, so she knew they suspected she had finally fell victim to the medication. It was a living hell lying completely still the way she had done, but now she saw it was all worth it. She knew they were coming to take her to another room to probe, poke and tinker with her body.

The two burly men, one white and the other black, dressed in white uniforms reached down, pulled her up, wrapped one of her arms around their necks and dragged her out of the room, completely disregarding the fact her bare feet were sliding across the padded floor.

With one eye cracked open ever so slightly, Fashawn watched as they lead her down a dimly lit corridor, and to her surprise, she saw she was in a place she had been before. Upon closer observation, she realized she was inside the Veteran's Hospital where she attended her therapy sessions. This was indeed a blessing from God.

In one swift and violent maneuver, Fashawn came to her feet while simultaneously slamming both men's heads together, dazing them. As if she never stopped moving, Fashawn grabbed the black guy by the back of his pants and shirt collar and rammed him into the wall headfirst. In a blink of an eye, she laid a spinning wheel kick to the white guy's chin, who was already coming at her. The blow dazed him again, and Shamara began pounding both men with a series of vicious head blows, while slamming their heads into the nearby wall. Her punches alternated back

255

and forth between the two, making sure each one didn't have a chance to regroup from the debilitating head blows. After a moment she saw both men were unconscious.

Breathing extremely hard, Fashawn saw the nearby stairwell and quickly dragged them inside. She stripped the white guy of his clothing since he was just about her size and put them on. The soft sole shoes were rather big, but they would have to do.

As she rushed down the stairs, Fashawn prayed it wasn't too late. Just as she hit the ground floor, she realized she needed a weapon and a ride. She peeked out of the stairwell and saw there were about a dozen or so people sitting in the waiting room.

As Fashawn slid out the stairwell door, and crossed the corridor heading for the main entrance, Fashawn did something she hadn't done in a very long time. She prayed to God, begging for him to provide a way.

As if in response to her hypocritical call for help from God, Fashawn saw the man at the admittance window staring at her strangely. When she was a few yards from the exit, Fashawn saw the man hastily picked up his phone, while nervously cutting his eyes at her.

*   *   *   *

Tommy cruised around the Church examining the outer structure carefully. Although he was very familiar with this location, it just made good sense to re-familiarize himself with the surroundings. He had spoke to T-Bone moments ago and knew there were now at least three people inside of the Church. T-Bone had informed him that just before he pulled up a man wearing an old green army fatigue jacket had entered the Church.

Tommy parked about a half a block down from the Church and approached, along with Kahmel, Slick and T-Bone. They all were fully armed with an assortment of weapons, including two compact Uzis.

"Remember," Tommy said to his three bodyguards. "Follow my lead."

$*$ $*$ $*$ $*$

Inside the Church, Shamara, her Uncle, Rodney and Frank took their positions. Minister Reid and Rodney stayed out front; Shamara stood near the hallway leading to the back of the Church, while Frank was in a back room watching for anyone trying to sneak up the rear. According to the plan constructed by Minister Reid, they would draw Tommy into a false sense of security and the first opportunity to end this he would take the lead.

$*$ $*$ $*$ $*$

Outside in back of the Church, three cars sat parked and the eight occupants stared at the windows and two doors. They were parked inside the Church's parking lot, but at the very far end.

Gizmo sat in the back seat of a black Audi and was becoming very impatient and bored. Although Gizmo received explicit instructions to stay inside the car and to do nothing until he got word from Kahmel or T-Bone, or until he heard gunshots, Gizmo's problematic personality wouldn't permit him to sit still.

Gizmo said to Demon, who sat in the passenger seat with Joe Ringo behind the wheel, "Yo' sun, we need to get closer. You know we don't rock like this. Come on, Demon, I'm steppin' to my business." He got out the car and so did Demon.

Joe didn't even attempt to beef, since none of them would've listened to him anyway. He was the new guy on the team.

Gizmo and Demon eased towards the Church.

Gizmo not only wanted to be nosy, but to also score some serious points for saving the day like he did that time when he foiled the robbery at their spot over on Claiborne Street in Newark.

*   *   *   *

Shamara was peeking around a corner just as Tommy entered. She had both guns in the ready and had her five clips tucked in her pockets in such a way that they were available for rapid retrieval. Her heart started pounding in her chest and the arousal wasn't connected to fear. She couldn't believe she felt something inside of her upon seeing him and it wasn't hate.

"Minister Reid!" Tommy said happily as he scanned the interior. He saw his men were doing the same. "I'm so glad you invited me here." He shook the Minister's hand and instantly noticed his nervousness. "I'm sorry it had to be at such a late hour of the evening, but you know how it is when you're trying to stay on top of a multi-million dollar empire."

"I understand clearly how it goes, Tommy," Minister Reid saw the other men were clearly holding heat and weren't concealing what they were holding. He cut is eye at Rodney and saw he didn't appreciate the grandstanding. "Listen, Tommy, I need your associates to restrain themselves with their firearms. This is—"

"These are my bodyguards, Earl," Tommy said with a smile, noticing these two old foggies were packing heat, but were trying to front like they weren't. He was still looking for Shamara and he noticed he could sense her presence. "It's their job to carry weapons." He locked eyes with Minister Reid and said. "What's the matter, Minister? What you so nervous about?"

Shamara had pulled back when she saw them closely examining the Church. Uncle Earl's advice was inside her head, but it wasn't sticking the way it should have, and she decided she was no longer going to continue ignoring her inner voice. She tucked her weapons and approached. She saw Tommy's expression of surprise and sensed it was a fake response.

258

"Shamara!?" Tommy said, causing everyone to turn and watch her approach. "What brings you here? I hope it's not to finish the job."

"I need to talk to you, Tommy." Shamara said as she stood next to her Uncle, who she saw was steaming with anger. "I feel a little awkward trying to tell you this—"

"That fake last name—Fox—Now that was a good one!" Tommy continued smiling. "Yah got me good with that one."

"Tommy, I know this sounds crazy, but we should try to resolve this like civilized people. If you could hear why I did what I—"

"Tommy Jr. told me to ask you, the next time I saw you, why did you shoot his daddy?" His voice was filled with serious sarcasm. "But, I wanna ask you something before you answer that." He saw she was all game by the sadness in her eyes. Despite the fact she tried to get at him, he was certain her heart was getting in the way and now was the time to fuck with her head. "After all the shit we been through, how could you flip out like that!?"

Shamara sighed as she noticed it was getting hard to look him in the eyes.

"And what's up with him Golden 9? You shot me, stole my shit, and then tried to shoot a brother again. And all I ever did for you was treat you good. Name one time I ever did you wrong—"

Sudden massive gunfire rang out from the back of the Church and everybody instantly reached for their weapons . . .

*   *   *   *

Moments earlier Gizmo and Demon eased up towards the Church with Uzis in their hands.

As the two moved towards the Church, Frankie saw them creeping. When they tried to open the door, Frankie rushed over to the other door, opened it, hastily stepped outside and spit off several shots from the AK-

259

47, dropping Demon, but missed Gizmo, who returned fire as he scurried to the nearby car.

Every single hitter outside was hurled instantly into full attack mode. Every hitter positioned in various places around the location moved rapidly towards the Church from all four directions. This was one of the signals. Tommy had made clear that they were to converge on the Church only if they received word from either him or Kahmel, or if any gunfire was heard.

*   *   *   *

Inside the Church, the place went up like a giant Rome Candle. The second the gunfire was heard every weapon inside the Church was pulled and was spitting flames.

Minister Reid pulled his gun, squeezing off shots aimed at Tommy as he ran for the podium.

Shamara pulled both of her weapons and started spitting bullets, hitting Slick in the forehead as his gun roamed. She simultaneously dove with her fingers still on the triggers as bullets flew everywhere.

Rodney had pulled his 9mm, fired four rapid rounds, hitting Kahmel in the leg, and T-Bone in the center of his chest (a perfect heart shot) but was struck twice (in the leg and the stomach) by Kahmel's Uzi that brought out a pain stricken scream.

Shamara scrambled towards the platform where the altar was located, firing both nines as Tommy and Kahmel continued firing at her.

Meanwhile, gunfire was going off in the back of the Church as if a full fledge war was in progress.

Minister Reid hastily moved from the podium to get to the first row of benches. He saw Kahmel firing at Shamara, took aim and blew a huge hole in the back of his head. Just as Minister Reid stood and was about to move, Tommy fired four shots, but only one tore a hole into the

Minister's unsuspecting body. Minister Reid hit the floor as if his life energy was violently snatched from his body. He grabbed his shoulder as he cringed in pain.

Suddenly, an army of eight Uzi totting men crashed through the front door of the Church.

Minister Reid and Rodney took aim from behind the wooden benches and picked off six of the eight men without any difficulty.

The two remaining men began spraying Uzi bullets in a wild and indiscriminate fashion, aiming at any and everything in the Church that looked like it had the potential to move, while completely oblivious of the fact that their boss was still in this place. The Uzi bullets ripped, tore and shredded everything they touched; glass, wood and plastic were strewed everywhere.

Rodney hollered when a stray bullet cut through his the lower back after it ricocheted off the wall. All the fight and the life were instantly knocked out of him.

"Stop shooting!" Tommy shouted, but noticed he was unable to yell over the loud gunfire. When there was a pause in between the gunfire, he screamed at the top of his lungs. "Stop shooting, Motherfucker!"

A deep, penetrating silence took hold of the Church.

"Yo', Tommy, you alright!?" Linny said with a smoking hot Uzi in his hand as he was crouched behind the admittance podium. "Say something man!"

"I'm good!" Tommy shouted. "What the fuck you shooting all crazy like that for?" He was surprised a stray bullet hadn't hit him.

*   *   *   *

In the back of the Church Frankie was kneeling behind a car, re-loading the banana clip as bullets ate at the fender near his face. He was in the parking lot, banging out with the five remaining thugs; three of them were laid stretched out on the pavement, including Gizmo and Demon.

Frankie felt alive! He was finally doing what he had dreamed of doing for years: stepping to these trifling, destructive ass, young drug dealing motherfuckers and showing them what getting busy was really all about. Twenty years ago he used to be a show-nuff hell raiser, but gave it all up when he gave himself completely to the grace of Jesus Christ. He slammed the clip in place, cocked the bullet into the chamber with the sliding bolt, peeked around the fender, ascertained the thugs' locations and decided to show them how a real wild cat stepped to the business.

Frankie stepped from behind the car with the assault rifle spitting spurts of rapid gunfire as he moved rapidly towards the cars where the five young wipper snappers were hiding behind.

When the five thugs saw what Frank was doing, and that he was coming for them and wasn't afraid of their bullets, they had the nerve to try to frantically flee.

Frank grinned as he noticed their fearful retreat was exciting him. *Don't start runnin' and hollerin' now mufucka!* Frank thought as he plucked off a guy in a black leather jacket who screamed in agony as the bullets violently knocked him off his feet. Frankie moved the assault rifle in a sweeping motion, spraying bullets as he picked off two more thugs.

Suddenly, a bullet struck Frankie in the hip and he went down, but continued firing his weapon as he mowed down the last two thugs.

                    *   *   *   *

Inside the Church, Linny looked around with wide eyes at all his homies sprawled out on the floor, all around him, apparently dead. The penetrating smell of gun smoke was heavy in the air, which served only to infuriate him more. He was furious at the fact Tommy had told him to be easy!? *Fuck this shit*, he decided, and ducked walked closer inside the

Church as he heard Shamara and Tommy talking. He gave Deadeye the signal to follow his lead.

Meanwhile, Tommy was talking to Shamara as they were hiding behind various objects. Tommy was behind the third row of benches, while Shamara was behind the platform where the altar stood.

"Shamara, why are you doing this to me!?" Tommy sounded genuinely hurt. "I told you I didn't mean to kill your peeps. What would you have done if a person had a gun to your mother's head, and said you either kill somebody else's mother, or your mother dies? Believe me, if I could take it all back I would. I've opened my heart to you! I loved you, and you know that shit, Shamara. What we had was special and you know that shit! If it makes any difference, I'm sorry Shamara for what happened to your mother and fa—"

"Don't believe him, Shamara!" Minister Reid shouted. "He's a lying piece of shit drug dealer! An enemy of our people; selling poison to them in the name of fattening his pockets!"

Linny smiled as he moved closer to the Minister, now knowing for certain where he was positioned.

"Look who's talking!?" Tommy's voice was saturated with bewilderment. "Name one black owned Church that's not stealing, selling out and exploiting black folks!? Don't get me to puttin' your shit on blast, Minister Reid. You ain't no saint in a position to be throwing bricks in a glass house."

Shamara didn't hear a response from her uncle, and knew there was a lot of truth to what Tommy had said, especially since she told her uncle the same thing on countless occasions.

"Shamara, you rolled with me," Tommy said softly. "You know what's really inside my heart. If I was a rotten to the core type of motherfucker, would I have donated all that money to those charities?

Would I have shown all that love to young folks? Would I have tried to make amends for what I did to your family? I wanna ask you something else. If you're a good person, with a pure heart and soul, where is the forgiveness? You shot me and I'm willing to forgive you, why can't you forgive me now!?"

Shamara felt herself falling in the opposite direction. That remark was the knockout blow that touched her heart. The painful truth of it all brought her to her knees. "You right, Tommy." She felt her inner voice telling her to go with this. Stop this madness, and end it right here and now, while she and her uncle were still alive. He just said he forgave her for shooting him. What more could they ask for!? "We can end this beef right here and now—"

BANG! BANG! BANG!

Linny sprung to his feet and sprayed a wave of bullets at Minster Reid who tried to scramble for safety, but was struck in the leg and screamed.

Shamara sprung to her feet with both of her fully loaded nines barking off a bombardment of bullets, striking Linny in the neck and the upper chest, but missing Deadeye.

Simultaneously, Deadeye opened fire just as Shamara stood up.

Shamara screamed when Deadeye's bullet struck her in the stomach. She stumbled to the floor, shocked by the overwhelming impact of the blow that damn near knocked her silly. She was amazed she was seeing stars; she was even more shock by the fact the bullet had shoved her in a violent fashion, and was burning as if a lit cigarette was inserted inside her gut.

Tommy screamed, "No!" He sprung to his feet and pumped off four shots into Deadeye, killing him instantly. Minster Reid tried to crawl towards the platform and Tommy canceled his contract with a bullet square to the side of his head.

Shamara saw what Tommy had done to Deadeye, but missed what he had done to her uncle, being that the Minster was in a location that was out of her line of vision.

"Shamara, oh, God, don't tell me you're hit!?" Tommy's voice was genuinely filled with alarm. "Where are you hit!?"

Shamara cringed in great pain. "The stomach." She still held onto one of her guns. The Golden 9 was in her right hand, while her other hand was clamped on the bullet wound that was spewing blood.

"Shamara, let me help you, please. You know I got mad love for you, girl. I loved you the moment I laid eyes on you. Let me help you; you're bleeding. Lemme get you to a hospital." Tommy saw she was cringing in great pain. "Look, Shamara, I'm disarming." He reached his gun out from behind the bench and dropped it to the floor. "I'm standing up with my hands in the air." He stepped out as he said he would.

Shamara's first instinct was not to trust him, but the rational side of her mind told her she had no choice. She was losing a lot of blood in a very rapid fashion and obviously needed help. "Okay, okay," She stood and tried to approach Tommy, but fell face first. The room felt like it was spinning and she noticed the Golden 9 had slipped from her grasp.

"Shamara," Tommy ran to her as though he was deeply concerned about her condition. "Be easy, you gotta preserve your energy. Come on, let me help you." He reached down, pulled her into his arms, sat on the nearby platform with her sitting next to him and embraced her. He then looked into her eyes and said softly, "Shamara, you don't know how much I missed you, boo." He gave her a deep tongue kiss. At first he noticed her lips were tensed and filled with resistance. He put some affection into the kiss and moments later she went with it, closing her eyes as though she was in paradise.

As Tommy kissed Shamara he smiled inwardly because he had this bitch just where he wanted her. He said he would do it to her ass in such a way that it would give him the ultimate pleasure and it was clear he was getting what he wanted. He would touch her heart and then kill her while she was locked in a state of blind affection. *This was the ultimate and proper way to shit on a cutthroat, ungrateful bitch!*

As Tommy put his all into the deep kiss, his hand inconspicuously slid down to the knife stashed in the leg holster fastened to his right leg. Once the knife was in his hand, he felt the weight of the weapon, twirled it in his hand until it was in its proper stabbing position, and his hand went up in the air, it went up, up and up. Just as the huge knife started descending downward . . . .

BANG! BANG!

The first bullet hit Tommy in the top of his head, splattering blood all over Shamara's face. The second bullet struck him in the temple region, tearing off a huge glob of flesh that landed on the floor next to Shamara.

Shamara was too shocked to even scream. She saw Tommy fall to the floor as she slowly looked up and saw Fashawn. She almost lost her mind with something far more powerful than fury. "Why the fuck you kill him!? We resolved it!? He apologized and he said he forgave me! And I forgave him!" She started crying. "You stupid crazy bitch! Why did you—"

"Look at his fuckin' hands." Fashawn said calmly as she moved closer to Shamara. "Turn him over and look at what the fuck is in his hand!" Fashawn rushed over and flipped Tommy onto his back with her foot.

266

As Tommy's lifeless body flipped over, Shamara saw the knife and an earthquake of horror mixed with shock erupted inside of her. She was literally speechless. Everything started moving in slow motion as the gravity of the situation started to register in her mind. *Oh, my god, this motherfucker was going to kill me!?*

"Come on! Let's get the fuck out of here" Fashawn tucked her gun in her front waist of her white pants and pulled Shamara onto her feet. "It's nothing short of a miracle the police ain't here yet."

Just as Shamara and Fashawn were rushing towards the back of the Church, the faint sounds of police sirens were heard.

CHAPTER # 25

FIRST ENDING

Five months later.

Shamara stood in front of the Bedford Hills visiting room gate as it slid open. She stepped through and gave the white male correction officer her pass. She was dress in green standard prison garb and state issued footwear. *Who could this be!?* This particular inquiry was the only thing that kept pulsating through her mind. She was sweating, since her system was racing with excitement. She was certain it wasn't her Uncle Earl's wife Tina. She had just came up to see her two weeks ago, and only visited her once a month. This was definitely a surprise visit.

After Shamara was pat frisked, the huge metal door was opened and she entered the visiting room floor, looking at the sea of faces sitting at the several rows of tables, but didn't detect any familiar faces. The smell of freshly popped butter-covered popcorn caressed her senses. Ever sense she stopped smoking she noticed all of her senses were heightened tremendously. She approached the desk and handed the pass to the heavyset black woman C.O. that had a face full of acne.

"You're at table seven, row four," The heavyset C.O. said.

Shamara looked in the direction she was instructed to go, and the sight she saw had instantly made her day. Fashawn waved at her and was dressed like a businesswoman. The sleek, snug fitting black suit and the white blouse brought out the shapely contorts of her youthful physique. Tears of enjoy almost burst from her. Shamara rushed to her life long friend.

Shamara embraced Fashawn and they took their seats. They immediately got the mundane issues out of the way and then dove into the heavier topics.

"So, what did those military people do to you?" Shamara said. "After you dropped me off at the hospital, you said you had to set things straight. Girl, you just disappeared. Now look at you. It's a whole new you."

"I stopped running," Fashawn said with a permanent glow on her face. "I went back to the VA hospital and explain why I escaped. I gave them some bogus ass story, but they wasn't trying to hear anything I had to say, and were about to Court Marshall me. I decided to put my foot down and end all the bullshit. I demanded to see Colonel Richter. After I spoke with him, I told him if he didn't clear me of all the bullshit, including the mind controlling shit they did to me overseas, I was going to start talking to the media. I wasn't gonna actually snitch him out, but hey, he didn't know that."

Shamara had a confused expression on her face. "Go to the media about what, Fashawn?"

Fashawn instantly realized she had never told Shamara the real deal about her so-called honorable discharge. She noticed that after she had undergone the hypnosis treatment and when she was back to herself, there were a lot of things she was getting mixed up. "Listen, when I was overseas, I agreed to be a part of a top secret experiment; some kind of brain washing experiment where they were hypnotizing us. They were paying real good money so I went for it, since they said there were no side effects and there were no medicines involved. After being hypnotized, I wasn't myself. It was like if I heard a certain phrase, and all of a sudden, I was like somewhere else. I was doing things I normally wouldn't do. I'll leave all the graphic stuff for another day. Eventually, my whole command was put under investigation for all the black bag operations we were engaged in, and to make a long story short, Colonel Richter pulled some strings and got most of us who were following his instructions off the hook from all the war crimes we were committing over there in Iraq."

"My god, Fashawn," Shamara sighed; she always suspected those military people had done something to her, but this was crazy. Now she saw her observations were correct when she was assuming the military was the root of Fashawn being so obsessed with turning everything into a mission.

"And what about you?" Fashawn smiled. "I can see despite the fact we didn't leave behind any evidence at the scene, they still snatched you up. What the hell happened!?"

"They found traces of my blood at the scene of the Church. When we wiped up those drops of blood, it wasn't thorough enough, I guess. But, the good thing is I only got two years in this place. I copped not to obstructing justice and tampering with crime scene evidence. They are mad as hell with me, girl, because I wouldn't tell them what happened. Shit, they could see it was self-defense, and it was clear as day that Tommy and his people were the aggressors. That's all they needed to know and they already knew that. So, I told them, if you know all this then it's obvious you don't need me to tell you what you already know."

The two laughed lightly.

"I guess two years ain't as bad as it could've been." Fashawn stared at Shamara with a crazy smile.

There was a long moment of silence as Fashawn smilingly stared at Shamara

Shamara saw the stare was becoming uncomfortably long and said, "Girl, why you staring at me like that!?"

Fashawn laughed good-naturedly. "I still can't believe, I walked up into that Church and saw you kissing this nigga, while he was about to stab your ass. I asked myself ten thousand times, how in the fuck that happened?" She laughed again. "And you still haven't told me how that happened."

Shamara shook her head, surprised she didn't feel embarrassed and realized Fashawn wouldn't understand. She decided to keep the explanation as painfully short and sweet as possible, and then move on with her life. "It's very simple. When your mind, body, and soul are correct, love is more powerful than hate, and forgiveness will win over the need for revenge any day."

ALTERNATE ENDING

Two days later.

Shamara felt someone calling her name; she was dreaming about the shoot out at her Uncle Earl's Church. She felt someone shaking her and the dream world started fading as she opened her eyes. Through a cloud of grogginess, she saw Fashawn staring down at her. She looked around and saw she was in a hospital bed. The smell of antiseptics galvanized her senses into action as the pain in her stomach shot to her brain and it all came back to her.

Shamara spoke with a crackling voice. "What you doing here, Fashawn?" She struggled to get into a semi-sitting position. "I thought you were on the run from those army guys?"

Fashawn's mind was all over the place. "Yeah, I'm good. But, you know I gotta come check on my peeps. Did the police come fuckin' with you yet?"

"They came asking me about the gunshot wound, but not about what happened at the Church. So far so good. I'm glad you snatched up my guns and wiped up those drops of blood I was about to leave behind. I'm just hoping and praying Frankie don't say anything crazy. I heard she's the only one who made it out alive." Shamara paused a moment as other issues came to the forefront of her mind. "My Aunt Tina is all messed up about what happened to my Uncle Earl." She suddenly felt the urge to cry and fought back the tears. "All I can do right now is hope they don't connect me to that crime scene."

"I think you'll be alright. We got this far, we'll make it the rest. You know the deal; proper planning always prevents poor performance."

"But, what about you!?" Shamara said adamantly. "Ain't those army people looking for you!?"

"They ain't too crazy about fuckin' with me any more. I know too much shit they don't need the media catching wind off. I sent them a kite the other day, telling them if they keep fuckin' with me, I'm gonna start talking."

Shamara had a confused expression. "Go to the media about what Fashawn?"

Fashawn instantly realized she had never told Shamara the real deal about her so-called honorable discharge. She decided it was time to stop all the ducking and weaving. "Listen, when I was overseas, I agreed to be a part of a top secret experiment; some kind of brain washing experiment bullshit where they were hypnotizing us. After being hypnotized, I wasn't myself. I was doing things that I normally wouldn't do. I'll leave all the graphic stuff for another day. Eventually, my whole command was put under investigation for all the black bag operations we were engaged in, and to make a long story short, Colonel Richter pulled some strings and got most of us who were following his instructions off the hook from all the war crimes we were committing over there in Iraq. They told me they recently brought in some specialists from DC to try to undo the dumb shit they did to us. They asked me to come in for some therapy shit to try to re-program me." She was about to mention that she was seriously thinking about taking them up on their offer because she was fiending for another mission, but figure that was a waste of words.

"My god, Fashawn," Shamara sighed. "They did all that to you over there?"

"Yeah, but I'm all good," Fashawn stared at Shamara with a locked jawed expression. "I still can't believe I walked up into that place and saw you kissing this nigga, while he was about to stab your ass. I asked myself ten thousand times, how in the fuck that happened?" She shook her head with clear disgust resonating through her bodily gestures. With an expression that said she was waiting to hear it, Fashawn inquired. "So, what happened?"

Shamara shook her head, and realized Fashawn would never understand. She decided to keep the explanation as painfully short and to the point as possible, and then move on with her life. "It's very simple. When your mind, body, and soul are correct, love is more powerful than hate, and forgiveness will win over the need for revenge any day."

THE END

<u>Vote for *The Canarsie Connection* Sequel!</u>
<u>Take part in the Raffle!</u>

This novel, as you can see, has two endings; the first ending and the alternate ending. They are diametrically different endings and each one has the potential of creating an entirely different sequel.

The Canarsie Connection 2 will be written, and you, the reader, can decide the direction this sequel will take. Should Part 2 be based on the first ending (Shamara in prison; Fashawn no longer running from the military) or the alternate ending (Shamara in the hospital; Fashawn running from the military)?

You, the reader, will decide this question by participating in the vote for *The Canarsie Connection* sequel. The ending that acquires the most votes will govern the direction the sequel will be written. All participants can vote by logging unto www.divinegentertainment.com and going to *The Canarsie Connection* page and vote. In order to vote, all participants must have a valid email address and must produce proof of purchase of *The Canarsie Connection*.

All readers who participate will not only decide the direction the sequel will take, but will also be included in a raffle where first, second and three place prizes will be awarded to the winners. Participants will also receive a coupon that will allow them to get 10% off the purchase of *The Canarsie Connection 2*.

The deadline for all voting will be May 30, 2014. *The Canarsie Connection 2,* will be releases and available for sell in the fall of 2014.

A book signing will be held shortly thereafter, where a raffle will be held, and the first, second and third place winners will be chosen. For more information, please log on to www.divinegentertainment.com, for participation details and rules.

Vote for *The Canarsie Connection* Sequel!
Win 1st, 2nd or 3rd place prizes!
Get a 10% discount on the sequel!

About the Author

Divine G is the founder and owner of Divine G Entertainment. He is a four-time PEN American Center award winning writer and the winner of the 2008 Tacenda Literary award for best play. He has been quoted by the United Nations and the New York Times.

Divine G recently produced, directed and starred in his debut short film consisting of a scene from his novel, Enigma of Love, which is currently being entered into various film festivals internationally. The film's trailer can be reviewed at
http://www.imdb.com/video/demo_reel/vi69708057/

He was employed as a carpenter for Lil Wayne on his 2013 AMW tour and is also hosting his own Internet Radio (The Divine G Show), which can be reviewed at
http://www.spreaker.com/show/the_divine_g_show.

Discover Other Titles by Divine G:

No Other Love - www.**amazon**.com/**Divine-G**./e/B001RZYN1Y

Enigma of Love - http://www.amazon.com/Enigma-Love-Divine-G-ebook/dp/B00C1Y13AY

Money Grip - http://www.amazon.com/Money-Grip-1-Divine-G-ebook/dp/B00BWEU92W

Money Grip 2 - http://www.amazon.com/Money-Grip-2-Volume/dp/1481924451

Baby Doll - http://www.amazon.com/Baby-Doll-Divine-G-ebook/dp/B00D55MZYQ

Upcoming Novels from Divine G

TGONG
(In bookstores Spring 2014)

Rayhiem Jones loved his community (Nubia Gold) so much he was willing to do whatever it took to clean it up. But he never thought his efforts to rid the community of drugs would cost him ten years in prison for a murder he did not commit. After finding out Jose Rodriguez (J.R.), the leader of Supranova, a vicious drug gang, had framed him for the murder, and upon his release from prison, Rayhiem is unable to simply put an H on his chest and handle it. Driven by a series of incomprehensible, reoccurring, life-long dreams, Rayhiem formulates a group that specializes in shutting down drug houses called . . . TGONG.

TIME-JACK
(In bookstores Spring 2014)

Calvin Thompson spent countless years mastering the field of Time Travel Technology and just when he is finally about to become the first official time traveler, a jealous co-worker, Eric Seabright, sends him back in time to the year 1831 in the deep south at the height of slavery.

With 4 months to make it to a Backlash zone (a safety component within the Time Machine that may transport him back to the future), Calvin struggles to overcome slavery, futuristic hit-men, and the demons inside of him that will not allow him to love and appreciate the people who are indispensable to his survival, his humanity and the victory of his journey.